PRAISE FOR GUNNAR STAALESEN

'Staalesen is one of my very favourite Scandinavian authors and this is a series with very sharp teeth' Ian Rankin

'The Norwegian Chandler' Jo Nesbø

'Not many books hook you in the first chapter – this one did, and never let go!' Mari Hannah

'Forty years into the Varg Veum odyssey, Staalesen is at the height of his storytelling powers' Crime Fiction Lover

'Staalesen continually reminds us why he is one of the finest of Nordic novelists' *Financial Times*

'Chilling and perilous results – all told in a pleasingly dry style' *Sunday Times*

'Staalesen does a masterful job of exposing the worst of Norwegian society in this highly disturbing entry' *Publishers Weekly*

'Employs Chandleresque similes with a Nordic Noir' *Wall Street Journal*

'Mature and captivating' *Herald Scotland*

'Well worth reading, with the rest of Staalesen's award-winning series' *New York Journal of Books*

'The readers … will feel drawn into the characters and their intertwined lives' Reviewing the Evidence

'Clearly translator Don Bartlett has an excellent understanding of Staalesen's writing. Haunting, dark and totally noir, a great read' *New Books Magazine*

'Big Sister is a vital contribution to the international body of P.I. literature. As noted, there are only two other writers that I know of who have achieved the depth of insight in detective writing that Staalesen has: Chandler, and Ross MacDonald ... Keep doing what you do, Varg. And never die. This weary world needs you more every day' *Mystery Tribune*

'The narrative never slows with Staalesen keeping the reveals coming thick and fast. Staaleson's Veum is accessible, reliable and intuitively inquisitive' Words Shortlist

'Another Varg, another quality read ... There's a lot to like in this novel but it's the writing and the sharp turn of phrase which I really enjoy' The Book Trail

'Staalesen was reportedly embarrassed when fellow crime writer Jo Nesbø labelled him a "Nordic Chandler" ... a beautifully constructed book, almost poetic, at times, in description, it's a well-earned title' The Literary Shed

'A quiet thriller of vivid descriptions of the towns and landscapes; it is a novel of characters and their traits, both good and bad. It is a novel with a contemporary feel that exudes from the pages and I loved it' My Bookish Blogspot

'*Big Sister* is a brilliant example of Nordic Noir, full of dark secrets and chilling characters ... asking for "just one more chapter" when you are trying to put the book down' Have Books Will Read

'Well paced and kept me hooked! I loved the story line and found myself addicted to the plot – I needed to find out how the book ended but also didn't want it to stop at the same time! It is more of an old-style crime thriller and I really enjoyed it' Donnas Book Blog

'Dark, thrilling, thoroughly absorbing and hugely enjoyable. A big recommend from me!' Emma's Bookish Corner

'This is a slow-paced story, but it was touching and so real that when I finished the book I wanted to read another case by detective Varg Veum ... Be prepared for a surprising book full of twists and a very sad story' Varietats

'An intricate web of lies, secrets, deceit and unspoken truths. It's the classic story of pulling at a thread and seeing the whole thing unravel, but what Gunnar and Don have been able to do is allow the unravelling to happen at a speed at which we can really feel everything come undone' The P Turners Book Blog

'It's emotional without being soppy, while taking the reader on an action-packed ride. The author doesn't placate the reader with happy endings, instead he forces them to stare into the face of reality' Cheryl M-M's Book Reviews

'The dark, evocative Norwegian setting is suitable for the novel, the perfect frame for the crimes at the centre of the story ... I will be recommending everyone to read this thrilling, dark, entertaining novel' Book after Book

'Hints of menace coupled with a chilling climate make this the perfect locational mystery. There is also an emotional element attached to these books, and that is extremely prevalent in *Big Sister*. Highly recommended!' Bibliophile Book Club

'A sharp and intelligent thriller that will delight noir fans and no doubt introduce many new readers to the name Gunnar Staalesen' The Shelf of Unread Books

'This is a beautifully balanced piece of writing, which leads you effortlessly through ... This is a thriller with quality running through its centre. It is thoughtful, incisive and observational – a real class act' Books, Life and Everything

'If you like a book that will have you guessing until the end, then this is the one for you' Vanessa Turns Pages

'This is a story that left me numb as it knocked the stuffing out of me. A brilliant read and flawless translation' Books from Dusk Till Dawn

'I enjoyed being kept on my toes throughout this novel! Nordic Noir is fast becoming one of my favourite subgenres, not least because of the amazing descriptions that really captured my imagination' Portable Magic

'There are some dark and emotional twists and turns … With an addictive plot, believable and relatable characters, this is a novel I highly recommend' Hooked from Page One

'Truly excellent … Magnificent stuff. Highly recommended' Beardy Book Blogger

'There is something just so fantastically absorbing about Staalesen's work that I'm always longing to read more … Every time I think I've read the best book I will in a year, Orenda drops a new Gunnar Staalesen that jumps straight to the top of the list' Mumbling about…

'The author builds up the powerful suspense with an expertise that is astounding, complex plotting, perfectly paced, provides a terrifying Nordic Noir journey' Chapter in my Life

'Gunner Staalesen has delivered a masterclass in storytelling and this book will delight existing fans and I hope draw new readers to Veum's world. It is heady stuff and compulsively addictive' Books Are My Cwtches

'Another intriguing and entertaining read' By The Letter Book Reviews

'Very fast-paced and suspenseful novel, filled with very intriguing characters and very surprising twists and turns, and I do strongly recommend to give this book a try' Book Inspector

ABOUT THE AUTHOR

One of the fathers of Nordic Noir, Gunnar Staalesen was born in Bergen, Norway, in 1947. He made his debut at the age of twenty-two with Seasons of Innocence and in 1977 he published the first book in the Varg Veum series. He is the author of over twenty titles, which have been published in twenty-four countries and sold over four million copies. Twelve film adaptations of his Varg Veum crime novels have appeared since 2007, starring the popular Norwegian actor Trond Espen Seim. Staalesen has won three Golden Pistols (including the Prize of Honour) and *Where Roses Never Die* won the 2017 Petrona Award for crime fiction. He lives with his wife in Bergen.

ABOUT THE TRANSLATOR

Don Bartlett completed an MA in Literary Translation at the University of East Anglia in 2000 and has since worked with a wide variety of Danish and Norwegian authors, including Jo Nesbø and Karl Ove Knausgaard. He has previously translated *The Consorts of Death, Cold Hearts, We Shall Inherit the Wind, Where Roses Never Die, Wolves in the Dark* and *Big Sister* in the Varg Veum series.

Wolves at the Door

GUNNAR STAALESEN

Translated by Don Bartlett

ORENDA BOOKS

Orenda Books
16 Carson Road
West Dulwich
London SE21 8HU
www.orendabooks.co.uk

First published in Norwegian as *Utenfor er hundene* by Gyldendal, 2018
First published in English by Orenda Books, 2019

ISBN 978-1-912374-41-0
eISBN 978-1-912374-42-7

The publication of this translation has been made possible through the
financial support of NORLA, Norwegian Literature Abroad.

Co-funded by the
Creative Europe Programme
of the European Union

Typeset in Arno by MacGuru Ltd
Printed and bound by CPI Group (UK) Ltd, Croydon CR0 4YY

For sales and distribution please contact *info@orendabooks.co.uk*

WOLVES AT THE DOOR

'For without are dogs, and sorcerers, and whoremongers, and murderers, and idolaters, and whosoever loveth and maketh a lie.'

(Revelations 22:15)

Bergen, Norway

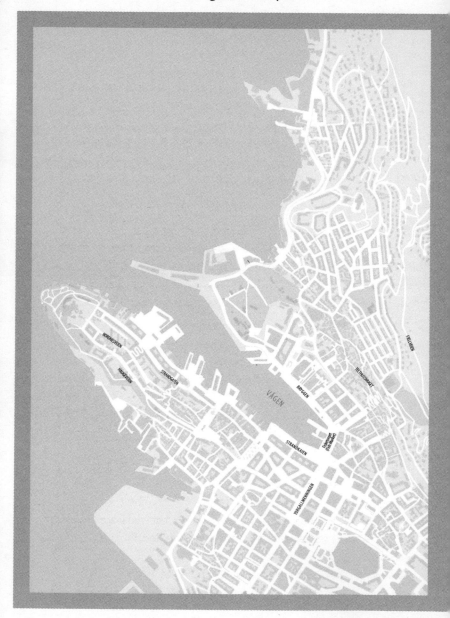

1

I heard the car before I saw it.

I had been on a little job for a married couple who lived in one of the new residential areas at the rear of Lagunen Shopping Centre. They had asked me to park discreetly when I visited them, and I was on my way back down to my Toyota when I heard a snarling engine just behind me.

I had enough time to turn around. The vehicle was coming straight at me with no indication that it was going to veer away. For a second or two I was paralysed. Then I reacted instinctively and hurled myself to the side. The car was so close to me that I felt a rush of air as it passed.

I fell into a pile of snow the JCB ploughs had left during the Yuletide break. Now it was the first Sunday in January and the weather was as cold as it had been since Christmas.

What the… ? I said to myself.

My heart pounding, more shocked than frightened, I sat up in the snow and stared at the tail lights of the car racing down at the same breakneck speed. It was much too far away for me to read the registration plate, but in the evening gloom the car looked grey, and if I wasn't much mistaken it was last year's model of the VW Golf. I watched the tail lights go past the shopping centre and out to Fanavegen, where it took a right into Bergen and disappeared behind the hills there.

I struggled to my feet and stepped onto the road. I looked up to make sure there were no more cars hurtling down at me and to see whether anyone was out walking who could confirm what had happened. But there was no one in the area between Lagunen and the petrol station before Fanavegen.

Hadn't the driver seen me or had he seen me all too well; in other words, had he intentionally tried to mow me down? Could it have anything to do with the case I had just solved? Hardly. It was so insignificant that the only people who might react to it would be the tax authorities, because my fee was so modest that there was virtually nothing left for them, even including VAT.

On the way to my Corolla it struck me there might be another link and this worried me. I became even more worried than I had been when I first noticed the two deaths: one in October, the other two months later.

I had made only a mental note of the first. After the second, I had a suspicion there was something fishy going on. In both obituaries the surviving families had used the words 'died suddenly and unexpectedly' and this is what set me thinking. 'Suddenly and unexpectedly' as in … murdered?

But there had been no mention of it in the newspapers I had seen. I hadn't met either of the two men, but their names – Per Haugen and Mikael Midtbø – had been seared into my memory.

Soon it would be a year and a half since we had, for a few dramatic autumn months, shared a similar fate: all three of us had been accused of the same crime. This was a period of my life I had consciously tried to repress. Now it all came flooding back.

When I reached my car, I unlocked the door, got behind the wheel and rewound the previous sixteen months, to the morning when I was woken by the police for what in the course of a few days would develop into the worst nightmare I had ever experienced, and I had been wide awake.

2

It had been an experience I would not have wished on my worst enemy.

I was taken to the police station and charged with being in possession of what they now called 'sexually explicit material' on my computers: films, pictures and books featuring child abuse. And I wasn't the only person to be charged. Three other men had been brought in for the same reason, and during a later interview I found out their names: Mikael Midtbø, Per Haugen and Karl Slåtthaug.

I knew of course that I was innocent and that someone had planted this material on my computers, but that convinced neither the police nor the legal system. After the initial hearing I was held in remand while the case was investigated further. During another interview at the police station I seized an opportunity to escape, and then the nightmare began in earnest. In a race against time I did what I could to get to the bottom of the case, in which the main issue was this: who hated me with such an intensity that they had hacked my computer and planted this material? I found the answer in a summer house in the village of Søre Øyane, Os Municipality, in a confrontation with four other individuals, all involved in the case in various ways.

However, one of them got away. Later that evening I was standing by a diving tower facing Bjørna fjord, searching in vain for a man who had slipped into the sea after being outed as one of the ringleaders in the case. Wave after wave of breakers crashed on the shore, the wind howled around my ears, but no one reappeared from the foaming waters. He had been swallowed up.

I managed to get off the slippery, sea-soaked rocks. Back on dry land I rang two people: first Sølvi, to say everything was in the process of resolving itself, then my lawyer, Vidar Waagenes, so he could help prevent those words from coming back to haunt me.

It hadn't been so easy. When I returned to the summer house I was arrested by armed police, unceremoniously handcuffed, led to a vehicle and delivered post haste to Bergen Police Station. The only information I managed to pass on was that they should start a search for a man in Bjørna fjord. I didn't find out until later whether that had been done. The orders from the operational commander, an officer I had never seen before, to the policemen taking me to the car had been short and sweet: This man has escaped remand before. Don't let him out of your sight for a second.

They didn't either, until they handed me over on the third floor of the police station, where the department head, Jakob E. Hamre, received me with a thick layer of repugnance daubed across his already-pale face. I made an attempt to clarify the situation for him, but he interrupted me with a raised hand: 'I think we'll wait until Waagenes is here, Veum, before we say anything.'

Fortunately, it wasn't long before Waagenes arrived and I was able to start explaining. In addition to Hamre, Inspector Bjarne Solheim took part in the interview. He glared at me sourly, and I could well understand why. It was fairly clear that he had been blamed for allowing me to abscond a few days earlier.

The interview was recorded. Solheim sat writing on his laptop and both Hamre and Waagenes took notes. Initially, they let me talk more or less without interruption as I tried to summarise a case that had its roots in the past.

We talked until late in the night. After a few hours a report came back to Hamre to say that the search for a man in Bjørna fjord had been unsuccessful, but they would continue looking as soon as there was daylight. 'The most important element of your proof is there,' Hamre had commented, but Waagenes protested at once: 'Not at all! Varg's furnished you with so much information that as soon as you've examined all the other detainees' computers and mobile phones there should be more than enough evidence for his statement.'

'Let's hope so. We'll have to rely on the experts here.'

'You've arrested the other three, I take it?' I asked, and Hamre nodded in a measured way.

'They're being interviewed, but we're unlikely to get through all the material tonight. You'd better prepare yourself to stay here longer until we feel we have a clear overview.'

'I object!' Waagenes exclaimed. 'You've both known Veum for many years…'

'Indeed,' Hamre mumbled with an eloquent sigh.

'It's utterly inconceivable that Varg would've downloaded sexually explicit material with his background as a child-welfare officer and a private investigator.'

'Don't forget the incriminating photos,' Hamre said.

'Which Varg has explained.'

'Exactly. *He* has explained. *Quod erat demonstrandum*, as we Latinists like to say.'

'Yes. And Mother Nille is a rock – Ludvig Holberg told us all we need to know about Latinists,' Waagenes commented drily.

But Hamre won the tug of war in the end. I was still formally charged and had to spend further days and nights on remand, interrupted only by more tedious interviews.

On the third day I was summoned to yet another interview, where the police lawyer Beate Bauge, Hamre and Waagenes were present. Bauge was as erect and disgruntled as she had been for all the hearings. The look she sent me before she started speaking told me her hand had been forced. However, the conclusion was clear. Preliminary examinations of the other detainees' computers had led to them taking the following decision: the charge against me had been withdrawn. After a short, dramatic pause she added: 'For the time being.' And she stressed that if any evidence to the contrary appeared I would have to expect to be brought in for further questioning.

It was as if snow was falling quietly inside me. I didn't erupt in whoops of joy and I didn't burst into tears. However, I did feel a huge amount of relief that they had at long last taken me at my word and that the other computers had corroborated what I had told them.

'And the other arrestees?' I asked warily.

'They'll stay on remand until they're indicted.'

'And Sigurd Svensbø? Has he been found?'

Bauge looked at Hamre, who shook his head.

'No. But our experience of missing persons at sea is that it can be a very long time before bodies wash ashore, if ever.'

'If ifs and ands were pots and pans there'd be no need for tinkers,' Bauge said with the same disgruntled expression she wore earlier, and there were no further comments.

I left the police station in the company of Vidar Waagenes. On the doorstep outside we exchanged glances. It was as though I still hadn't realised I was free, that I could do whatever I wanted – whether that was to go home, down to my office, visit Sølvi or catch the next plane to wherever in the world. In the end, Waagenes and I went for an early lunch at Holbergstuen, as of old.

But that was almost a year and a half ago. Now something had happened that had brought the case back to life. The first thing I did when I got into my office on Monday morning was ring Hamre, albeit with extreme reluctance.

3

Since the events of that autumn I'd worked on one big case, and an incidental consequence of it still lay in the bottom drawer of my desk, in an unopened envelope postmarked the Public Health Institute. I had sat weighing this in my hand many times without taking the decision to open it. In it I imagined was the result of the tests I had requested the DNA registry office perform: I'd sent a few strands of long-deceased saxophonist Leif Pedersen's hair and one of mine. If the tests proved to be positive, I had a new father. If not, I would have to assume that the likewise deceased tram conductor, Anders Veum, was still my biological father. For some reason I had a strong aversion to opening the letter. After all, I had grown up with the tram conductor. He was my father figure, inasmuch as I had one. The saxophonist had come out of left field, holding his instrument, for which I had a special affection, although I never knew why.

Besides, I had quite a different problem now. Hamre hadn't exactly been delighted to hear from me. And his mood didn't improve when I told him why I wanted to talk to him and what the case was about. But he cleared the decks for a meeting in his office half an hour later. 'Half an hour? That's quick.' 'That's when I have some time, Veum.' 'The sooner, the better,' I answered, and twenty minutes later I was on my way.

There were still remnants of the snow that fell before Christmas on the edge of the pavements. The mountainsides around the town were a painting in black and white. I had celebrated Christmas Eve with Sølvi and Helene at their place in Saudalskleivane. On New Year's Eve Sølvi had invited some friends round. I had been as discreet as possible and remained in the background, but raised my glass of champagne at midnight with the other guests. The turn of the year had never been high on the list of occasions I wanted to celebrate. I had spent most of them in solitary majesty, except for my loyal companions – a bottle of aquavit and the rain.

I only moved back to Telthussmuget when the New Year weekend, and what had reminded me of a good old-fashioned Christmas holiday, was over. It was definitely over when on a Sunday in January I just managed to avoid being mown down by a car that had undoubtedly had me in its sights. Even now, walking to the police station the day after, I looked twice both ways when I crossed the road, Torgallmenningen first, then Domkirkegaten.

Hamre sent Solheim down to reception to collect me. He still didn't appear to have forgiven me. I noticed that he had assumed a new style. His once very untidy hair was shaven down to a classical crew cut, like a subordinate officer in the sixties, when I myself was doing my national service. As he was hardly likely to have planned a military career, I took this as a clear sign that he envisaged himself climbing up the hierarchy of Bergen Police Station, where the length of your hair was perhaps still a factor.

Hamre, on the other hand, was the same as always, only even paler, like an overexposed photograph in which the white dominated. The sole feature to break this sameness was the grey of his tailored suit. There had always been a classical elegance about Hamre, whom I had known in our usual ping-pong way since the late seventies. Basic arithmetic told me that he must have been getting on for pensionable age in the police, which the tired expression on his face reinforced.

He received me with a kind of resignation, pointing to the free chair on the visitor's side of his desk. 'Take a seat. Can we offer you anything? A cup of coffee? The force's finest, lukewarm since seven o'clock this morning.'

'No, thank you. I sleep badly enough as it is.'

'Now, don't say I didn't offer you a cup, Veum.'

Solheim sat down on the third chair in the room, at the side of the desk, on which he placed his laptop. He raised his gaze and looked at me, as laconic as a court reporter at the start of a long hearing.

'What did you say on the phone? You want to report someone? What for?'

'Someone tried to run me over last night, behind Lagunen.'

'Oh, yes? Can you give us any details?'

I told him the little I knew. It wasn't much.

He motioned to Solheim to take notes, which he did with poorly concealed irony. 'A VW Golf, probably grey, last year's model, no registration number. Did you catch all of that, Bjarne?'

Solheim nodded.

'Any suspicions about who it could've been?'

'Not yet.'

He turned the words over in his mind. 'Not yet. Hmmm. But it was my understanding that you were worried about the deaths of two of your co-accused in the big child porn case in 2002.'

'The charges against me were dropped.'

'Yes, of course. We remember. Under a cloud of doubt. The star witness from Bjørna fjord still hasn't appeared, as far as I've been able to establish.'

'No, but … Do we want to go through all of this again?'

'No, no, no,' he said, quickly. 'That was just an icebreaker, to get us in the right mood. How long have we known each other, Veum?'

'I was thinking the same myself. Our paths first crossed during a case in 1978. So, in my head that makes it about a quarter of a century ago.'

'In mine, too. Twenty-six years ago to be absolutely accurate. And do you know what?'

'It feels as though it were yesterday?'

He pointed to a calendar of the neutral variety on the wall. 'Can you see the red circle around the thirtieth of January?'

I followed the direction indicated by his index finger. 'Yes.'

'That's a Friday by the way. And it'll be my last day in the police force.'

'I had an idea something like that was coming.'

'And let me put it this way, as civilly as possible. The less I see of you this month, the better. In the future, in ten to fifteen years, we can have a glass of beer together in a suitable watering hole and chat about the good old days, but right now ... No, thank you. In this building your name's synonymous with trouble, but of course you know that yourself. You just don't care.'

Solheim was following our conversation with what looked suspiciously like an amused glint in his eyes. Hamre concluded his monologue. 'So let's get down to brass tacks and finish this as fast as we can. You wish to make an official complaint about an unknown person, or unknown persons, who, according to you, at ten o'clock last night tried to run you over, at such and such an address in Fana, the Bergen district in question.'

'Yes.'

'Did you catch that, Bjarne?'

Solheim elevated his fingers from the keyboard as a sign that this was already documented.

'Then I promise we'll look at this more closely. How many such cars do you think there are in the Bergen region, Bjarne?'

'Mmm.' He took his time. 'Probably several hundred.'

'If we collate a list of all the registered owners I'm sure we can email it to Veum to see if he recognises any of them, can't we?'

'I'll do that. After all, we have his email address.' He smirked.

'Laurel and Hardy on a new adventure,' I said. 'You don't seem to be taking this very seriously.'

Hamre sent me a stern look. 'We take every single complaint we receive seriously. It's only a lack of capacity that prevents us from clearing up all of them. And, of course, how much information we're given.' He raised his eyebrows sardonically, almost as a challenge to me to bat the ball back.

'And what about the two deaths?'

'Yes, tell us some more about them. I asked Bjarne to dig up what we have on both cases.'

'In other words, you've opened files on them?'

'We have, after the duty doctor's report. A sudden death's a sudden death. So ... what can you tell us?'

I took out my notepad and opened it. Both obituaries were there. I laid them down in front of Hamre on the desk so that he could examine them for himself, if he felt the need.

'So, there are two deaths. One in October, the second in December. Both obituaries say the deaths were sudden and unexpected.'

'One of the adjectives is redundant, if you ask me.'

'Let's take the more recent death first. The man's name was Mikael Midtbø and he died on the third of December. According to the obituary, he left behind two persons, both women, but it isn't clear from the text what their relationships to him were. One's called Svanhild and the other Astrid.'

Solheim tapped on his laptop. 'That's correct. His partner and her daughter.' After a glance towards Hamre he added: 'A relatively new relationship. When we investigated the case in 2002 he still had an address in Frekhaug.'

I noted that on my pad. 'And what do you know about the death itself?'

Hamre looked at Solheim. 'Accidental death. A fall, wasn't it?'

'Yes. From the tenth storey of a housing block in Dag Hammarskjølds vei.'

There was a tiny pause before I spoke up again. 'And you're sure this was an accident?'

The two policemen exchanged glances. Hamre nodded to Solheim and let him answer. 'We questioned some people, of course, and we carried out our own investigations. But, as I'm sure you know, if we're talking suicide, we always keep mum with regard to communicating with the media and so on.'

'And did you conclude it was?'

'Yes, we did.'

'And what did you base your conclusion on?'

'We talked to his partner, some neighbours and an eyewitness.'

'An eyewitness?'

'Yes, indeed. A woman was passing below with a pram; Midtbø hit the ground only a few metres from her.'

'She saw the impact, in other words, but not the fall itself?'

'Yes, and she was quite shocked, naturally enough.'

Hamre coughed. 'His partner also expressed the view that Midtbø had been unstable in the time leading up to the fall.'

Solheim nodded. 'Ever since the police action he'd been depressed and irritable. Like certain others...' He snatched a quick glance at me. 'He'd proclaimed his innocence. But there was evidence against him too, images, and he didn't get any support from his then wife, who separated from him while he was on remand.'

'I assume you checked the alibis of all those involved?'

Hamre sent me a condescending glare and nodded once more to Solheim. 'Of course. This happened at approximately twelve o'clock. His partner was at work, which colleagues corroborated. Her daughter was at school. We even checked out his ex-wife, to be on the safe side.'

'No one else who might've had a grudge against him?'

'Loads probably, if we take a broader perspective, but ... There was no evidence to suggest that he hadn't decided to end his life, on an impulse maybe, bearing in mind the method and the time of day—'

Hamre interrupted. 'If there are any sudden new developments, we can pick up where we left off. That's where we are now. Nothing's written in stone on this one.'

'In which case it would be a gravestone,' I muttered under my breath. Aloud, I said: 'Something new *has* come up.'

'Oh, yes?'

'The attempt to run me over!'

'Mm. Shall we look at the second case first?' He gestured towards the two obituaries. 'As far as that one's concerned ... Per Haugen was an elderly man, seventy-two years old. He was found dead on the Eidsvågsnes headland at Frøviken bay, where he used to go fishing in the morning almost every day. The autopsy report gave as the cause of death drowning in combination with a heart attack.'

'No external signs of violence?'

'None.'

'So you didn't launch an investigation?'

'We talked to his wife. It was her who told us about his fishing. Otherwise he never went out during the day.'

'They were still married, I take it?'

Hamre nodded.

'Children?'

Solheim tapped away. Without raising his eyes from the screen, he said: 'Two grown-up children. A son and a daughter. Two grandchildren. Neither of the Haugens' children had any contact with their parents. The daughter was a witness and told the court about how she'd been abused. But it was so long ago that the court couldn't take that into account in their sentencing.'

'She sacrificed herself for no purpose, in other words.'

'You could put it like that.'

'But both of them were imprisoned, Midtbø and Haugen? And then they were out again by the autumn?'

Hamre sent me a bitter look. 'They weren't given long sentences, and good parts of them were conditional. With regard to Haugen, age must've played a part. Both defence counsels referred to the withdrawal of the charges against you – or an earlier suspect, as they called you – as a form of precedence. That's what's often so desperate about these cases. The strict requirements for forensic evidence. Maybe someone had hacked into their computers, too? This kind of thing is meat and drink for a defence counsel of the right calibre, and here they definitely received a high degree of support from the court.'

'Well, don't blame me! I *was* innocent.'

'We've accepted that. Our own computer experts convinced us. May I emphasise "our own"?'

'Thank you.'

'But back to the case. At best it's our word against theirs. Images are damning primarily if they're of the suspects' own children – or of others in their circle of acquaintances – and they're recognisable. If not ...' He leaned forwards. 'We don't have the resources to get to the bottom of these cases. But no one should feel safe. We're improving. Technology's improving, even in the police force. I'm afraid we can only see the tip of the iceberg here. If you ask me, there's pure evil out there. In the whole of my police career nothing has shaken me more than meeting the guilty parties in cases such as this one, with children as young as infants victims of sexual abuse.'

'I don't think I've ever met pure evil, Hamre. If so, it must've been purely pathological.'

'Well, I'm sure it'd be hard for a social worker like you to understand that such evil exists. But we – Bjarne and I, and many of our colleagues – see the victims of this, and for us there's no other explanation.'

'Absolutely. I share your revulsion and have myself met such victims, back in my social-welfare days, but … Well, there's a third person on the list too. Karl Slåtthaug, the fourth man to be charged in 2002. Do you know anything about him? Surely he didn't get off so lightly, did he?'

'Oh, no? He was let off the hook too. Didn't even have to report to the police station!' Hamre's face was flushed. 'Bloody defence counsels! Sometimes you wonder what people are like inside.'

'He's left town, I hear,' Solheim said.

'Oh, yes?' Hamre turned to his colleague.

'Far?' I asked.

'Vestfold. Tønsberg, unless I'm much mistaken.'

'And he's alive?'

Solheim shrugged. 'For all I know, yes.'

Hamre took over. 'As you can see, Veum, we're not complete idiots in the police. We have the usual suspects under surveillance, even if they move away from the district.'

'Perhaps he should be given a warning, at least?'

'A warning? That someone might crash their car into him? If only they had.'

We sat for a moment looking at each other. In the end, I said: 'You don't mean that.'

'No? You warn him then. In many ways you're closer to him.'

The atmosphere in the room was beginning to become oppressive. I made an attempt to change the focus. 'Re: my own case. There were three men charged at first. But during the operation in Bjørna fjord three more were arrested. The professionals, if I can put it like that. Where are they?'

He looked at me sombrely. 'They're still on remand, but there are appeals in hand for all three of them, so don't be surprised if you bump into one of them in the street during the next six months or so.'

'Two of them were involved in murder.'

'Which wasn't that easy to prove so long afterwards. You probably have enemies out there, Veum. Maybe you should get used to taking a long, hard look before you cross the street for some time to come.'

'At any rate, I cleared up the case. What if I hadn't done the investigating myself?'

'After absconding from remand. Thank you very much. You shouldn't underestimate the likelihood that we would've come to the same result if we'd been allowed to do our job in peace. You are, and have always been, what Americans call "a pain in the ass", Veum.'

'They have ointment for that, Hamre.'

Solheim sat tight-lipped listening. I could see his brain overheating, but he said nothing. Not this time, either. The look he gave me was eloquent enough.

I spread my arms in conciliation. 'Well … what if I find out there's really a link between these two deaths, and neither of them died of natural causes…?'

Hamre smacked both hands down hard on his desk and rose halfway out of his chair. 'Let me make one thing absolutely clear to you, Veum. You won't find out anything. If I see you just once in my office before the thirtieth of January I'll have you hauled before the bloody court again, even if it costs me half my pension!'

'For that money you could just about buy a semi-decent midfielder for FC Brann.'

'There are already two corpses here. We don't want any more.'

'Ah, you're thinking about me after all, I can hear. You're taking my complaint seriously, are you?'

Hamre looked at Solheim, desperate. 'What shall we do with this character? Hang him up to dry and let the flies feed off him?'

We eyed each other. We were both clearly in a droll frame of mind.

'You can go now, Veum. I think we've finished talking.'

'Can I expect to hear from you regarding my complaint?'

He waved an arm, resigned. 'You'll hear from us.'

I stood up and put on my winter coat. '*Alea jacta est,* as the late Julius once said.'

Hamre turned to Solheim. 'Would you accompany him out?'

Solheim rose to his feet. 'With pleasure.'

I raised a hand to Hamre. 'Enjoy your retirement. A beer in ten to fifteen years, wasn't that what you said? Deal.'

'Let's make it twenty,' he said, smiling wryly and shooing me away.

Solheim accompanied me onto the pavement, without saying so much as a single word of any kind. However, there was one thing I was sure of. I might never meet Hamre again. But Solheim shouldn't feel too safe. Our paths would cross for certain. That was a guarantee signed and sealed in blood.

4

The cloud cover was high and white, like a dull bell jar over the town. I stuffed my hands deep into my coat pockets as I strolled back to the office after the meeting with Hamre and Solheim.

Back at my post on the third floor I checked the answer machine and saw that no one had asked after me while I was away. Surprise, surprise. I put on the kettle in the hope of brewing a better coffee than I had been offered at the police station.

While I was waiting for the water to boil I took out my notepad, laid the two obituaries out in front of me on the desk and read the notes I had made during the conversation.

Both obituaries were very simple. Not only did they use the same language – 'died suddenly and unexpectedly' – but there were remarkably few surviving relatives. Under Mikael Midtbø's name there were only two: Svanhild and Astrid. Followed by information about the funeral, which was to take place in Fyllingsdalen Church, and a final postscript: 'Please don't bring any flowers. The church ceremony will conclude proceedings.' His ex-wife and children were conspicuous by their absence. Per Haugen's obituary was equally laconic. In his, too, there were only two names: Tora and Hans. After Hans, 'brother-in-law' was written in brackets. There was nothing about flowers, but here too the funeral ceremony terminated in the church, in Biskopshavn.

It was clear that neither Mikael Midtbø nor Per Haugen was considered worthy of a commemorative speech, not even by their closest family, but I was not unaware that some people would have gladly danced on their graves. The absence of overt grief from the surviving family told its own story.

There was a marked age difference between the two deceased.

Haugen was to some extent old enough for the police to have no problem declaring that he had died of natural causes. As for Midtbø, however … a fall from the tenth storey of a block of flats in Fyllingsdalen. Mm. I would have made further enquiries. But my days were filled with leisure; clients weren't beating a path to my door. The job in Fana had been the only one in the last fortnight. The workload was probably greater in Domkirkegaten, at the police station.

The kettle was boiling. I took a filter, measured the required amount of coffee and poured the water. The aroma of freshly brewed coffee spread through the room like the perfume of an exotic woman, dark-skinned, big smile. On looking more closely, however, I saw her back was bent from lifting far-too-heavy sacks on a plantation in Brazil for what was a pittance when compared with the sums at which her employer in Bergen and in other places was quoted on the stock market. So perhaps her smile wasn't that big after all. But the coffee was good, no two ways about that.

I poured myself a cup, took it with me to the computer, booted up and began to search for two people by the names of Svanhild and Astrid in Dag Hammarskjølds vei, 5144 Fyllingsdalen. I couldn't find an Astrid, but a Svanhild, surname Olsvik, appeared, with an address in what I thought was one of the high-rises by Fyllingsdalen Cemetery. She had a mobile phone and a landline. I jotted down both numbers.

While I was at it I searched for the surname Midtbø in Frekhaug. Only one name came up: Haldis Midtbø – she also had two telephone numbers. As I clearly had the wind behind me, I tried Haugen too. Per and Tora Haugen lived in Brunestykket, not far from Frøviken bay, where his body had been found. Here there was only a landline number. His brother-in-law, Hans, would have to wait, as I had only his Christian name.

Cup of coffee in hand, I stared out of the window. The snow lay like a bridal veil over Mount Rundemanen. Bryggen, on the other side of Vågen bay, was conspicuously deserted. The tourist season was months away and Bergensers had other things to do than go for a stroll. Most were probably doing what I was doing – staying indoors in heated offices, shops, or at home. Only the fittest were skiing in the nearest mountains.

I had several options to choose from. I could shut the office for the day, go home, fetch my skis from the cellar, carry them on my back and head for the hills as well. But I wouldn't make much money if I did that.

Or I could ring one of the phone numbers I had jotted down and blindly pursue an investigation no one had asked me to set in motion. I wouldn't earn much from this either, as I was my own employer. On the other hand, I had every reason to be on the alert. The failed bid to run me over the previous evening was still firmly in my mind. There could, for example, be a third way of engineering 'a natural death', even if a hit-and-run job would probably make the police sit up and take notice more than they had done in the Midtbø and Haugen cases.

I got to my feet, went over to the worktop and poured myself another coffee. When I sat down I opened the lowest drawer to the left and gave the bottle of aquavit a reassuring pat on the back. 'Out of sight, but not out of mind,' I said to it. But this wasn't a day for aquavit. Not yet.

I rang Svanhild Olsvik's home number. No answer.

I rang her mobile phone. She answered.

5

She didn't sound very friendly.

I told her who I was and said I had been asked to investigate her late partner's death.

She barked: 'Who by?'

'I can't tell you.'

'Hah! It'll be that bitch, I bet.'

'May I visit you at home?'

'Absolutely not.'

'Somewhere else then?'

'I can't see what the point is. It's more than a month since it happened, and the police closed the case ages ago.'

'Too early maybe?'

'Too early! What do you mean by that?'

'There are … a few loose ends. I can explain when we meet.'

'*If* we meet.'

'You must be interested in knowing what happened. Or…?'

'Or what?'

I could have answered: *Or perhaps you know already*. But I didn't. I said: 'You must've asked yourself a few questions afterwards, surely? And your daughter? How did she react to the drama?'

'You bloody keep my daughter right out of this!'

'By all means. It's you I want to talk to.'

'OK then. But it'll have to be somewhere with lots of people around. The café in the square inside Oasen. Could you be there in … half an hour?'

I did a quick mental calculation. 'I can jump on a bus. Give me a bit more time in case I'm unlucky with the schedule.'

'Three quarters of an hour. Not a second more.'

'And how…?'

But she had already hung up. I would have to hope I knew who she was when I got there.

In fact, catching a bus was the best option. I put my computer on standby, pulled out the plug of the kettle, slipped on my winter coat and rushed off. The services to Fyllingsdalen went through Olav Kyrres gate and I jumped on a bus at the last moment, so in fact I was able to alight by Oasen within the thirty minutes she had first suggested. I ran through the entrance by the office of the insurance company that had given me plenty of jobs, that was until a few years ago, when my contact moved to pastures new and the link was lost, which meant my financial status sank a few more notches.

A long corridor with a view into one of the supermarket chains in the mall led to the large square in the centre of the massive building. They had planted a few palm trees in large containers to give the impression that you were in the middle of the natural phenomenon the mall was named after. For me, the name Oasen had never appealed. Most of Fyllingsdalen was greener than the brick desert here. But then the shopping centre known as Lagunen was no sheltered idyll either. The choice of names for malls in the Bergen region owed more to a yearning for sunnier climes than what they were: overcrowded ant hills paying their dues to commercialism.

I stood at the entrance to the café that occupied a large part of the square and looked around, obviously searching for someone I knew – or didn't know. I met the gaze of a robust, dark-haired woman sitting in the middle of the room and wearing black glasses and black clothes, from her jumper to her velvet trousers. She glared at me and I seemed to recognise the voice on the phone in her eyes.

I looked at her with raised eyebrows and she returned a belligerent glare. It had to be her. 'Svanhild Olsvik?'

She nodded.

There was a free chair at her table. She had an empty cup of coffee in front of her. 'I'll go and get a coffee. Would you like a refill?'

She shook her head. 'I'll be off soon.'

'I won't be a moment.'

I joined the queue at the counter, poured myself a coffee from the machine and ended up behind an elderly Bergensian lady at the cash till. She was so immersed in her account of her grandchild's merits that I just elbowed in, threw the money on the counter and said to the listening head that she could keep whatever was left over, which she accepted absent-mindedly, sweeping the money into her apron pocket without even so much as a question as to whether I wanted a receipt.

I hurried back, coffee spilling into the saucer, sat down on the free chair and adopted my most charming expression. 'I apologise for bothering you during your working day.'

She shrugged. 'It's over.'

'What's your job?'

'Cleaning consultant,' she answered with a defiant look, in case I should be so bold as to call her job anything else. 'I can't understand why I'm talking to you.'

'I'll be as brief as possible. Let's get straight to the point. Your partner, Mikael Midtbø, died after falling from the tenth floor of the block where you live. The police have called it a suicide. Is that your view, too?'

Her face, if possible, stiffened even more. 'My view? What do you mean?'

'Well … that's quite a brutal way of taking your life. Most people would choose another method.'

'What do you mean? That he … ? That someone pushed him off?'

'Possibly.'

'Surely the police would've investigated the case further, wouldn't they? All they did was to talk to me – twice – and then nothing happened until I received a phone call telling me they'd decided it was suicide.'

'And you were happy with that?'

'If there was anyone who wanted to kill him it was that bitch, but he would've never let her in after all the trouble she's caused.'

'That bitch, as you call her. Are you referring to his ex-wife?'

'She was the one who started all the rumours about him. You can bet your bottom dollar she's the one who reported him to the police, too. She wanted to make sure she kept the kids. And to do that, she used the dirtiest of all the lies.'

Her face had loosened up now. Muscles twitched, her eyes wandered from side to side and her whole body was in motion. It was obvious that this was a matter that engaged her. She made a powerful impression in all ways. A large woman she may have been, but there was nothing flabby or limp about her. She seemed more like a bundle of muscle, a well-trained heavyweight wrestler. I could truly imagine the energy with which she set about the floors as a cleaning consultant.

'Right. Did they keep in touch?'

'Touch! He was banned from visiting his children. If he was ever seen near where they lived in Frekhaug, she would ring the police. And she never showed her face out here of course, as I was trying to tell you.' She shifted uneasily. 'But now I've got to go.'

'Wait a minute. If we assume the police are right – in other words, that it was suicide – did you notice anything that pointed in that direction, in the time before he died? Was he depressed, quick-tempered, unstable?'

She pulled a long face. 'Depressed, quick-tempered, unstable? You talk like a social worker.'

'Well...'

Then she appeared to remember something. Her expression changed, from aggressive to more thoughtful. 'Though something did change in him after he received a phone call.'

'A phone call? Who from?'

'"Do you believe in demons, Svanhild?" he said. "Get away," I said. "Demons?" "Yes," he said. "As much as I believe in the devil and hell," I said. Then Astrid came home from school and there was no more talk about that, until the evening when she'd gone to bed. "What did you mean about demons earlier today?" I asked him. Then he looked, like, well, scared and he said: "There's a pastor coming here tomorrow. He can help me," he said. "A pastor?" I said. "A bloody priest? What do you want with him?" "Well, he insisted," he said, and so I said he should just ring and cancel, but then he didn't want to talk about it any more. But I could see it was on his mind for the rest of the evening, even while we were watching a decent action film on TV. And the following day it happened.'

'He fell to his death?'

'Yes, but now I've really got to go. I must be at home when Astrid comes.'

'OK. Mm … did you tell the police this? About the phone call?'

'I don't remember. Maybe.' She stood up, took a big, dark-blue puffer jacket from the back of her chair and put it on. 'You'd better ask them.'

'Which school does your daughter go to? Løvås?'

She immediately leaned over me. Towering above me, her girth increased by the puffer jacket, with the nastiest expression I had seen since I was an army recruit, she made an even more aggressive impression than before, bordering on dangerous. 'That's got bugger-all to do with you. If you go anywhere near my daughter I'll fucking well report you. Have you got that?'

'Loud and clear,' I said. *Sergeant*, I added, in my head, but that was where it stayed. No reason for any slips of the tongue.

With long, bouncing strides she disappeared from the café and left in the same direction from which I had entered the mall. I stayed put and finally tasted the coffee, which had died a silent death in the meantime, and tasted like it.

But now I had something to chew on. I took out my notepad and wrote a single word on it: *Pastor*. After some deliberation I added a question mark. I wanted to know a bit more about him.

6

Emerging from the mall, I stopped and looked around. In many ways I liked the way Fyllingsdalen was organised. Possibly that had something to do with the expanse of flat space, but it was much better laid out than the district to the north of Bergen, Åsane. This local mall was within walking distance for quite a lot of the area's inhabitants. You could see them on their pilgrimages with their roller bags, all the elderly women – and some men – who had been to Oasen to shop or were on their way there. Young mothers with prams full of shopping and some students carrying plastic bags bulging with beer cans – and perhaps the odd soup packet or two – completed the picture.

The two high-rises by the cemetery towered up against the rear of Mount Løvstakken and the range of hills leading to the suburb of Krohnegården, and they were close enough for me to stroll along one of the paths in their direction. There was a chance I might fall victim to a flying tackle from Svanhild Olsvik, but I had to take that risk. After all, I was in a line of business where you had to be prepared to live dangerously.

When I arrived at the correct block, I took in the façade. This wasn't the first time I had been here. In the early seventies, while I was still in social welfare, I had visited a woman here – Johnny-boy's mother – who had been stripped of her parental rights. It wasn't a happy memory, and I quickly repressed it.

At the front of the building the balconies faced west. Once again it struck me that I would probably have chosen a less brutal form of suicide than jumping from the tenth storey to the ground, without even considering that a young mother might be passing by with a pram, according to what Solheim had told me.

In my mind I tried to imagine him lying on the ground and the extent of his injuries. Had he landed head first, which would have caused fatal damage? On his side? Or on his legs, with no chance of remaining upright, like a pole vaulter after an unassailable world record, forty metres up ... and down? A chill ran through me, at the mere thought of it.

He had asked his partner if she believed in demons. Was he afraid that he himself was possessed by them? Experience told me that people who felt they were possessed by demons could do the most gruesome things, to themselves and others. Was that what had happened? Had he heard a voice telling him to jump? Was this unknown guest, the pastor, the person who had evoked the demon, as some preachers were in the habit of doing, even in such enlightened times as our own? Was jumping the only way of exorcising the demon or silencing the voice? In which case, what was the legal position of the pastor? Would the police consider taking this further? Would I ... ?

While I was standing lost in thought, a little schoolgirl traipsed up the last part of the path from Løvåsen. She walked with her eyes staring downwards, dragging her feet, as though she had absolutely no desire to go where she was going. She was wearing a blue anorak with a leather collar and dark-brown trousers, possibly cords. On her back she was carrying a light-coloured faux-leather satchel.

As she came into the square she appeared to be walking even more slowly and she looked neither left nor right. There was a sullen, noticeably sad expression on her face. In front of me I saw a textbook victim of bullying on her way home from school, without a girlfriend, an outcast from the herd, with no one but adults to relate to.

I couldn't be sure, but the body shape and the way she walked reminded me of Svanhild Olsvik. Her gait was far from bouncy, but her body had the same robust frame, even though she was barely eight or nine years old.

I stood watching her. There was nothing to suggest she had noticed a man standing near her. When she reached the entrance to the block, she seemed to hesitate there too, ever so slightly. Then she raised her hand, opened the door and went in.

Through the glass in the door I watched her walk through and press a button by the lift. Shortly afterwards, the door opened, she stepped inside, the door closed again, and she rose, not exactly to heaven, at any rate not yet, and she wouldn't be going there with her mother at her side either, now that I recalled her mother's language.

Unconsciously, I raised my eyes as the lift rose. When I reached the tenth floor I caught a glimpse of a movement in one of the windows, a head darting back so as not to be seen. But she wasn't fast enough and I saw who it was.

Heaven would have to wait. I went back to Oasen.

7

Back in my office I flipped through the notes I had made during my visit to Fyllingsdalen. I sat looking at one word: *Pastor?* Beside it I had written: *Demons?*

I didn't discount the possibility that some preacher had convinced Mikael Midtbø that he was possessed by demons and that this was perhaps a good enough reason for him to throw himself into the abyss. Wasn't there, somewhere in the Bible, a story about Jesus delivering a man from a legion of evil spirits and transferring them into a herd of pigs that rushed down a steep bank into a lake and drowned? But more important than that, if this pastor were involved, could he be traced?

I took a risk, called the police and asked for Solheim. When he came to the phone, he said acidly: 'Veum? You didn't waste any time.'

'I have just one question. I was chatting to Svanhild Olsvik, Mikael Midtbø's partner.'

'Were you indeed?' His sarcasm almost scorched the line. 'Didn't Hamre tell you to steer clear of all this?'

'He did, but the way I see things, this case has a personal dimension now. Have you got the list of the Golfs in the Bergen area?'

'Not yet. But we've started the process.'

'My question is: did Svanhild Olsvik tell you about a pastor who had rung Mikael Midtbø and arranged to meet him the day before he died?'

He went silent. I could hear him tapping on his keyboard. 'No-o. There's nothing about it here anyway.'

'Right. She wasn't sure whether she'd told you or not. Don't you think this sounds interesting? Worth having a closer look?'

'A phone call from a pastor the day before Midtbø died? Well, I've made a note of it now. I'll confer with Hamre.'

'Would be great if you took it further. After all, your resources are much better than mine for things like this.'

'Tell me something we don't know, Veum.'

'Get Telenor to find the caller's number and the name of the caller.'

'You don't have to tell us how to do our jobs. I've made a note. Thank you.'

With that he hung up.

I continued to muse. It would be interesting to have a word with 'that bitch' in Frekhaug, that was if she was willing to talk to me. Strictly speaking, no one had commissioned me, apart from myself, which meant my enquiries had as much authority as a greenfly had at a gathering of crows.

I found the note I had made on Haldis Midtbø and called one of the two numbers – the mobile. There was a voicemail that said she couldn't take the call right now and asked me to leave a message. I tried the landline number, but there was no answerphone and the ringing went on and on until I twigged there was no reason to wait any longer. Then I called the mobile again and asked her to contact me.

I wasn't particularly optimistic about getting a response and I was right. She didn't call back.

I went back to the list of numbers I'd made earlier in the day. Tora Haugen answered after a few rings. Her voice sounded reedy and anxious. 'Yes, who is it?'

'The name's Veum. Am I talking to fru Tora Haugen?'

'Yes, but I'm not married. I'm a … widow.'

'Yes, I know. My condolences.'

'Thank you.'

I thought on my feet. 'I'm making some enquiries about your late husband's death.'

'Enquiries? Are you the police?'

'No, but I'm a kind of investigator. Private.'

'I see.' Her intonation didn't change. There was something monotonous, impersonal, about the way she spoke.

'Is there any chance I could have a chat with you? Face to face.'

'When?'

'Well, whenever is convenient for you.'

'Tomorrow morning, maybe.'

'OK, fine. I'll make a note. At around eleven?'

'Yes. Have you got my address?'

'Brunestykket. You're in one of the high-rises, aren't you?'

'Yes. On the second floor. You can ring downstairs.'

'Let's say that's arranged then.'

'Yes.'

We rang off. I made a note and hoped she had done the same.

Strategically, I realised there was no point in annoying Haldis Midtbø with another call now. I would give her until after working hours and think about trying her again in the evening.

Outside my windows darkness was beginning to fall. January is a lustreless month. The town still had Christmas decorations up, but it was as though all the glitter had lost its shine. The Christmas trees were dropping their needles, behind shopfronts staff were doing the stocktaking, Bergensians were either back at school or at work, and as for myself, I felt like a Christmas gift that had been returned to sender because of an incomplete address. Not many idle days have to pass before depression hits me like a low-pressure system from the west, and there is no shortage of those.

After celebrating Christmas and New Year with Sølvi and Helene I had decided to stay at home for a couple of days. Helena would soon be twelve and still hadn't completely come to terms with this man who came and went without any fixed routine. I could clearly see in her eyes that it wouldn't be long before I took the deceased father's place in her head or heart, or wherever it was deceased fathers resided.

Instead I went home and cooked myself a simple meal: pieces of chicken in a sweet-and-sour sauce. Afterwards I secured my skis to my back, walked to Proms gate and caught the Fløibane funicular. There was something liberating about living in Norway's second-biggest city and winter being only a seven-minute ride in a cable car away from ski slopes that waited discreetly for weeks after the last remnants of snow had disappeared from the streets of Bergen.

I usually walked up to Halvdan Griegs vei and branched off onto the floodlit trail. There, I could do two loops, an upper and a lower one. Apart from the danger of being sent flying by fitness-crazy business managers training for the Birken race or groups of local company staff who didn't go any further than the Kvamskogen circuit, at this time of the evening you could ski in fairly lonesome splendour up there among the snow-covered spruce trees. The cloud cover had broken and between the drifting clouds appeared a surprisingly large crescent of the moon, closer to the earth than at other times of the year. Once again it struck me that our loyal satellite probably saw more than most of us guessed. It was just a shame that it never revealed its secrets, but allowed us to find out everything on our own, as far as that was at all possible.

There was a virgin purity about the snowy countryside up there that filled my body with a composure it rarely felt – there was invariably an unanswered phone call to follow up.

I had skied halfway down towards the Skansemyre residential area before the snow became so thin that the undersides of even my old wooden skis began to suffer. I took them off and carried them on my back over the last section, past the sign saying that a competition had been organised on this ski-jumping hill in 1948, on Midsummer's Eve of all days; mind you, with snow transported from Finse, 1,222 metres above sea level. There were still some rocks sitting at the start position, recalling past fearless spirits, the memory of which would soon be preserved only by the sign down near the road.

Once at home, I took a shower, poured a glass of dark lager and a little snifter of aquavit and dialled Haldis Midtbø's number again. When she answered she sounded as amiable as Svanhild Olsvik had. It occurred to me that perhaps it was this kind of woman the men in their lives had preferred: dragons, as a friend of mine used to call them.

'Yes,' she barked.

'Good evening. I'm sorry to disturb you, but—'

'What was the name?'

'Veum. Varg Veum.'

'I don't want anything.'

'I left a message on your voicemail earlier today.'

'I don't respond to public surveys.'

'No, neither do I. Or at least it would have to be a very—'

Once again she interrupted me. 'Get to the point.'

'This concerns your late husband.'

'I have no late husband.'

'No? Well, I apologise. Of course I should've started by … Weren't you married to Mikael Midtbø?'

'My ex-husband.'

'Yes, but you do know that he's dead, don't you?'

'Let me make myself clear. This is a closed chapter in my life. Was there anything else?'

'You're aware of how he died?'

'I suppose he died like the pig he was.'

'After a fall from the tenth floor of—'

'Listen, whatever your name is…'

'Veum.'

'Veum, the pig I was married to caused me enough problems in my life. If he'd fallen from the tenth floor and I'd seen him, I'd have happily picked him up and thrown him off the tenth floor again.'

'Again?'

'What?'

'Thrown him off again? To me that sounds as if you were there when it happened.'

That silenced her, for a while anyway. Then came an ice-cold: 'What do you mean?'

It was my turn to weigh my words. 'Well, actually what I mean is … if you were willing to have a little chat with me … that at any rate would free you of any possible suspicion hanging over your head.'

'Suspicion? Tell me, who are you actually?'

'Varg Veum. I'm a private investigator.'

'Investigator?'

'Yes, with years of experience of child-abuse cases. I'm sure that's something you wouldn't mind talking to me about.'

Her voice changed tone. 'I see. But then it would have to be … No, the safest is probably that we … that you come here. To us, here at home. But it can't be before the children have gone to bed. Tomorrow, at around this time.'

'Nine o'clock?'

'Something like that. And, Veum … my husband will be here.'

'Your…?'

'My present husband.'

'I see. That's fine, of course. Then we have an arrangement.'

'Yes,' she replied curtly and rang off. It was only afterwards it struck me that she hadn't given me her address, but it would be online anyway, and I assumed it would be correct.

At this point I was fairly satisfied with the results of the day's activities. I had two appointments the following day, so I wasn't going to be idle then either. Because that was another hallmark of January: the month when everything went quiet, waiting for something to happen. In February, if not before.

8

The arrangement I had made with Tora Haugen was that I should be at hers at eleven. I left in good time, parked in Helleveien and ambled over to the characteristic high-rises of Brunestykket.

I remembered well seeing them being built. From Nordnes peninsula we could look straight out to the Helleneset headland. In the early sixties something was growing there that we had never seen before. 'They've got loads of them in Junaiten,' one of my former classmates told us – Piddien, who had been to sea for the first time, and was home after sixteen months and acted as if he were an old salt. 'Skyscrapers,' he added, significantly, and sent a long arc of spit in their direction. 'You can take a lift up to the top and see all the way to Nordnes, heh, heh.'

Later we heard credible rumours that these buildings were built in such a way that they swayed in the wind. We told each other we were the lucky ones, living safely in Fritznersmuget, or at a pinch in one of the new housing blocks that rose from the ruins after the war, and not in a house that could make you seasick. Anyway, they had lifts in the Seafarers' Care Home and the Troye building by Tollbodallmenningen, if that was what took our fancy.

The building site had been given the name Brunestykket, the 'brown bit', after a piece of land where local farmers never managed to get anything to grow. Situated on one of the town's windiest headlands, the location was not perfect. During the first years after they were built, there were reports of cladding coming loose in gales and storms, and rain seeping into the apartments. Later, quite a lot of repairs were done, apparently with variable success.

From the outside the blocks looked sturdy enough, at any rate, but then I had never been in one until now. I found the name P. Haugen beside one of the bells at the front and assumed the P stood for Per. The door was locked. I rang and waited for an answer. Surprisingly enough a man's deep voice answered, but before I could ask if I was in the right place, the lock buzzed and the same voice said: 'Come on up. We're on the second floor.'

I entered a large hallway with panoramic windows facing the sea. I had a choice between the lift and stairs. As I was only going to the second floor I took the staircase.

The man waiting for me in the doorway was wearing dark-grey trousers and a red-checked shirt under a dark-blue cardigan. He was in his stockinged feet and definitely gave the impression he belonged there. I guessed he was around my age, perhaps a few years older. He had dark, combed-back hair with long streaks of grey. The deep folds on both sides of his broad mouth evoked comparisons with a congenial bloodhound. He stood there with a patient, but not unfriendly, expression on his face, waiting for me to reach the landing.

On my way up the last steps, I slowed down and said: 'I have a meeting with Tora Haugen.'

He nodded. 'I know. I'm her brother. She's not so keen on meeting strangers any more.' When I reached the top he extended a hand. 'Hans Storebø.' His dialect placed him in the coastal area to the west of Bergen – Øygarden or further south.

We shook hands. 'Varg Veum.'

'Interesting name. Tora said you were an investigator.'

'That's correct.'

'For the police?'

'No. Private.'

He arched big, bushy eyebrows the same colour as his hair. 'Really? This is about my brother-in-law, is it?'

I confirmed it was and looked towards the doorway behind him.

He took the hint and half turned. 'Yes, do come in.'

He pointed to a coat stand inside the door where I could hang my jacket. I followed his example and slipped off my shoes, quickly checking that I hadn't put on the socks with toe ventilation this morning, and followed him through the narrow hallway, a round mirror on one side and cupboard doors on the other. Before we entered the sitting room he turned to me and said in a low voice: 'She's been deeply affected by this situation. She might seem a little incoherent.'

'I see.'

'She's having a thorough medical examination later this week, but, well, there's some reason for concern.'

I nodded without saying anything and we continued inside.

The windows in the slightly old-fashioned sitting room faced Byfjord to the south-west, so that you could see, in widescreen format and over a large distance, the rainclouds this morning's radio weather forecast had promised us for later in the day. The dark teak furniture with rose patterns in discreet colours gave an impression of the thirties rather than the sixties, so I assumed the Haugens had brought the furniture from somewhere else, either when the building was new or at a later point.

A table was set with coffee and pastries for three. There was a small selection of cakes and biscuits in a glass stemmed dish in the middle of the table. Tora Haugen resembled a little bird, sitting, slightly stooped, at the end of the table. She looked up anxiously as we entered. She was dressed in black and white: black trousers and a white cotton sweater. Her face was narrow and lean, her hair completely white. If her brother looked like a bloodhound, she reminded me of an anaemic lap dog, barely able to raise its head to look at us.

Hans Storebø showed me in, and when he talked to his sister it was with clear diction and more slowly than he had spoken to me. 'This is herr Veum, Tora. He's come to ask you a few questions.'

'Oh?' she said, seeming a little surprised.

'We spoke on the phone yesterday,' I said amiably.

'Ah …' She thought for a moment. 'That's true. Please take a seat.'

I established that she was one of the last survivors of the time when Norwegians used the polite form of address and told myself I would have to try and adapt.

'A cup of coffee?' Storebø asked, taking a white Thermos flask from the table. I nodded and he filled three cups. Another glance. 'Sugar? Cream?'

'No, thank you.'

He put a splash of cream in his sister's cup, used a pair of tongs to put two sugar cubes in his own, and we sat down on either side of Tora Haugen, him with his back to the window, me facing the view. It was impressive even in grey weather. I could just imagine what it would be like from the top floor.

Storebø focused on me again. 'What was it you wanted to know, Veum?'

'Well…' I shared my attention between the two of them. Tora Haugen still looked surprised, as though she didn't quite understand who I was or what I was doing here. 'I wanted to ask about the circumstances of her husband's death.' I looked straight at her. 'Your husband died suddenly, didn't he? There were no warning signs?'

She continued to look at me. Then she nodded gently. 'Yes, Per's dead.' She appeared to be pensive. 'He died on me. When was it again?' She gazed at her brother.

'In October, Tora,' he said with a fleeting glance in my direction.

'Yes, that's what I have noted down, too.' I nodded emphatically. 'My condolences.'

The shadow of a smile flitted across her face and was gone as quickly as it had come. 'He was buried in Biskopshavn. That's our church.'

Hans Storebø nodded in agreement, but without saying a word.

'But when he died … My understanding was that it was early in the morning and that he … That they found him down by the sea?'

She looked at me with big, light-blue eyes. 'He was Sjur Gabriel.'

Now it was my turn to look surprised. 'By which you mean?' I had slipped into the informal form and corrected myself.

Her brother coughed. 'What she means is … I don't know how well acquainted you are with Amalie Skram's *The Hellemyr People*, Veum.'

'Well, we read it at school.'

'Yes, I suppose most people in this part of the country did. So of course you know it comprises four classic novels. But it's said that

Amalie Skram had living models for the characters of Sjur Gabriel and Oline Hellemyren. They're supposed to have lived not far from here, up in what we call Fagerdalen nowadays. Even now you can see the remains of Olaplassen – the small farm they lived in. And they probably had their boatshed down in what's known as Frøviken, where my brother-in-law regularly used to go fishing in the morning. Just like Sjur Gabriel in the books, although he fished in the fjord. Still, that's what she means. He never went out during the rest of the day. She had to go to the shop, however heavy her bags were. Well, I tried to give her a hand, but I don't live in town, do I, so…'

'Was it like that for many years? Him not going out, I mean.'

'No. It started with the case a couple of years ago, as you know yourself, otherwise you wouldn't be here, I suppose.'

I nodded. 'He isolated himself, in other words?'

'Yes. People stared at him. They obviously knew who he was and what he'd done, most of them. That sort of thing spreads through a community in no time at all. Before that, he was the outgoing type, kind to everyone, big and … small.' The last word came after some hesitation, as though he didn't want to go too deeply into that side of things.

'And then he was found in Frøviken – he'd either drowned or had a turn, I was told.'

'Yes. They couldn't say what came first, but I think they said the most likely scenario was that he'd had a turn, perhaps a heart attack, and fell into the sea. And then he drowned.'

I looked at Tora Haugen. She was gazing at the fjord with a faraway expression in her eyes, as though she hadn't been following what we had been saying.

I lowered my voice and said: 'Do you know if he'd received any threats? Leading up to the incident.'

He sighed. 'Well, he didn't say anything. And as far as I know, there was nothing in writing either. I've been through her papers and haven't found anything there.'

I faced Tora again. 'Fru Haugen,' I said to catch her attention, and she turned meekly in my direction. 'Tora … Fru Haugen, can you remember if you received a visit before your husband ... died? An unexpected visitor? Or someone you didn't know?'

'My husband? What do you mean?' She looked to the side. 'He's gone now, Per has. He won't be coming back.'

I looked at Storebø again, and he sent me an eloquent look back while vaguely nodding and gesturing with one hand, a movement he completed by grasping the coffee cup, raising it to his mouth and taking the last sip.

He set down the cup, glanced at me and said: 'Bit more, Veum?'

'No, thanks. I think that's enough. Mm ... a pastor. Does that ring any bells?'

He looked at me in surprise. 'A pastor? The parish priest, do you mean? He officiated when Per was buried. He'd been here and talked to Tora, but I was present too. Beyond that I have no idea what you're after.'

'Alright. You might not know ... your brother-in-law's death is not the only one this autumn. One of his co-accused suffered the same fate.'

'Really? No, I didn't know.'

'And he was a much younger man, not yet forty.'

He looked serious. 'Yes, life can take many turns if you don't know how to steer it.'

I glanced quickly at Tora before concentrating on him again. 'I was wondering ... I'd like to go to Frøviken to see where he was found. Would you be interested in joining me?' As he appeared to hesitate, I said in a hushed voice: 'There are a few things we perhaps ought to talk about without her present.'

He studied me thoughtfully. Then he nodded. 'Yes, I understand. Of course I'll join you.' He pulled his chair back from the table and stood up. In a loud, clear voice he addressed his sister again: 'I'm going for a little walk with herr Veum, Tora. We won't be long. I'll be back soon.'

'That's fine,' she said in the same delicate tone she'd had all the time. It was like a child's voice, as though the elderly woman was returning to where she had once been, a time of innocence far from all the trivialities of the day and life's many turns, to which her brother had just referred.

I stood up, but she remained seated. I shook her hand before leaving. It was a limp handshake, as if life was ebbing out of her, with a kind of resigned serenity, the way some people are when their partner has died and they themselves will soon follow.

Without another word Hans Storebø and I walked together to the hallway. We shared a shoe horn and put on our outdoor clothes, then strolled down the stairs and out.

9

As soon as we were outside the building, I said to Hans Storebø: 'There are a number of unanswered questions that I thought we might run through without your sister being present.'

'I understand.'

'I never met Per Haugen. But I know of his case. Can you give me a picture of the person he was?'

He showed visible signs of disapproval. 'Let me put it like this, Veum. When he was alive, as time went on, I had very little to do with my brother-in-law. It would perhaps be more correct to say there was no contact at all. It's only now, after his death, that I have proper contact with Tora again.'

'And the reason for the break was…?'

'Well, we were very different types. I felt that early on. Nevertheless … it was only when all this came up that I saw behind his façade. There was something calculating, something distant about the way he treated people. His children … he didn't seem to have a relationship with them, either. It was mostly Tora who took care of everything … at home and otherwise.'

'There are two children, I gather.'

He motioned with his head for us to start walking. We did, and then he answered: 'Yes. Knut and Laila. They moved out of the family home years ago.'

'I didn't see their names in the obituary.'

'No, and there are reasons for that, of course.'

'The daughter testified against her father in court and described how he abused her when she was young.'

'Yes, that was tragic to hear.'

'Were you in court?'

'Yes, but only with the utmost reluctance. I felt I had to support my sister. This was, as you can imagine, a desperate situation for her. Behind the stiff mask, the man was a swine, basically. They said Laila's testimony was past the statute of limitations, so it had no significance for the outcome of the case.'

'Yes, I heard.'

We had reached the point where the border between Bergen and Åsane had been until the two municipalities merged in 1972. From here we looked up Fagerdalen valley. Some way up the long straight you could still glimpse the old path above the hills to the town. Directly in front of us was the lake known as Hellevete, after the modest mountain behind it, a name local people soon changed to Helvete – 'Hell'.

We paused there.

'My sister and I had a rather special upbringing, Veum.'

'Oh, yes?'

'The first year of our lives was spent in Telavåg. In 1942, when the Germans razed villages and arrested all the men aged between sixteen and sixty, Mum, Tora and I were first sent to Storetveit and then to Framnes in the Hardanger region. Dad died in Sachsenhausen in 1944, and Mum was never the same again. Tora was also marked by this.' He raised his voice. 'I would've wished her a better husband than Per Haugen.'

I allowed the gravity of what Hans told me to sink in before I continued, gently. 'But … if there was sexual abuse going on in the family home how could Tora not have noticed?'

He scanned the flat, grey surface of the lake. On the northern side of the water there was a private dwelling-cum-storehouse. Further in, towards the valley, were the buildings of a big timber company. Then he turned back to me. 'Tora's a simple soul. I think it was very easy for her not to see what was going on under her nose. She believed in the goodness of people, even after Telavåg.'

'And the children … ?'

'As I said before, they moved out as soon as they could.'

'Are you in contact with them?'

'No, I'm afraid not. It's Tora I'm in contact with, and there's no communication between her and the children any more. It's an utterly tragic situation. I'd like to meet them, but … it is as it is.'

'Do you know what they do for a living?'

'I think Knut's followed in his father's footsteps. He works for a computer company, from what I understand. Wife and children. Laila, she … I'm not sure. She was some sort of model when she was younger.'

'A model?'

'Yes, the kind you see advertising women's clothes and suchlike. Local stuff. She may've done catwalk modelling as well. Then she got married, but what her surname is I have no idea.'

'That won't be difficult to find out.'

'I'm sure it won't.'

Slowly we made our way towards the headland. Soon we came to a side road sloping down towards Frøviken.

'What do you do, Storebø?'

'Nothing to shout about. I have a little farm. Some sheep. I'm alone, so that's good enough for me.'

'In Telavåg?'

'No, we never went back. Further south, towards Klokkarvik.'

'And your brother-in-law? You said Knut was following in his footsteps?'

'Well, in a way, yes. He ran a small electronics company, in town. Not much to shout about either, but it made ends meet.'

'And Tora?'

'She was a housewife when the children were small. Later she worked on a till at a supermarket in Sandviken.'

We were almost down by the sea now. Frøviken had been a popular bathing resort before the war and Bergen Swimming Club had had a hut on the Midtnes promontory in the south of the bay. Now some concrete steps and a single concrete pillar were all that was left of it. The slopes around were overgrown and there was little to remind anyone that once upon a time this had been a small marina.

We were almost down by the water's edge. From here we could see across to Herdle fjord, which lay grey and apparently lifeless between the island communities of Askøy and Holsnøy. There wasn't a lot of traffic on the fjord on a Tuesday morning at the beginning of January, only a little cargo boat chugging alongside the land north of Florvåg, heading for Bergen.

'This is where he was found, I'm told, isn't it?'

'Yes. I don't know any more than what I heard afterwards. But apparently another fisherman found him. I say, fisherman; they were both hobby fishermen, anglers, I suppose. Per had never shown much enthusiasm before, but after he was released from prison it was about the only thing he was interested in. Tora said he got up early in the morning, took his fishing rod and a couple of empty plastic bags for the catch, and after a few hours, never later than eight, he came home, usually with cod and podleys in his bags.'

'This second man, was he a neighbour?'

Hans shrugged. 'Someone from the district anyway. When he got here Per was lying on the shingle on the beach, head down in the water, so the man knew at once there'd been an accident. He pulled him out and rang A&E. An ambulance arrived quickly, but they said straightaway there was nothing they could do. He was dead.'

'You don't know the name of this man?'

'No.'

There was a sadness about Hans Storebø as he stood there gazing at the bay where his brother-in-law had lost his life a few months before. But it appeared it wasn't the thought of Per Haugen that was making him sad. It was more the thought of a wasted life, a life lived at the expense of others, scarring those who were exposed to him and survived.

Then he turned to face me again. 'You didn't say … What's your angle in all of this? Has someone commissioned you?'

'I can't answer that.'

'But … does someone suspect there's been an, erm, a criminal act here? That his death wasn't natural?'

'I'm afraid I can't answer that, either. But, as I told you before, there's

been another death this autumn, another man who was found guilty
... of the same crime. Some people think there may be a connection
between these deaths. That's about it.'

He studied me. 'And one of these people is you?'

'Among other things.'

'Well...' He flung out his arms. 'Don't let me stand in your way. If
you find someone did it with intent ... you should give him a medal, if
you ask me.' He spat symbolically into the sea. 'Nobody's missed him.
There was hardly anyone at the funeral. Tora, me, a few neighbours.'

'And the parish priest.'

'Yes, naturally enough.' He eyed me with surprise. 'Of course the
priest was there.'

'Perhaps I can have a little chat with him, too.'

'Doubt you'll get much out of it, but ... go ahead.' He raised his arm
and looked at his wristwatch. 'Now, I'm afraid I'll have to get back to
Tora. I have to see if there's any shopping I can do for her. She has her
lunch delivered to the door by her home help, but she may want something from the shops, too.'

'Many thanks for taking the time to talk to me. It was a useful chat.'

'Keep me posted if you find anything out.'

'Will do.'

We walked together into Helleveien. I got into my car parked by the
block of flats in Brunestykket. He disappeared into the building. I sat
for a while looking at the door, half expecting him to reappear, like a
jack-in-a-box.

But he didn't. I started the car and pointed my nose towards town.
I hadn't thought so far ahead. They might not have a pastor in Biskopshavn church, but they did have a parish priest. And they kept office
hours, didn't they?

10

Biskopshavn Church was built in 1966, doubtless to meet the need for ecclesiastic activity among the fast-growing population of Ytre Sandviken in the 1950s and 1960s. It was shaped like a boatshed and perched attractively on the top of a crag above the actual Biskopshavn, the bishop's harbour, which was mentioned as early as in the 1200s, in Snorre's kings' sagas.

The parish registry was in the east of the church, attached to the large vestry. The priest, Bjarte Nyland, turned out to be an easy-going fellow of my age with a white Father Christmas beard, thick hair and a friendly smile. He showed me into his office. We sat down on a small sofa by a nest of tables with just enough room for the two cups of coffee he had brought with him from the secretarial office.

'How can I help you, Veum?' he asked in a sonorous tone, which must have sounded good from the pulpit.

'I'm investigating a death. A person by the name of Per Haugen, for whom you performed the funeral in October.'

His face became serious. 'Yes, I won't forget that one in a hurry. At funerals you do occasionally talk to an almost empty room, but then they're solitary individuals, life's lost sheep, people who have often lived in the most abject loneliness, unseen, unnoticed by anyone.' He looked at me, as if to make sure I understood what he was talking about. To confirm I had, I nodded. 'What is unusual in this case was that he did have a family. A wife, children, grandchildren...' He stretched for the coffee cup. 'No contact with any of them. Well, apart from his wife, that is.'

He raised the coffee cup to his mouth and took a sip.

'I don't know if anyone explained the background to you?'

He set the cup down again and nodded. 'Yes, one of the employees here told me. Neither of them was a regular churchgoer, so they were new to me.' He paused. 'I tried discreetly to ask his wife if there was anything she wanted to talk to me about – as we do on such occasions: ask if there's anything people want the priest to emphasise in his speech. Personal memories, something about the deceased's character and personality. But there was nothing. She was very upset by the death, it seemed, and the result was an extremely brief mention of Haugen before we went on with the standard texts and rounded off the ceremony. She didn't even want to choose the psalms, so the organist and I selected some of the more usual ones.'

'There weren't many people in church, I understand.'

'No. Fru Haugen had her brother with her, fortunately. He seemed like a reliable sort. Otherwise there was no one from the family. Just a few others. A couple of neighbours perhaps. An ex-colleague.' He smiled wryly. 'We don't exactly do a roll-call, so this is just my interpretation of who they might've been.'

It was my turn to taste the coffee.

'You're a private investigator, you said. Does this mean that there's something suspicious about the death?'

'Let me put it like this: there have been two deaths among three men convicted of possessing sexual images of children. These are cases that arouse strong emotions in people. Child abuse – you can hardly imagine anything worse.'

'No.' He looked at me sadly. 'It's so far from what we can imagine. Have you got any children?'

'A grown-up son and a small grandchild. But they live in Oslo.'

'As a priest you have an insight into so many lives. Even if we have no Catholic customs such as confession in the Norwegian church, it does happen that some people come to the priest with their confessions. If you have no one else to confide in, a priest may be the very last resort. During my career I've met people with a need to confess something or other. Some of them have admitted the kind of thing we're talking about now. Their urges were simply too strong for them and they preyed on children who were close to them. Their own, the neighbours', the children they met in connection with sport, a variety of situations. But precisely because of the closeness to the victims it's harder to bear when it – in some cases – comes out. Imagine a small village or a suburb of a town, a sports team. You're exposed forever. You'll never be the same again, neither in your own, nor in others' eyes. For many there's only one way out.' He heaved a sigh and said no more.

'You're referring to … suicide?'

He nodded.

'And that might also be what happened to Haugen?'

'Quite possibly.'

'Of course you have a point. But the circumstances and this second death … I don't know … In fact it's described as suicide by the police. In Haugen's case the incident was shelved as an accident. My problem is, however, that I think these two deaths are conspicuously close in time, and there may be a common motive behind both of them.'

'*Thou hast seen all their vengeance.*'

'What?'

'Lamentations: chapter three, verse sixty.'

'Exactly. As I said earlier. Strong emotions.'

'But I don't think I can help you in this particular case, Veum.'

'Never mind. Thank you for your time.'

On my way out of Biskopshavn Church and down to where I had parked the Corolla I drew a black line through my hypothesis that Bjarte Nyland could be the unknown pastor in this, for the time being, somewhat nebulous mystery. I would have to pursue my investigations elsewhere. Top of the list was Per Haugen's children.

11

Over the last decade, tracing people had become much easier than it once was. It was no longer necessary to have a good friend at the national registration office. You could go a long way with a co-operative computer and a talent for finding your way through the many labyrinthine highways and byways of the internet.

I drove back to Bergen, left my car in the multi-storey car park in Markeveien, walked down to the office and started my search.

In those cases where I had people's full names it was even easier. I knew the son's name: Knut Haugen. The sister's name was Laila. According to their uncle she had married, but he didn't know if she'd taken her husband's name.

I searched the Yellow Pages for Knut Haugen. I found only one person in Bergen with that name. The address was Nystuveien, on the mountain above Bellevue. I tried searching 'Knut Haugen' and 'IT'. This gave me several hits. Knut Haugen appeared as the general manager of the IT company BI-IT. It had a chic logo and the text said the first two letters stood for Bergen International. On one webpage showing impressive yearly results his face was wreathed in a broad smile. On another he looked at least as pleased after signing a new contract with a big concern in the health service, and on a third he was giving a thumbs-up to the appointment of a creative, young games developer. There, he was mentioned as an investor and the company name was different. I confidently assumed this was my man. I noted down the street number in Nystuveien and the office address of the company, in Bryggen.

Then I searched several sources for a Laila Haugen in the local area, without any luck. I tried her mother's name, in case she had taken it, but with no luck there, either. So I would have to hope her brother could help, and aimed for a meeting with him initially.

As I was finishing my searches the telephone rang. I picked up and said: 'Hello, Veum here.'

No one answered.

'Hello? Anyone there?'

All I could hear was a car horn in the background, as if the caller was in the traffic somewhere. Then the line went dead.

I looked at the phone display. There was a short message: 'Unknown number'.

I shrugged and put the phone back in my pocket with a slightly queasy sensation in my stomach. But I ignored it and continued what I was doing.

There was still a good deal of the day left before my appointment with Haldis Midtbø in Frekhaug. I had a suspicion Knut Haugen was unlikely to be willing to talk about his father. In my experience, in cases such as his, making prior arrangements met with little success. A direct approach would be more effective, and Bryggen was close enough for me to see it from my office.

At the end of the nineteenth century the town council decided that all of Bryggen – or Tyskebryggen, 'German Wharf', as it was called at that time – should be demolished and replaced with tall brick buildings in the architectural style of Lübeck. When large parts of Bergen centre burned down in January 1916 they had got as far as Nikolaikirkeallmenningen. Then they had to employ all their construction capacity to rebuild the razed areas in the centre. This prevented the rest of Bryggen from being demolished before 1920. The timber houses stayed put.

BI-IT resided in one of the brick buildings between Nikolaikirkeallmenningen and the Hanseatic Museum. I found the company name on the list of the tenants facing the street. They were on the second floor and to maintain my fitness I took the stairs up.

A solid wooden door with a neatly carved rhombus pattern on the front panel led into the company premises, but the door was locked, and I had to ring a bell to contact them.

A woman's voice came over the loudspeaker above the doorbells. 'Yes?'

I said, 'Veum here,' which was true. And it turned out to be enough. The lock buzzed, I pressed the handle, opened the door and went in.

I entered an elegant reception area that was more reminiscent of a shipping company than an IT business. The furniture for visitors was, if not Louis Seize, then definitely King Oscar II of Sweden, not that I would claim to know anything at all about that sort of thing. At any rate it looked very exclusive.

The person I assumed owned the voice was a woman in her late twenties with close-cropped fair hair and frameless glasses with thin steel arms. She was dressed in what some Norwegians after the turn of the millennium called *casual*: faded denim jeans decorated with what looked like small diamonds, hopefully made of glass, and a loose, waisted blouse in light-coloured cotton with a very discreet neckline that revealed none of what was inside. She had no visible workplace in the office, but stood waiting for me in the middle of the floor. 'The name was … ?' she said, looking at me with big blue eyes from behind the lenses.

'Veum. Knut Haugen, is he in?'

She sent me a measured look. 'Have you got an appointment?'

'No, but I won't be long.'

'And this is about … ?'

I smiled disarmingly. 'That's a little too complicated to explain.'

Her expression altered from measured to sceptical. 'Then I think you should contact him in some other way. By email or something like that.'

'It's about his family.'

'Really?'

'I think I'll have to explain it to him personally.'

She appeared to be thinking. Then she said: 'Well, wait here and I'll find out.'

She disappeared down the corridor and I waited. Some ancient sea charts hung on the walls, which gave me an even stronger sense of being in a shipping office. Perhaps it had been one once and they had simply taken it over. There was a lot to suggest that growth in IT was greater than in shipping at the moment.

She returned with a man I recognised from the photos I had seen on the net. He was around forty, dressed in a dark suit, white shirt and tie, like an estate agent or a financial consultant. His hair was short, his face quite square, his body rounded, and when he came over to me I could confirm he was no more than 1.70 metres in height.

Our eyes met. He regarded me in a way that betrayed no emotion. 'What's this about?'

The woman still stood beside him. I gestured in her direction. 'I don't know if your colleague said?'

He shook his head.

'I think we should discuss this in private.'

His face, if possible, became even squarer, as though his jaw muscles were tensed to repel reality.

The woman immediately excused herself. 'Don't let me stand in your way.' She flashed a quick smile at Haugen, ignored me and disappeared into an office to the left of the entrance, closing the door behind her. However, it was made of glass and I saw her sit down behind a desk and signal with one quick glance that she knew how to talk straight if anything untoward happened out here.

Knut Haugen narrowed his eyes and squinted ominously. 'What was the name, did you say?'

'Veum. Varg Veum. I'm a private investigator.'

His lips seemed to turn inwards, making his mouth one thin, compressed line. Sound emerged only with difficulty. 'Private investigator?'

'I'm carrying out investigations regarding your father's death.'

The familiar refrain was repeated. 'Investigations? On whose behalf, may I ask?'

'I'm afraid I can't say.'

'Then we have nothing to talk about.'

I took a short cut. 'No? You'd rather have the police on your doorstep, would you?'

'The police!' For a moment he seemed almost angry.

'You know very well your father was investigated and even served time recently.'

His eyes narrowed even further, if possible. He became more and more reminiscent of a stick drawing. Two horizontal lines at the top, one under his nose, square head, not a circle. His voice sounded compressed as well. 'I haven't had any contact with my father for many years.'

'No. So I understand. Neither your name, nor your sister's, was in the obituary.'

'Keep my sister out of this!'

'What—?'

'She's suffered enough as it is.'

I flashed a look down the corridor behind him. 'Why don't we sit down and chat about this more comfortably?'

'I have nothing to…'

A man came from another office into the corridor. He walked in our direction, then turned into a side room through an open door, with a quick glance at us. Straight afterwards we heard the sound of a photocopier starting up.

Haugen stopped talking. He looked sullenly at me. 'Alright then. Fifteen minutes. Not a second more.' He spun on his heel and set off for his office without beckoning me to follow.

I did anyway. He walked ahead of me into his office, strode over to the desk and sat down, with his back to the magnificent view across Vågen to my office. If we got to know each other better, we could stand in our windows and wave to each other.

He didn't say I could sit down in one of the chairs facing him, but I took the liberty. I knew that, here, there was no time to lose.

'Your father…'

'As I told you outside, I haven't had any contact with either of my parents in twenty years, since I left for the military.'

'No contact at all? Not even with your mother?'

'No.'

'And what was the reason for that?'

'That's got nothing to do with you or anyone else.'

'Haugen, the point is that I haven't come to this meeting completely unprepared.'

'We are not in a meeting.'

I ignored his objection. 'Your sister testified against your father in court.'

'They forced her to.'

'Forced? Who did?'

He flung up his arms. 'The police! The prosecution counsel. How the hell do I know?'

'She testified anyway.'

'It caused her even more harm.'

'What do you mean?'

'He's done a spell inside, you say? For what and for how long? He's … he was already out on the bloody street again this summer.'

'Your sister's case was considered past the statute of limitations.'

'Yes, right. The statute of limitations. A ruined life – can that ever be past the statute of limitations? I don't doubt that his defence counsel had a few things to say. But he wasn't the victim here.'

'Neither was—'

'There were many others. Real victims.'

'And do you consider yourself one of them?'

He jumped up from his chair. 'Me? I wasn't … I had nothing to do with them any longer.'

'But before that? Before you moved out?'

He turned to the side and looked across the bay. Out there was *Statsraad Lehmkuhl,* the stately three-masted barque, at the quay. Further out we could glimpse Skolten, the cruise-ship terminal, and the tip of Nordnes, the gateway to Vågen, one side fronted with old warehouses, the other with functionalist buildings from the 1920s.

He seemed to be considering his answer. Then he turned to me again. 'Both my sister and I moved out as soon as we were old enough. My father … Well, yes. And my mother must've been blind. We have no reason to thank them, either of us. Was there anything else?'

'Do you know how your father died?'

'I heard he'd drowned, but that didn't cause me to have a nervous breakdown.'

'Who told you?'

'The police. They rang me.'

'And what did they say?'

'Just that. He'd drowned. I don't know if it was my mother or my uncle who'd told them we no longer had anything to do with them. They knew about my sister's case. They asked me a few questions, but to me this all seemed to be a matter of form. They clearly didn't have any suspicion that this was anything other than an accident.'

'And what do you think?'

He quickly ran his tongue over his lips, pinched his mouth and stared stiffly at me. In the end, he said: 'If someone smashed the guy over the head with a hard object and threw him into the sea, they should be given a reward.' It struck me that he was repeating what Hans Storebø had said earlier in the day, if not word for word. It confirmed more or less what I had suspected: there was more than one person wanting to dance on Per Haugen's grave rather than shed tears over his demise. If I had to draw up a list of suspects I was afraid it would be very long, much longer than I had the capacity to cover.

He looked at his watch demonstratively and stood up. 'And now our time's up.'

I realised I wasn't going to get a great deal more out of him. Before leaving, I asked: 'Your sister … What's her surname?'

'Keep her out of this, I said.'

We stood staring at each other. I didn't budge an inch.

Once again he flung up his arms. 'Bratteli. Now just clear off, will you.'

I followed his advice and cleared off. I waved to the woman in the secretarial office, but she didn't wave back. I didn't feel very popular either. About the same as Per Haugen, I thought. But for completely different reasons.

12

Back in the office, I booted up the computer and began a search for Laila Bratteli. All I found was an address and a mobile phone number. Apart from that, she was completely off the news radar, at least on the net and by name. When I looked for discussion of the court case in local newspapers I found her referred to twice, but only as 'the grown-up daughter of Per Haugen' who had 'made serious accusations against her father of abusing her sexually and from a very young age'.

Her address was Adolph Bergs vei in Landås. I rang her phone number. She answered, but didn't say anything. In the background I could hear what I thought was the sound of a radio and one of the extremely wearing advertising channels.

'Hello? Laila Bratteli? Are you there?'

Then the line went dead.

I dialled the number again, but now she wouldn't answer. The phone just rang and rang. There wasn't even an answerphone message. Perhaps she only replied to voices she recognised. At any rate she didn't want to talk to me.

I could do what I usually did: take the cheeky approach – go and ring her doorbell. If nothing else, at least I would find out where she lived. There wasn't a lot else to do before my trip to Frekhaug that evening.

I nodded to the woman at the hotel reception desk I had to pass in order to leave the building or access my office after the recent renovation work. She smiled back cheerfully. I had no idea what they thought of me. Probably they took me for a hobgoblin, the kind that comes with a house and you never get rid of.

I went to my car in Markeveien and drove to Landås. Once there I parked in Chicago. The old nickname from the 1950s and 1960s for the lower end of Adolph Bergs vei was still used, at least by people of my age. In earlier decades the clientele had been of the more motley variety, although the colour tended more towards grey. During my social-welfare years it wasn't that uncommon for us to come out here after expressions of concern from neighbours or teachers. More often than not we sorted out the situation without too drastic an encroachment on their everyday life. Now my impression of the street was that the arrival of our new Norwegians was evident in a more colourful way than in most other places in town. Vibrant hijabs brightened up the street in a totally different way from the earlier residents' headwear or lack of similar.

The three blocks of flats differed architecturally from most of the others in Bergen. The flats each had two floors and there were entrances to them either from street level or via an external gallery on the second floor. A staircase at each end led up to the gallery. I found the right street number, but searched in vain for a Laila Bratteli on any of the lists of residents. Most of the names were foreign too. I walked from door to door reading the nameplates. On the second floor there was a door without any sign at all, only an empty holder where the name could be slid in. From the half-open window of the neighbouring flat issued the unmistakeable smell of oriental spices, and I felt my stomach rumble, reminding me that I hadn't eaten anything since the biscuits at Tora Haugen's earlier in the day.

I stood in front of the anonymous door. I turned my head and placed my better ear against it, in the hope that I might recognise the radio noises I had heard on the phone before. Not a sound reached me.

There was only one thing to do. I rang the doorbell, but I didn't hear anything this time, either. It wouldn't have surprised me if it had been disconnected. Laila Bratteli clearly did whatever she could to avoid confronting circumstances over which she had no control.

While I was there I dialled her phone number. Again I put my ear to the door, but I couldn't hear any ringing sounds inside. In the end I tapped on the door with my knuckles, tentatively at first, then I knocked harder and with increasing volume.

This time I provoked a reaction, but not the one I had been expecting. The door of the next-door flat opened. A dark-skinned man with a black beard, glistening hair of the same hue, large metal-framed glasses, red shirt and dark-brown trousers appeared in the doorway. 'Now you people just leave the poor woman in peace! If not, I'll call the police.' He spoke Norwegian with only a tiny suggestion of an accent.

'I've never been here before. Have other people tried to talk to her?'

'Tried? They're here at all hours, but she refuses to open up. And we know who's probably behind it. It's her ex-husband. He never gives up.'

'My name's Veum. Varg Veum. I haven't come here to bother her.'

'Ghulam Mohammed,' he said, with a slight bow of the head.

'Do you have any contact with her? Laila Bratteli?'

'Not me. But my wife, Fatima, does. The two of them talk. They have a cup of tea together now and then, at the mall. Not often, but a few times a month maybe.'

'Is your wife in now?'

'No, she's in town, shopping.'

'If I come back later today, or tomorrow, could I have a few words with your wife?'

He eyed me sceptically. 'I don't know. I can ask her.'

'Or could she help me to contact Laila?'

'I'll ask.'

I produced one of my business cards. 'This is my name, phone number and whatever else you might need to contact me. Tell me when it's convenient for me to come back or give it to Laila Bratteli, and ask her to contact me directly if she wants.'

He took the card, read everything on it and then looked up again. 'Private investigator?'

'Yes.'

'First time I see that.'

'OK. You mentioned her ex-husband…'

'Yes.'

'Do you know what his name is? Other than Bratteli?'

He projected his lower lip and waggled it from side to side, as a sign that he was thinking. 'Bjarne or Bjarte? One of the two, I think.'

I nodded and made a mental note.

'She hasn't had an easy life,' he said. 'From what I've been told.'

'Yes, that's exactly what I'm trying to find out, but…' I opened my palms. 'You'll be doing me a big favour if you – or your wife – can ask her to get in touch with me.'

He nodded again. Holding the card demonstratively in the air, he withdrew into the doorway. 'We will try. I have understood.'

He closed the door quietly after him.

I stood for a few moments staring at the door Laila Bratteli was hiding behind. Walking back to my car I heard the echo of a song from a radio play about Dickie Dick Dickens in my head: '*Oh Chicago, my Chicago…*'

I turned and looked up at the windows I assumed belonged to Laila's flat. There wasn't a sign of life on either floor. The blinds were drawn and not one of them moved, in case she was peering between the slats. That gave me even more incentive to talk to her. Or to her husband, for that matter.

13

Once again I sat down at my computer.

I still had an ambivalent attitude towards it. On the one hand, it had become an almost indispensable tool of my trade. It was unbelievable how much you could find out with it and if a search proved to be difficult there was, at best, help elsewhere. On the other, I had personal experience of how it could be abused by those with malicious intent. Since then I had been very careful about what emails I answered and what links I opened, unless I felt a hundred percent secure about the sender, and often not even then.

But now I was back searching for another name. It wasn't long before I had a hit with Bjarne Bratteli – his address and phone number, landline and mobile. Further searches revealed only a link to the tax lists for several years, 2002 the most recent. His income didn't suggest that he had a particularly lucrative job, and I was unable to establish what it was.

I tried the landline first. No one picked up. I rang the mobile number. He answered, but there was lots of background noise; it sounded like children playing, and clearly he found it difficult to hear what I was saying. At length we agreed I would call him later. Preferably after nine, but I said that unfortunately I was busy then.

'What about tomorrow?'

'I'm calling about your ex-wife. Laila.'

He seemed to have moved away from the worst of the noise. 'Oh, yes? Anything serious?'

'No, no. I just can't contact her.'

'Yes, tell me about it. But why do you want to see me?'

'To have a chat.'

'How busy are you this evening?'

'Hard to say.'

'Anyway, you can call me any time until twelve. Midnight. Now I have to ring off.' Before he did, I heard a child screaming in the background. Then everything went quiet.

I made a note of where he lived, in Nye Sandviksvei. That meant I could possibly pay him a call after I had been to Frekhaug. Or, as he had himself suggested, the day afterwards.

I continued searching. There was another name from among my co-accused a year and a half ago: Karl Slåtthaug. According to the police, he had moved to Tønsberg. I entered his name on the screen and searched.

It appeared in various news stories. Most of them were several years old. Some I remembered from the last time I searched for his name. He had organised collections for street children, in Europe and South America. He had taken part in debates about child welfare and had written several newspaper articles on the same topic. In addition, he was very committed to environmental issues and was referred to as one of the leading lights behind an environment party that for unknown reasons never came into being.

Luckily – I had to concede on my own behalf – no names were mentioned when he, I, Mikael Midtbø and Per Haugen were in the same boat for a few weeks in September 2002, so there were no articles associated with him. The most recent one, however, caused a chill to run down my spine. Five months ago, in August, there was an article in *Tønsbergs Blad,* showing him with a broad smile on his face standing alongside a woman flanked by another man. What made me react was the headline:

'PRIVATE CHILD REFUGEE CENTRE
ESTABLISHED IN TØNSBERG'.

The centre was obviously situated in a rural setting, judging by the background in the picture. An initiative calling itself BiT, Barnemotta-ket i Tønsberg – child reception centre in Tønsberg – had, so the article ran, financed and organised a centre for orphaned refugee children. Here they would do the best they could to integrate the children into the local milieu and into society in general. Physical activity, schooling and culture were the priorities. The director of the centre was ... Karl Slåtthaug.

I felt an immediate urge to grab the telephone next to me. Didn't they know what they were doing in Tønsberg? Didn't they conduct background checks on the staff they employed? And who was behind this private initiative?

I jotted down the names of the two other people in the photo: Anne Kristine Kaldnes and Pål Vassbotn. She was fair-haired and looked like a classic social worker, with round glasses, a light-coloured shirt, denim jeans and a purple scarf hanging loosely around her neck. He looked like an estate agent, a young man in a dark suit, white shirt and tie. The way I interpreted the photo, the distribution of roles was clear: from right to left, sponsor, idealist and director. There were no children visible, but the article also said the first would be coming at the end of the month, in other words, August.

On the newspaper's website, I searched for the word 'Barnemottaket', but there were no more hits. I entered the two other names. Anne Kristine Kaldnes came up as a member of an organising committee for the Women's Day in Tønsberg in 1999 and as a speaker on the theme of refugee children somewhere else. There was a photo of Pål Vassbotn as a new customer support officer at Nøtterø Savings Bank and a short bio that said little more than that he had the right professional background and had studied at the BI Business School in Oslo.

Tønsberg was a town of which I had only peripheral knowledge. Of course I knew that Slottsfjellet Tower was the town's emblem and that the historical connection between Bergen and Tønsberg had been important, not least during Håkon Håkonsson's reign, when his daughter, Kristina of Tunsberg, was a central figure. I had been there a couple of times, but only in transit and even that had been quite a number of years ago.

The only person I knew in Tønsberg was a lawyer I had been in touch with now and then. I had carried out some investigations for him in Bergen. The last time was around a year ago – in connection with a case about a medicine spiked with red saffron. I searched my mobile for his telephone number.

He answered after three or four rings. 'F-f-oyn.' It was him. I remembered now. He had an occasional stammer.

'Veum here.'

'The Bergen Veum?'

'Yes. Happy New Year.'

'Thanks. S-same to you.' After a slight pause he continued: 'How can I help you? I assume you're not ringing to wish me a h-h-happy New Year.'

'You're absolutely correct. I'm working on a case with a possible lead in Tønsberg.'

'I see. Anything interesting?'

'Does the name Karl Slåtthaug mean anything to you?'

'N–oo. Can't say it does.'

'What about Anne Kristine Kaldnes?'

He hesitated. 'Kaldnes … I think I've met someone with that name. A child-welfare case a few years ago.'

'Sounds like the right person.'

'A feminist virago. Could that be her?'

'Depends on your definition, but from the photo I found on the *Tønsberg Blad* webpage, she's probably a feminist.'

'Social worker is my guess.' He was chuckling.

'Don't laugh at social workers. I was one myself.'

'Well, well. Is this a child-welfare case as well?'

'Not necessarily. I have another name. Pål Vassbotn.'

'Don't know him.'

'Employed by Nøtterø Savings Bank.'

'Doesn't mean a thing to me.'

'And then there's another institution. BiT they call themselves. Barnemottaket in Tønsberg.'

'Yes, I know about them. But not much. They're out by Olsrød.'

'Karl Slåtthaug's the director. The other two are both involved in the project, in one way or another. You haven't heard anything about the business? Does it do what it's supposed to do? No – what shall I say? – rumours circulating in town?'

'Now you're whetting my curiosity, Veum. Rumours about what?'

'Karl Slåtthaug's from Bergen and he has a very bad CV. Let me put it like that.'

'Worse than yours?' Again the low chuckle.

'Much worse. To be frank, I'm quite shocked that anyone there would employ him. At any rate, they can't have asked the police for a record check.'

'That type of institution should have done so, really.'

'Yes, indeed they should.'

'Listen, Veum, I'll put my ear to the ground, see if anyone's heard anything, but I doubt they have. Otherwise it would've reached my ears. Sometimes I walk past there when I'm out with the dog in the evening. I'll keep my eye on the place and make some enquiries about this … Slåtthaug, was that the name?'

'Yes. Karl.'

I could hear him making notes and then we rang off. I was happy with this. Foyn was a man I could trust. If there was anything to find out, I was confident he would do it.

So there was little else I could do other than get some food down me before leaving for Frekhaug. The day had been a lot busier than I had imagined. And it wasn't over yet. Frekhaug is a village situated by a fjord and as the old folks say: where there's life, there's hope.

14

If you have lived for long enough in one place, over the years you have been almost everywhere in the town and its environs. Usually I had only seen Frekhaug from a distance as I passed over Nordhordland Bridge. My sole remaining memory of the area was the time before Nordhordland Bridge and the one between Flatøy and Holsnøy were built. Frekhaug was connected to the mainland by the Salhus ferry. I had once spent a rainy June night in my car because I had missed the last ferry across the fjord, a classic situation for most Vestlanders in fact, before the highway authorities began to build bridges to even the smallest skerry off the coast.

The bridges that appeared in the 1990s had in reality turned Frekhaug into a suburb of Bergen, which was reflected in the building style. The small homesteads were replaced by terraced and detached houses in a variety of price brackets. With the help of a road map I found my way to where Haldis Midtbø lived: a terraced house in the area between the centre of Frekhaug and the old ferry quay.

I was there as close to nine as it was possible to be. I could see a woman I assumed was her at the window, watching me park by a sign saying *Guests*. When I got out of the car she moved away from the window and stood in the doorway as I approached the house. 'The children are in bed,' she said in a low voice, stepping aside to allow me in.

I entered a cosy hallway where a staircase led up to the floor above. She drew my attention to a clothes stand. I removed my winter jacket, which she took and hung up. Then she nodded towards the stairs and motioned for me to follow her up. 'Their bedroom is downstairs,' she said in a slightly more normal voice when we were at the top. Along a bright corridor with a number of doors, several of them ajar, we came into the sitting room. It had large windows overlooking the fjord, with the ferry quay on the opposite side and the floodlit church and town of Salhus shining at us in the darkness.

Haldis Midtbø was a thin woman. Her reddish hair was knotted into a ponytail and she was wearing a dark-blue jumper and light-brown cord trousers. She had dark bags under her eyes, pale skin and a slightly nervous disposition. The tired expression in her eyes suggested a lack of sleep or that this was the end of a long day.

The furniture in the room was simple and practical; the pictures on the walls were decent prints and lithographs, most with easily recognisable coastal-landscape motifs. A shelving unit and a TV screen vied for attention along one wall, where a door led to the south-facing garden. Outside I saw some sparse bushes and a pile of snow.

'My husband'll be back later. He's been held up by a meeting.'

'That's fine. It's you I want to talk to anyway.'

Her eyes wandered. 'Yes, but as I told you on the phone yesterday, I've put everything to do with what Mikael did behind me. I can't bear to think about it. What he did to our own children! To the neighbour's! But for the fact that I have a good job here, we'd have gone miles and miles away and never returned.'

'What do you do?'

'I'm a primary-school teacher. I'm with children every single day. Just the thought of what some of them might've been subjected to by those responsible for them! It's absolutely disgusting.'

'And what was your husband charged with? I mean … the precise terms?'

'What he was charged with? It came out at the trial that he was involved with some kind of network sending pictures of naked children all over the world.' She inhaled deeply and a low sob emerged before she could continue. 'He'd taken photos of our children while they were in the bathtub here, or in the sea in Spain, and what was worse – while they were sleeping.'

'Did you see these pictures?'

'I was questioned, too. Can you imagine? A primary-school teacher.

I could've been suspected too, of being connected with that!' Tears sprang from her eyes and she had to swallow hard before she could go on. 'Yes, I did see some of the pictures. He'd been in their room while they were asleep, pulled off their pyjamas and taken photos. And not only of them. I recognised two of Anne's friends, girls. They were seven or eight years old then. One of the fathers was furious. He came to our door brandishing a wooden bat, and if Mikael hadn't already been in remand, God knows what would've happened to him.'

'I see. What's his name?' I asked as casually as possible.

But she was in her stride now. 'Stiansen. They live here, they're our next-door neighbours.' She gesticulated towards the window and outside. Then she seemed to catch herself. In a whisper she added: 'And I completely understood him.'

'You were quite forthright when I talked to you yesterday.'

'Yes, well … I apologise, but … I get so mad whenever I think about what…' She flashed a weary smile. 'My tongue runs away with me.'

'And you never suspected this was going on before?'

She blushed. 'Not at all! Do you think I would've let this sort of thing go on?'

'No, I was only … It's always surprising that such terrible things can happen within the four walls of a home without the perpetrator's partner realising.'

'Yes; for me it came like a bolt out of the blue. I had no idea until the police were at our door early one morning, even before we'd left for school, the children and I. And then they took him with them. Mikael, that is.'

'He was at home? What was his job?'

'He was a car salesman, but at that time he was unemployed.'

'And how did the children react?'

'They were as shocked as I was. Anne started howling. Klaus sat shaking, pale as a sheet.'

'I suppose you … I suppose the police asked if you'd suspected any more had happened than just taking photos?'

'What could I say? I didn't have a clue what was going on!'

'No, of course. Tell me – what happened afterwards? You got divorced, I understand?'

She eyed me coldly. 'As soon as I realised the gravity of the case I filed for a legal separation. We were divorced in the autumn.'

'But you've kept your old surname?'

'For practical reasons initially.'

'And I understand you have a new man now?'

'Yes.'

As she didn't elaborate, I continued: 'And the children. Did you reach some agreement over them?'

Her eyes widened. 'Are you crazy? Surely you don't think I would leave them with him. Not for so much as a second! I denied him access and my solicitor supported me. There was quite a row of course, but the last thing I told Mikael was: sue me then!'

'You met?'

'We had a meeting with our solicitors present, yes.'

'Did anything else happen?'

'Well, he didn't sue me before he died.'

'No...'

She sent me an accusatory glare. 'But I had no doubt I'd win the case, if that's what you're thinking.'

'He had a new partner as well.'

'New? He'd known her long before this blew up.'

'Oh, yes?'

'She's nothing but a tart. She had a flat in Flaktveit in Åsane, where she lived with her daughter. Retrospectively, I've heard there was a long line of men at her door, at all hours of the day and night, and all types. Mikael was one of them. Her poor daughter. God knows what she's been through!'

'Your husband was one of them? How...?'

'My ex-husband! A colleague of mine lived nearby. She saw him several times.'

'And she told you?'

'Not until afterwards, when all this other stuff came up. She hadn't said anything, she said, to spare me.' She grimaced to show me what she thought about being spared.

'When was the last time you saw your … late ex-husband?'

'At the meeting, in September. With our solicitors present.'

'You didn't meet him later?'

'He used to ring me and give me an earful. In the end I stopped picking up when I saw his number. Then he tried ringing with her phone. I fell for it once. Then there was peace.'

'And in December he died.'

She nodded. I could almost see how she was struggling to suppress a smile. It crept into her eyes anyway.

A door slammed on the floor below.

'Here he comes; Magne.'

After a little while we heard footsteps on the stairs. A rather short man came in, grey, from his short, thinning hair to the plain, workaday suit. There was something pale and faded about his face too, as though it had been hung out to dry for too long. The grey shirt with the round white collar gave away his profession. He was a priest.

15

The atmosphere turned awkward, as if I was a secret lover on a visit and he had caught us unawares.

He crossed the sitting-room floor, which seemed very large all of a sudden as I stood up. We shook hands. He had a handshake as firm as a jellyfish. His eyes were a pale light blue. It was as if he were in a badly exposed black-and-white film. 'Magne Molstad,' he said with a faint touch of Sunnmøre dialect in his intonation, an exiled Ålesunder for all I knew, a very last remnant of the ash from the town fire of 1904.

'Varg Veum,' I said, and not even he could refrain from smiling at my name.

'Actually we've finished,' Haldis Midtbø said. She had stood up, too.

'Not quite,' I said. 'I suppose I ought to congratulate you. You're as good as newly-weds, aren't you?'

Magne Molstad wrapped his arm around his wife's shoulders and gave a thin-lipped smile. 'In November. It's changed the life of someone who was becoming an old bachelor.'

'But you've known each other a while?'

'Some people probably thought it happened too fast, but ... I'm a priest in Lindås and we met each other in a professional context. I've visited the school where she works many times. I held the Christmas church service there this year, for example.'

'The priest in Lindås? Does that mean to say you're in Lindås Church?'

'No, we're peripatetic, so I cover several churches as part of my job.'

'Are you sometimes in Fyllingsdalen?'

He opened his mouth and stood like this for a few seconds, like a fish taken from an aquarium to be shown to others. 'What? Fyllingsdalen? Why?'

Haldis looked at me suspiciously, but she didn't seem to understand what I was driving at, either.

'Well, according to his partner, Mikael Midtbø, your wife's late husband – ex-husband – was expecting a visit from a priest the day he died.'

'Is that so?'

'You can't trust her,' Haldis said vehemently. 'She's lying. She never says a word of truth.'

'A pastor, she said.'

'Well, that's a rather old-fashioned term. We don't use it any more. Pastor Molstad, ho, ho, ho.' A dry chuckle escaped his lips.

'So it wasn't you?'

'To tell the truth, I've never met him. We didn't move in the same circles.'

Haldis seemed to move even closer to him and stared at him with a form of gratitude in her eyes.

'You never met Mikael Midtbø?' I asked.

'No.'

'Didn't you hear what he said? He never met him and I've put that part of my life behind me forever.' Haldis appeared almost exultant. 'And even more now he's dead.'

'But your children. Don't they miss their father?'

'A father who committed such abuse? What do you think?'

'Both the police and you say the only thing that's certain is that he took these photos and passed them on. That's serious enough, of course, but I'd still maintain that physical abuse is even more serious, which is also reflected in the sentences meted out.' She opened her mouth to answer, but I was quicker. 'Were your children ever questioned?'

Tears flowed from her eyes, and I watched Molstad tighten his arm around her shoulders. 'Yes and no. A policewoman came here and spoke to them, but she was very careful in her choice of words, she said.'

'You weren't present?'

'No. It was just her and the children.'

'Do you remember what the police officer's name was?'

'Does it matter?' She looked around the room as if the answer hung in the air somewhere. 'Borgersen, Bergesen, something like that.'

'Annemette Bergesen?'

'Probably.' She looked at me impatiently, 'Can we draw this to a close? I have to be at school early tomorrow morning and need to get to bed.'

I nodded. 'I'm going. Thank you for talking to me.' I shifted my gaze to Magne Molstad. 'This is my card. Contact me should anything occur to you.'

He examined the card I was holding out to him. 'What's this supposed to be?' He waved a hand in the direction of the card. 'I don't need this.'

'No?'

'No. I agree with Haldis. This is a closed chapter in her life, and it was never part of mine.'

'Not even the preface?'

His mouth twitched as if to tell me that he didn't find that remark funny. He was right about that. But it was him who accompanied me down and outside while she stayed upstairs.

'Not just between the two of us either?' I said in a last-ditch attempt.

He shook his head slowly. 'You don't give in, do you.' After waiting for an answer from me, he added: 'The answer's still the same. No. No contact.'

I got into my car. Life had taught me one thing: I didn't trust anyone, not even priests. I cast a glance at the neighbouring house, where Stiansen was supposed to live. Some of the windows were lit; however, it was too late to make an unannounced call. For all I knew, he might be swinging the bat in readiness and was simply dying to use it.

16

It had just passed ten o'clock when I called Bjarne Bratteli to see if it was still alright for me to drop by later in the evening.

He hesitated before answering. 'OK then. When will you be here?'

'In about half an hour.'

'Fine. Ring the bell downstairs.' He told me the address, but I already had it on my notepad.

The clouds were beginning to break as I passed Nordhordland Bridge. Above Veten, the highest mountain in Åsane, I glimpsed a few scattered stars, like crushed fragments of glass on black velvet. On the motorway the last queues of the night had dissipated and I had an open road all the way to where I turned off by the entrance to Fløyfell Tunnel. I stopped for the lights at the bottom of the hill.

I parked in Nye Sandviksvei and followed the house numbers up the street. I found B. Bratteli on one of the nameplates by the entrance to the correct house. I rang the bell beside his name. His voice sounded in the loudspeaker, I introduced myself, the lock buzzed, I opened the door and went in.

Bjarne Bratteli lived on the seaward side of Nye Sandviksvei and on the second floor. Above the roofs of the housing development in Skuteviken, some of the oldest timber constructions in Bergen, he could see straight out to Europe's largest freezer in Bontelabo, which was also where, in the summer, the cruisers docked. Now there was an oil rig laid up at the quay.

He received me dressed in a red-checked flannel shirt hanging over black denim jeans. He was in his late thirties, with slightly untidy gingery hair and a red tone to his skin, as though he had just come out of a sauna. The explanation was provided when I entered his tiny sitting room. An old-fashioned stove glowed against a firewall and the room temperature was closer to thirty degrees than twenty.

'Cold, are you?' I asked, with a wry grin.

'If you had a job that meant you were outdoors most of the day, you'd be cold too at this time of the year.'

'What's your job?'

'I'm a kindergarten assistant.'

That explained the background noise when I talked to him on the phone earlier in the day. 'But it's a pleasant job, isn't it?'

'If you say so. I was working in the North Sea before, but I had an accident at work and was refused permission to go back. So it had to be a land job instead, and after some to-ing and fro-ing that's where I ended up.'

'OK. Were you physically hurt?'

'Well, I can't do heavy work any more, so … But you didn't come here to talk about me, I suppose?'

'No, this is about – as far as I understand – your ex-wife, Laila.' I sent him an enquiring look, but he didn't comment. 'I've tried in a variety of ways to contact her, but she seems to have simply isolated herself. She won't answer the phone. She doesn't open the door when I ring the bell. The only person she has some contact with is her neighbour, Fatima.'

'Tell me something I don't know. I can't get in touch with her, either.'

'How long is it since you were divorced?'

'Less than a year. She testified in a court case, against her father, and since then she seems to have completely changed character. It was impossible to be in the same house with her any more.' He paused. 'But you still haven't told me who you are and what you're actually after.'

'You know my name. I'm a private investigator and I'm making some enquiries in the wake of the very case your wife testified in.'

He looked sceptical. 'Really? Enquiries for whom?'

This time I decided to be frank with him. 'For myself actually.'

'And what … ? Ah, were you one of those involved – I'm thinking … the parents?'

I was immediately a little more reticent. 'There are so many types of victim in a case like this, Bratteli.'

'Indeed there are. One of them's right here. I lost my wife because of it.'

'Can you tell me a bit about Laila?'

He hesitated. Then his expression changed again. 'But why are we standing here? Sit yourself down and I'll get ... A glass of beer?'

'No, thank you. I'm driving.'

'A Farris mineral water then?'

'Sounds good.'

He left the room and I heard a fridge door open and close. I looked around. Yes, she had lived here alright. The interior had a feminine touch – in the choice of colours and the artificial flower arrangements hanging from the walls. A big framed photo showed a young, blonde woman with a short skirt and an elegant blouse. She was leaning against a tree in Ole Bulls plass, with the bandstand in Byparken and Mount Ulriken in the background. Some other photos, of a more popular nature, were of animals: a setter with its ears pricked up in one, a huddle of kittens in another and a pair of lions under a tall tree in a third.

In a conspicuous break with the feminine style, the whole room was cluttered. Clothes were strewn over chairs, several of them near the stove, probably to dry after a wash. On the shelving unit there were piles of DVDs and a heap of men's glossy magazines. The only books I could see were a Swedish Biltema catalogue and a telephone directory. On the top shelf there was some advanced photo equipment and a small film camera.

He returned with a bottle for each of us, beer for himself and a Farris for me. No glasses.

I motioned towards the big photograph on the wall. 'Is that her?'

He nodded. 'When I first met her. She was a good-looking girl. Fun to be with. A model. Actually that's an advertising photo. It was printed in *Bergens Tidende*, but we managed to order a copy. That's all I've bloody got left of her. A photo on the wall!'

'What happened?'

'Well, what did happen? In the first years it was great. We lived together for a couple of years before we got married. I worked on a rig. She had her jobs here. As well as a model, she was a secretary in an advertising agency. A receptionist, you might say. But ... she wasn't comfortable with herself. There was something quite deep inside her, something dark and secret, which she never told me about. Not until ... well, this business with her father came up. The police called her in and there was one hell of a commotion.'

'But you were back on land then?'

'What? Ah, you're thinking about the accident. Yes, I'd been working at the kindergarten for more than a year when all this blew up. But then she lost it. It was as if a dam had broken. She told me about all her experiences as a young girl, with her father, and you can imagine ... And there was me working with children five days a week. It wasn't exactly good to hear.'

'No, I can imagine.'

'And then the problems really started. For us, I mean. She began to drink. She called work and told them she was ill, and when I came home from the kindergarten she was often completely plastered. I got her to see a doctor, but he just prescribed pills. For her nerves. Gradually she began to combine pills with alcohol, and then she was totally out of control. I did what I could to help her. I took all the days off from work I could, but there's a limit, and as time went on she started going out to drink, too. After she'd agreed to testify, she pulled herself together for a few weeks so that she could make a relatively credible impression. But then it turned out that what she had to say would have no effect on the outcome, and that completely unhinged her. She turned aggressive, violent ...' He stared gloomily into the distance.

'Do you mean she became violent towards you?'

'She was like a thing possessed. All men were the same, she said. She was going to kill us all. Several times she ran into the kitchen and came back brandishing a knife. Waving it in front of my face. In the end, I hardly dared close my eyes in bed until I knew she was asleep. I had to hide the knives, as far as I was able. We split up eventually and she moved out.' After a short pause he added: 'It was my flat, you see, at first.'

'But … the neighbours up in Landås told me that people were at her door day and night, but she didn't let anyone in. And that you were behind that.'

'I was behind it? That must be a misunderstanding. I've barely been there myself and after a while I gave up. I just wanted to make sure she was managing, more or less. But I remember her neighbour. A grumpy sort. Came out and said I'd disturbed his afternoon nap. He looked like an afternoon nap the way he was standing! He was a foreigner, too.'

'Well, he may've misunderstood then. But … who else would want to contact her, and so often?'

His eyes narrowed. 'I prefer not to think about that. The way she was going at it at the end I imagine she racked up a substantial debt in the most dangerous of markets. That's where you'll have to look if you want to find the people going to her door.'

'Drugs?'

'Pills anyway. And you can soon build up quite a debt with these people if your doctor's realised it's time to call it a day.'

'There are other doctors.'

'Yes, and there is, as I said, a market.'

'I'd hoped you'd be able to help me contact her.'

He gestured despairingly. 'I wish I could. And I can try, of course. But she doesn't answer when she hears it's me calling. She just puts down the phone. I could stand outside the house where she lives and wait, but what's the point? If she doesn't want any help, fair enough. I only want to help. I loved her for Christ's sake! We got on well.'

'Until the business with her father?'

'Yes. If people of that ilk only knew how many victims they create. Can you imagine?' Sitting there, beer bottle in hand, he did look desperate, as though it was the only fixed point in his life now.

'Well,' I said, 'I won't bother you any further. If I manage to get in touch with her I'll put in a word for you and ask her to contact you herself.'

'You can try,' he said, resigned. 'But I doubt she will.'

I drank up the Farris and got to my feet. He accompanied me out, and we parted without saying much more. I was frightened I had left him in a far worse mood than when I arrived. I wasn't that cheerful myself. I felt a strange unease in my body and the Farris definitely wasn't strong enough to eradicate that.

I carefully looked both ways before getting into my car and pulling away from the kerb. But there was no grey VW Golf waiting for me in the shadow of Mount Rothaugen. Most people, and cars, had snuggled down for the night, and I didn't see much traffic on my short drive to Øvre Blekevei, where I parked, strolled down to Telthussmuget and let myself in.

I ended the day with the classic two glasses of aquavit, one for each leg. I rang Sølvi and told her what I was doing.

'Any money in it?' she asked.

'Not that I'm aware of,' I replied.

17

The first thing I did when I arrived in my office the following day was to ring Bjarne Solheim and ask him if they had made any progress with the list of registered VW Golfs in the district. He answered that they had been promised it this morning and would consider emailing me a copy as soon as they had it.

I thanked him and sat staring out of the window. January is a quiet month in all ways. The Christmas celebrations are over. The sales are the only thing that brings people to the shops, and most people relax their New Year's resolutions until they are so palatable that they can be swallowed without resistance and are gone forever – or at least until the following New Year's Eve. All the indications were that it was going to be a slightly overcast day. The low sun lay like a projector lamp in the east, casting golden light over the roofs in the Vågsbunnen district and across Bryggen dock. There it reflected on the windows of BI-IT, so much so that I couldn't see whether it was Knut Haugen or his colleague waving to me. Then again, it was highly improbable that they would.

I returned to my notes. After what I had discovered, there was now one person at the top of my list. From our meeting two days ago I knew when she usually finished work.

This time I decided to arrive unannounced. I parked in the guest bay in one of the other blocks and walked the last stretch to the high-rise in Dag Hammarskjølds vei. I opened the front door and took the lift up to the tenth floor. There seemed to be a trend among the people I visited: to hide behind doors with no nameplates. I soon realised this was the case here, too. I stood with my back to the peephole in the door after I had rung.

It wasn't long before I heard noises inside and the door opened with a crash. I turned and met her eyes.

'What the hell do you want?' Svanhild Olsvik barked at me, as charmingly as on the previous occasion. 'Didn't we say all we had to say on Monday?'

'Not entirely. Something new's come up. May I come in?'

Lightning flashed behind her glasses. 'No!'

'May I make an appointment then?'

'Appointment? What the fuck are you talking about?'

'Do you still take appointments?'

'Take appointments? What are you suggesting?'

'You can make up your own mind. Either you let me in now or I'll phone the police, the vice unit, and then they'll pay you a call instead.'

She paled visibly, except for two bright-red flushes that had appeared at the top of her cheeks. Mute, she stepped to the side, left the door open and tossed her head towards the flat. I followed her in.

She seemed to be wearing the same clothes as the last time we met: a black jumper and black cord trousers. She talked all the way into the sitting room. 'Don't think you can just come here and spout a load of shit because you reckon you are someone. I suppose this is that bitch you've been talking to or what?'

She spun round, causing me almost to bump into her. I stopped equally quickly, feeling that it wouldn't take much for her to sink her teeth into me. The flushes had spread, like a contagious rash.

I stepped aside and looked around. Bare walls, apart from a big poster entitled *Leeds United 1998*. It was a picture of the whole team, and I recognised the blond hair of a former Viking Stavanger player among them. The poster was attached to the wall with tape and hung slightly askew.

Otherwise the furniture looked as if it had been picked up from a Salvation Army shop on a rainy day. In a pile in one corner was a little dollhouse surrounded by oversized dolls, like Alices in Wonderland after eating the cake that made them grow. Large windows opened onto a breath-taking view. You could see to Oasen and even further. One door led to the balcony where Mikael Midtbø had thrown himself off, if I gave credence to that version of events. It was closed now.

I looked at this big woman. I didn't feel at all confident about what might happen if she went for me. 'Tell me … when did you meet Mikael Midtbø, and how?'

'That's got bugger-all to do with you.'

'You used to live in Flaktveit, I've been told.'

'You've been told, have you? What the hell do you think you're doing? Are you investigating me?'

'Why did you move?'

'I move where I bloody like.'

'Listen … you have a young daughter.'

'Yes, and so what? I take good care of her.'

'I sincerely hope you do. It didn't look like it the other day.'

'Didn't look like it! Have you been snooping on her, too?'

'I happened to see her as she was arriving home from school.'

'Happened! Hah! How did you know it was her?'

'Are there that many girls of her age here?'

She didn't answer, but pursed her lips. Her eyes looked as if they might pop out of her head.

'I've heard you described as at best a rather frivolous woman.'

'Heard you described! Isn't that what I said? You've been talking to that bitch. I'll kill her!'

'Do you usually kill people you don't like?'

She made a move towards me. Her muscles swelled visibly in her neck, probably in the rest of her body, too. I straightened up, ready to offer resistance if she went on the attack.

But she didn't attack me physically. She stood so close to me that I could smell an artificial fragrance coming from her mouth, as though she had just spat out some chewing gum. 'I'll tell you what, Veum. I've been asking around a bit too. I know a few people who've told me I just have to contact them if I need someone beaten up. If that's what you're after, just say the word.'

'Did you contact one of them before Midtbø took the big dive, perhaps?'

This time she poked a stubby finger into my chest, but without much weight behind it. 'You're living bloody dangerously, Veum. If someone takes my daughter, you'll be top of my to-kill list.'

'Why would anyone take your daughter?'

'They've threatened it before. The child-welfare bastards.'

'But you were allowed to keep her, I see.'

'Yes, just imagine that. My solicitor helped me. I can easily set him on you as well.'

'What? Don't you know there's a law to keep that sort on a leash?'

'Eh? What are you talking about?'

I hadn't been mistaken. She had absolutely no sense of humour. 'At any rate you've piqued my curiosity. If it's true what they say – that you had men queueing outside your door in Flaktveit...'

'Queueing outside my door? Have you been talking to those crazy neighbours? There was no bloody queue.'

'Well, in that case ... if you moved here, with Midtbø, is it conceivable that one of them might've been jealous?'

'One of them? Jealous? Are you trying to make some kind of drama out of this as well now? I can easily get one of them to take care of you.'

'In that case I ... I can just return the threat. If anything happens to me, you're bound to lose her.' I patted my internal breast pocket. 'I've recorded everything you've said. So don't try anything.' It was a bluff of course, but I assumed she wasn't going to frisk me.

We stood glowering at each other, like two professional boxers the day before a championship fight. The mistake was that we each represented our own weight class and I was not at all sure that mine was the heavier of the two.

'Where's your daughter now?'

'At school. And don't you dare wait for her today as well. If you do...' She broke off.

I carried on: 'Will you kill me?'

'Go to hell!'

'Svanhild, so many people have recommended I go there, but I've never been tempted. Do you think it's an all-inclusive trip? If so, you might consider it yourself.'

She made a sweeping gesture with her hand towards the door. 'Out!'

I saw no reason to object, but made a small deviation as I walked past her. She hadn't intimidated me. Anyone could mouth off. But she had given me something to think about. If Mikael Midtbø had been killed, there could be many candidates for the job out there. Here, they wouldn't even have needed a bat. But whether the same person had seen to Per Haugen was a very different matter. And what about the driver of the grey VW Golf three days ago?

Was there any connection at all? In order to find out the answers, my only option was to continue my investigations, even if it meant going to Tønsberg to get the full picture of this case.

18

From Fyllingsdalen I took the shortest route to Slettebakken. I turned into Adolph Bergs vei and parked a little closer to the relevant block than the last time. The temperature was three or four degrees above zero; normal for Bergen in January.

I hadn't made any attempt to ring in advance this time, either. I looked up at what I had worked out were Laila Bratteli's windows. The blinds were drawn, as on my previous visit, and it was hard to see if there were any lights on behind them. I went up to the second floor and onto the gallery.

I laid my ear against her door. Not a sound. I rang the bell. Nothing happened. I repeated the action, but without much hope. I might just as well have been selling sand in the Sahara. The result would have been the same.

Then I went to the adjacent flat and rang the bell. It didn't take long for Ghulam Mohammad to appear in the doorway. When he recognised me he rolled his eyes. 'Can't you leave her in peace?' he protested.

I reiterated what I had said the previous time. 'I don't want to torment her. I just want to ask a few questions. They're not even about her; it's her father I want to ask about.'

'Her father?' He straightened his large glasses and eyed me sharply.

'Yes. It's too long to explain … Has anyone else been here since my visit?' When he didn't answer, I added: 'Was anyone here yesterday?'

'Yes. No. No one came after you.' He studied me thoughtfully, as though I had aroused his suspicions again.

'Well, I spoke to her ex-husband last night. He said it wasn't him at her door, but probably people she owed money. Have you, or your wife, observed … ? Does she still take pills?'

His eyes went walkabout.

I seized the opportunity. 'I see. Does your wife know about this?'

'Fatima, she…' He paused.

'I gave you my card yesterday. I'm a private investigator. If Laila's in that kind of trouble, I may be able to help her.'

'Really?' He looked at me in surprise. 'How?'

Well, I would have loved to know that myself. But I stuck to my guns. 'I know the milieu. If nothing else, I can tip off the police.'

'Uhuh.' Again he was considering his options. 'Fatima says she's been to the doctor's with her now and then. To a number of surgeries. Usually Laila was in a bad mood afterwards, but sometimes things went better. When the doctor gave her a prescription and Fatima accompanied her to the chemist's. There's a branch here.' He nodded in the direction of Sletten Shopping Centre.

'Is your wife in now?'

'No, they … She's out.'

'Out with … Laila?'

His jaw muscles writhed as if he had a nest of vipers under his skin.

'Last time you told me they occasionally go out for a cup of tea.'

'Yes.' He shrugged. 'I don't know.'

'But they did go out together?'

He nodded silently and pressed his lips together, as a sign that I wasn't going to get a word out of him. For a moment or two we stood eyeing each other. Then I nodded, thanked him and said I would try the shopping centre. If I didn't see them, my message was the same as before. If Fatima could pass on the message, I would very much like to have a few words with Laila, and there was nothing to worry about. Not any more, as her father was no longer alive and couldn't do anything to her at all.

I walked the two minutes it took to reach the shopping centre. Sletten was the original name, but it had been radically rebuilt since the sixties, when it had been new, and now it offered a lot more than shopping. There was underground parking too – and I saw them coming up from there.

I realised at once it was them. A muscle-bound man in a dark-brown leather jacket was engaged in a heated conversation with a woman wearing a red windcheater with the hood over her head, while a plump foreign woman in a long, brown winter cloak with her hair hidden under a dark-green hijab vainly tried to separate them. I recognised the man. His name was Bjørn Hårkløv and he was a debt collector I had crossed swords with before, or at least exchanged punches. The last time I saw him he had tried to drag me into a room in Skuteviken to finish me off. Now he had a firm grip on the shoulders of the Norwegian woman and was berating her while jerking her backwards and forwards so hard, she seemed to dangle from his great big fists.

I quickened my pace, shouting: 'Hey, hey, hey. What's going on here?'

They turned to face me, all three of them, the foreign woman with an expression of gratitude, the woman in the windcheater with one of despair, and Hårkløv with visible annoyance at being interrupted.

When he saw who it was, his square jaw churned and his biceps looked as if they might burst the seams of his leather jacket. 'Veum! What the fuck has this got to do with you? Just clear off. This is none of your business.'

I continued walking until I was standing right in front of him. 'In fact it is. I have a meeting with Laila now, which you're holding up, so unless *you* clear off I won't be responsible for what might happen.' I was right. I wouldn't be responsible for anything. The worst-case scenario was that I would end up at A&E, but I'd always had a big mouth, and it had helped me out of scrapes before. 'I don't think you should behave like this in broad daylight and imagine you can walk away scot-free.'

He released his grip on Laila Bratteli and brutally shoved her away. She tumbled into Fatima's arms while he focused his full attention on me.

'And who do you think's going to stop me? You? That fucking bitch's up to her ears in debt and it increases by ten thousand for every day that passes. If you fancy helping her, let's see the colour of your money. Ninety thousand today, a hundred tomorrow!'

Laila Bratteli sobbed beside us. 'He's lying! That's a lie!' Her voice cracked. 'I owe forty … maximum.'

He sent her a vicious glare. 'Forty a week ago. A hundred thousand tomorrow.' He turned back to me. From the corner of my eye I saw Fatima pull Laila away. He shifted his attention to them. 'Hey! Don't you bloody try to sneak off!' He gestured towards them. I moved two steps to the side and stood between them, tensing my stomach muscles as hard as I could and trying to keep his eyes focused on mine.

The last-mentioned succeeded. But he was so close to me that I had trouble focusing. Now it was *my* shoulders he had grabbed, but I lifted my arms and struck out and I was free.

We were no longer alone. More people had come out of the shopping centre, among them a man in a security guard's uniform who looked as if he had barely left school. 'Hey you! What's all this?' he shouted; at least his voice had broken.

Hårkløv changed focus once again. 'Ask this twat. He was trying to pick a fight with me.'

'I broke up a physical assault,' I said and looked at the young security guard with a teacherly air. 'This fellow attacked two women.'

'Shall I call the police?' the guard asked.

'The hell you can,' Hårkløv said, trying to share his attention between us.

'No one at home in hell,' I said.

'Eh?'

'Well, you're here, aren't you.'

He watched Fatima and Laila make their escape. They were by Wiers-Jenssens vei and about to cross the street towards Adolph Bergs vei. He eyed those of us around him with contempt. Then he started walking in the same direction. Once again I took a few steps and stood between him and them. It was safer now, with a handful of witnesses around.

'You stay here!' I said with conviction.

The guard held a phone in the air. 'I'm ringing the police.'

'Go to hell, the whole lot of you!' He turned on his heel, headed for the slope down to the car park and was gone.

The guard appeared uncertain what to do. 'Shall I ring?'

I shrugged. 'As you like.' I gave him my card. 'You can give them this if they want my name.'

'Varg Veum?'

'Correct.'

He extended a hand. 'Kalle Blomkvist.'

'Is that really your name? As in Astrid Lindgren's *Master Detective*?'

'Yes. Anything wrong with it?'

'Nope. Nothing at all. Welcome to the club.'

He looked down at the underground car park. 'And the crook? Do you know what his name is?'

'Bjørn Hårkløv. Well-known heavy.'

He nodded knowingly, as if it was something he had learned on the course for security guards. 'Let's leave it at that then, for now.'

There was a scream of tyres deep underground and from below came a black Audi with darkened windows. I didn't have a second's doubt about who the driver was. Because of the crowd that he himself had attracted he had to brake as he passed and he sounded the horn at anyone who was slow to move. With some satisfaction I noticed Kalle Blomkvist take a photo of his number plate with his mobile phone. He smirked to me: 'That's him on record.'

The Audi swung right, into Wiers-Jenssens vei.

'Good. Let me just …' I turned and jogged after the car. I reached the street just in time to see him enter Adolph Bergs vei. I speeded up and rounded the corner a few seconds later. He had pulled up outside the block where Laila and Fatima lived.

He opened the car door and stepped out. On spotting me, he stopped. 'Are you following me?'

'My car's here.'

'You *want* a beating, don't you.'

Now I had almost caught up with him. I came to a halt a few metres away. 'Not really. At any rate we can wait for the police to come.'

'That asshole didn't call them, did he?'

'They said they were on their way.'

His face darkened. He cast a final glance at the house where she lived. Then he abruptly turned, jumped into his car and started it up without a word of farewell. He drove down the street, well above the local speed limit.

I went into the block again and up to the second floor. This time I rang Mohammad's bell. I heard footsteps inside and a pause before he opened the door.

'Has Fatima told you what happened?'

He nodded.

'Where is she?'

'They're here, both of them.'

'Could you ask Laila if she's willing to talk to me now?'

He nodded and closed the door. I waited. After a short while the door opened again. 'You can come in,' he said. 'She'll see you.'

19

A kind of semi-darkness lay over the flat I entered. In the hallway the floor covering, furniture and furnishings were Scandinavian design, but when we entered the sitting room it was like walking into a different culture. On the floors there were oriental carpets in red, black and gold. On the walls, bright textiles, a mixture of appliqué and embroidery. In the centre of one wall, facing me as I went in, was a fabric with a black background and hanging threads of gold, like golden rain, and at the bottom some enormous crowns of purple flowers opening to the sun that was rarely there. The low furniture was covered with cushions in various patterns, some of them almost modernist in form, others an expression of a thousand-year old culture of such decorative beauty that it took my breath away. Permeating all of this was a faint fragrance of exotic spices.

The only element to disrupt this atmosphere was the sound of a radio in an adjacent room. Instead of extra-terrestrial tones from bamboo flutes, drums and zither what I heard was the news on NRK Hordaland.

The two women were sitting on the sofa. Fatima held her arms comfortingly around Laila, who was huddled up and leaning forwards, barely raising her eyes when I appeared. There was not much that reminded me of the good-looking, straight-backed woman I had seen in the photo on the wall of Bjarne Bratteli's flat. The blonde hair, which presumably had been bleached at the time, had become darker, and looked tangled and unkempt. Her face was lean and her mouth twitched at the corners. Her skin was sallow, but when she opened her mouth, her teeth were surprisingly neat and attractive, like an enamel reminder of the person she had once been.

'Thank you for your help,' she said in a voice so low it was barely audible.

'My pleasure.'

'Fatima,' Ghulam said in a peremptory tone.

She looked up, met his eyes, slowly let go of Laila with a solicitous pat on her shoulder and stood up. She didn't look at me, but went to the door of the adjacent room.

'We'll make some tea in the kitchen,' Ghulam said. 'So you can talk undisturbed.' He looked at Laila, as if to reassure her. 'We are out here. If there is anything, just say.' He turned his attention to me, sent me a serious look and then accompanied his wife into the kitchen. He closed the door quietly behind him and the somewhat noisy pop music that followed the news on NRK Hordaland became muffled and was eventually switched off.

Laila watched me shyly as I pulled out a chair, straightened the cushion on it and sat on the opposite side of the low, black, varnished table that separated us. She stared at me expectantly, unsure who I was or what I wanted from her.

'Let me say right from the start: I'm on your side. Whatever has happened in your life and whatever created the problems you now clearly have, I'll do everything in my power to help you. My name's Varg Veum. I'm a private investigator, but my background is in child welfare. I know everything about what can happen to children behind closed doors, sadly. I know what traumas it can cause and I know how difficult it can be to recover from such experiences.'

She nodded gently and ran the tip of her tongue over her dry lips and the red rash at the edges of her mouth.

'The reason I've been trying to get hold of you over the last couple of days is that for a variety of reasons I've decided to investigate your father's death.' I hastened to add: 'And I've already spoken to your mother and brother. And your uncle.'

She looked at me vacantly. In the same low voice, she said: 'I see.'

'I understand that this is difficult for you to talk about.'

She nodded, as before. There was something shrunken and cowed about her, as though what she really wanted was to curl up into a foetal position and never re-emerge. 'Mm,' she mumbled.

'But you've recovered from this before. You had recovered. I was shown a photo of you, as a model, and nothing seemed to bother you then.'

Her mouth twitched, but she still didn't say anything.

'Your husband also said you were completely different when you first met. It was after you testified against your father that—'

She made a sudden swatting gesture, as if to interrupt me. 'Stop! I don't want to hear about that pig!'

'No, I understand this is difficult.'

There was a knock at the door from the kitchen. Fatima came in holding a tray. She set it down on the table, passed a large china cup and a plate to each of us and poured tea from a pot. Then she proffered a bowl of small, rectangular cakes. I took one and tasted it. It was both sweet and sour. I recognised raisins and candied peel in the dark-brown cake, which reminded me vaguely of those of my boyhood, from the Smith-Sivertsen bakery in Nordnesveien. Then she withdrew with a kindly smile, to the doorway, where Ghulam was waiting for her.

Laila helped herself to a cake, too. We each took a sip of tea, which tasted of syrup, ginger and a spice I was unable to identify. We sat in silence until we had eaten a cake and taken a few more sips of tea.

'Neither you, nor your brother, wanted your names to appear in the obituary when your father died.'

'No. Knut rang me to tell me he'd died ...'

'And you agreed not to have your names published?'

She spoke slowly and with long pauses between her sentences. 'Yes. Why should we? Neither of us had good memories of him. It wasn't just me who was abused. Knut was, too.'

'What! He was abused, too?'

She suddenly raised her head and seemed to straighten up. 'And my best friend! She committed suicide. Later. When she was grown up. It was sick. Absolutely sick. If...'

As she didn't carry on, I said: 'Yes? If... ?'

She almost seemed to get some colour in her face. 'If these brutes only realised the consequences of their actions. We're all victims. Knut. Me. Marthe.'

'Marthe was your best friend?'

'She caught the bus to Kleppestø, and then she walked back, to the middle of Askøy Bridge, and jumped off.'

'Right.'

She came to life now. 'She'd been at home with us. There were probably no more than five or six of us. Playing with our dolls. Then he came in and asked if we'd like to play a different game. I said no. I didn't want to because I knew what he wanted. But Marthe didn't know, and she said yes. And I had to sit in the waiting room and wait.'

'Waiting room?'

'Yes, while she saw the doctor.'

'Afterwards she came out looking stunned, and then it was my turn, even though I kept refusing. But I was spanked, on my bare bottom, and then you had to pretend nothing had happened while he did what he did.' There were flashes of anger in her eyes now. 'He was a pig, a horrible, revolting pig. Him dying was the least that should've happened. We should've tortured him to death, slowly.'

Warily, I said: 'Do you know how he died?'

'Knut told me. He drowned. Pigs can't swim, can they.'

'To be honest, I don't know. But Marthe … she didn't say anything at home?'

'Don't you understand? It had been our idea, he said. And he would tell everyone that. So we had to keep this secret. It was our fault, after all. He said this so many times that in the end we believed it. We agreed we wouldn't tell anyone. Not Lise or Jorunn or any of the others in the class. No one. And then it just carried on.'

'For both of you?'

'Marthe stopped coming to ours after a while. But when I met her many years afterwards, in Nygårdsparken, we realised there was a reason for us to be there, for both of us. The same reason. But she … she was on much harder stuff than I was. Heroin. Amphetamines. I just took … pills. And spirits. Beer when I couldn't afford spirits. And then one day she was gone. It was several weeks before we heard what had happened. Someone had seen her on the bridge.'

'Tragic.'

'Yes.'

'And your mother; where was she while all this was going on?'

'I don't have a mother.'

'But—'

'I don't have a mother, I'm telling you. In court she said she didn't notice anything and she didn't believe a word I said. I'm not going to her funeral, either.'

'But your brother's managed well. He has a good job. And you managed well, too, for a long time.'

'Yes. So?'

'Well … I was only thinking aloud. Tell me something: how did you become a model?'

She straightened up a little more. Now she was sitting upright on the sofa and looked me straight in the face, but she was unable to hide what she was thinking. In her look I saw the same contempt with which she viewed all men. And still it was difficult to recognise the beautiful woman from the studio photograph. There seemed to be something awry and distorted about her whole face as she said: 'You're stupid pigs, all of you!'

'Not all of us, perhaps,' I said softly.

'Oh, yes, you are. But some of you haven't revealed your true selves yet.' She studied me defiantly. 'I discovered at secondary school that I looked quite good. And then I didn't let him have what he wanted. I slapped him and started to scream. And then I told … my mother.'

'You told her what he'd done?'

'Yes, but she was no longer my mother. She just said I shouldn't tell anyone else. It would bring shame over us all. Shame! That's all she was bothered about. And what about me? Nothing.'

I could visualise the slightly confused elderly woman I had met in the high-rise in Brunestykket, but I couldn't imagine her twenty to twenty-five years younger and the mother of a teenage girl who told her about things Laila's father – her husband – had done.

'I moved out as soon as I could. Got myself a bedsit. Got a job in an advertising agency. They were the ones who saw I was cut out to be … a model. First of all in ads, but also in fashion shows.' There was a new gleam in her eyes and her lips moved as though they couldn't resist a smile. 'I had them round my little finger, all the old pigs sitting in the front row and grinning. The cocky photographers who thought they were world champions behind a camera, just because they spent an hour on the photo-shoot instead of five minutes. My colleagues at the agency, whether they were married or not, they tried it on anyway. But they never got this far, not a single bloody one of the bastards.' She pointed to her groin and spread her legs. 'Until I chose one myself. One who had to leave for an oil rig, so that I could be left in peace for those weeks at least. But, of course, he turned out to be a pig as well.'

'Now you're referring to Bjarne Bratteli, your husband, are you?'

'My ex-husband! I never want to see him again. He's been ringing at the door too, but he can burn in hell, like my father … and all the other pigs.'

'But he said … He told me he came here because he was worried about you. He said he still loved you and that you'd got on well together.'

'Hah! He's lying, as you all do. I caught him, you know. Caught him red-handed.'

'Oh, yes? How?'

'Perhaps you don't know what his job is? He had to stop working on the rig and so he got a job at a kindergarten. And there the pig in him came to the fore.'

'You don't mean … ?'

'I caught him one evening at his computer. He didn't close the photos quickly enough, so I saw what he was looking at. They were of young children, in all sorts of positions. And he'd probably taken some of the photos himself … at the kindergarten.'

'But … but you reported him, I suppose?'

'What good would that do? I'd seen how I'd been treated in court, hadn't I. My father's defence lawyer, a real slippery sod, he made out everything I said was just fantasy. I was the kind who dreamt things up and many years later presented them as facts. "Just remember what her mother said when she testified," he said. My mother! I have no mother.'

'To be frank, if you found this out about your husband and didn't report it, then … that's like your own mother shutting her eyes to what she'd seen.'

She opened and closed her mouth. 'Like my mother? I only know that there would've been another pig sitting on the other side of a desk, if I'd reported him. A police pig. A lawyer pig. A psychologist pig. I've seen through the lot of you. The whole damn pack of you.'

It wouldn't be long before she was foaming around her mouth. I let her calm down while I kept an eye on the kitchen door in case the Seventh Cavalry should reappear.

'So that's what made you snap?'

She looked at me blankly, as though she had suddenly exhausted all her energy and anger. 'Snap?'

'Go on pills?'

She released another little smile, the wry sort this time. 'Pills? I've been taking them for years. But I had to do it secretly. When I caught Bjarne red-handed I just went for it big time. I knocked back pills and booze. Actually I suppose it must've been an attempt to kill myself, the long way. Not jumping from Askøy Bridge and being done with it. Just like that. But destroying myself slowly and laboriously.'

'You threatened your husband with a knife, he told me.'

'I should've bloody skewered him. Like I should've drowned my father. And thrown my mother from the balcony.'

'Thrown your mother from…?'

'Yes! They should've got their punishment, the whole bloody lot of them. And the person who did away with them should receive a medal. Do you understand?'

'Yes, I think I do, in a way. If you mean—'

'No, you don't! You're a pig, too.'

'Well … One last thing, Laila.'

She eyed me suspiciously.

'These people you owe money. The man I stopped harassing you in

Sletten. Bjørn Hårkløv. I know him from the past. They'll be back of course. You won't get rid of them, however rarely you venture out. And the next time there'll probably be no one around to help you, as I was.'

'So what?'

'Have you got any names of these people? Perhaps I can help you.'

'How? By giving them money? Or by beating them up?'

'I can set the police on them.'

'Right. I'm sure that'll help a lot. Just like it did with my father. They'll be out on the streets again after a few months, a year, at the most. And surely you don't think I'll get much sympathy from the cops or anyone else? A druggie, an alky. But there's one thing I'll never be: a whore. That's what they wanted. They wanted me to sell myself, then the debt would soon be paid off. When I refused they started using force. Talking about how the debt would grow from day to day. But no one will have me! Not one of you bloody pigs.'

'I don't know what to say, Laila.'

'Don't say anything at all. You can just sling your hook. I've said thank you.' She tossed her head. 'Don't imagine you're getting anything else as thanks.' She raised her voice. 'Fatima!'

It took them two seconds to come through the kitchen door, both Fatima and Ghulam. 'Yes?' Ghulam said. 'What is it?'

She looked at him wearily. 'He's leaving. And I want to go home.'

He bobbed his head slowly, as if to a little child. 'He's leaving. We'll accompany you home. OK.'

'Accompany?' I queried.

'Perhaps you don't think she still needs protection?'

'Yes, I do. Unfortunately. And you'll provide it?'

'It's better than nothing.'

And he was right of course. Anything was better than nothing. I should leave, yes. But he should take care. With what he had hanging between his legs, he was in the pig family, too. We weren't free from taint, any of us.

20

I sat in my car for a while, made some notes, read through some of the old ones, put question marks in a couple of places and wondered who to visit to find answers.

Before driving off I set up two meetings. My old social-services colleague Cathrine Leivestad could see me in her office in Strømgaten. Inspector Annemette Bergesen sounded a great deal more sceptical and she definitely didn't want to talk to me at the police station. When I described the case I was working on and mentioned a couple of names she agreed to a brief chat at the café in the railway station at sixteen hundred hours, as she put it.

I parked at the top of Bygarasjen, a multi-storey car park approximately halfway between the two meeting places. The time before I was due to see Cathrine I spent at her local public library. I sat down at a microfilm reader, found the Bergen newspapers from October and December 2003 and looked to see what had been written about the two fatalities. There wasn't much. Both incidents were mentioned in short single-column articles, in *Bergens Tidende* and *Bergens Avis*. In both papers the headline of the one about Mikael Midtbø's death was 'Fall in Fyllingsdalen'. Per Haugen's death was described as 'Accidental Drowning in Frøviken' in *BT* and 'Man Found Drowned' in *BA*. Here they had added an archive photo of Frøviken as an illustration. It was obvious that neither newspaper entertained a suspicion that this was anything other than what the police had concluded: a suicide and an accident.

I still had a little time and located the same newspapers' reports on the court cases against Midtbø and Haugen, which ran almost in parallel during January 2003, to see if there were any more details than those I had found on the net. *BA* had gone in for a fairly large spread about 'the daughter's testimony' against her father in the Haugen case, but they also quoted the defence counsel's comment that this was so long ago that legally it was time-barred and for that reason should be ignored at the trial. Since Haugen had been released from prison in July it was clear that the court had done exactly that. I noted down the name of his lawyer: Kristoffer Kleve.

Cathrine Leivestad smiled amiably at me when I arrived at her office, a couple of minutes before the agreed time. 'As punctual as always, Varg.'

'I daren't be anything else. I've learned that if I'm not, the person I'm meeting has seized their opportunity and done a runner.'

'Not me though?'

'No, not you.'

We hugged and I sat down on the client's chair, facing her across the desk. We had started in social services at about the same time. She had remained there for all these years. I had literally been shown the door after five. She had aged visibly over that time, and I didn't doubt for a second that the same was true of me. She had kept her long hair, but today it was gathered at the nape of her neck, which emphasised her lean facial features. Whenever we met there was a kind of resigned exchange of looks: you again? And: the world hasn't got any better since last we met. We swapped a couple of quick updates on how things were going. All fine on her side. Could be worse, on mine.

She was as efficient as always and got straight to the point. 'You asked me to check whether we had anything on a woman called Svanhild Olsvik.' She peered over the top of the computer. In a neutral tone she said: 'You know I can't tell you anything, Varg.'

I nodded. 'Yes.'

We sat looking at each other for a few seconds, as if to establish the principle. Then she flashed me a little smile. 'However…' she shifted her gaze back to the screen '…we have a note here. Some expressions of concern from neighbours where she lives … or lived. In Flaktveit. Two of my younger colleagues paid her a call at home and inspected her living conditions. But no decision was reached.'

'Everything was in perfect order?'

'Well ... she has a daughter and the concerns were with reference to her. My colleagues' notes say that she appeared quiet, shy and slightly withdrawn. But there was nothing to suggest any form of abuse. She went to school as normal, her diet seemed good; in short there were no obvious signs that we should step in.'

'What were the expressions of concern?'

She smiled ironically. 'Frequent visits from a variety of men at night. But, as you know, men aren't forbidden from visiting in a normal housing co-op. We conferred with the police, but they had nothing on her.'

'I'll have a word with them later. You know ... as I told you on the phone ... this is an investigation I'm undertaking on the back of a child-abuse case I was myself dragged into about a year and a half ago. One of the other men, Mikael Midtbø, to all outward appearances, took his own life in December by jumping from the tenth floor of the block where he lived in Fyllingsdalen. Svanhild Olsvik had moved in with him and taken her daughter along. If you had a daughter, would you enter into a relationship with a man who's been convicted of ... if not abuse, then spreading explicit images of child abuse via the net?'

'Hardly,' she said drily. 'And did she know about his background?'

'He's supposed to have been one of her regulars, I was told.'

'By whom?'

'Well ... his ex-wife.'

'And you know how much you can rely on that kind of evidence?'

'At any rate, the court found in favour of her as the sole provider for their two children. He wasn't even given visiting rights.'

'Right.' She nodded gravely. 'That's bound to cause trouble.'

'Exactly. But this time it was him who came to grief. In the sense that he lost his life. Whether it was self-inflicted or not.'

'Well...'

'Have you got anything on him? Mikael Midtbø?'

Again she smiled ironically as she tapped his name in. She read through what came up and typed. 'Mm. Not much. Something about some girls in the neighbourhood. But that was after you...' she looked up '...were arrested, all of you.'

I refrained from commenting, and she carried on: 'A neighbour, Carl Fredrik Stiansen, insisted that Midtbø should never be allowed to have any kind of contact with his own children or any others, and that was for perpetuity. We referred him to the police. But we made a note here, in case the matter should land back on our desk.'

'You didn't consider imposing any preventative measures?'

'We got in touch with fru Midtbø. Haldis is her Christian name, but she said she didn't need any help, and we didn't take any further action.'

She clicked on the screen and cast a glance at the clock on the wall behind me. I took the hint, thanked her for her help, gave her another hug and headed for my next meeting.

At 15.55 I was waiting in the railway café, ready to talk to Annemette Bergesen at sixteen hundred hours. She arrived at 15.59 in her immediately recognisable energetic style, scanned the room, located me, nodded, confirmed I already had a cup of coffee in front of me, and went to the counter to get one for herself. She came over, set the cup down on the table and occupied the free chair opposite me. She was out of uniform and wearing a dark, calf-length winter coat and dark-blue jeans.

'Veum,' she stated.

'Bergesen,' I nodded back.

'This meeting is off the record, but you said you had a tip-off for me.'

'Yes, I do, if you have one for me.'

She eyed me coldly. 'In our government department we don't do bartering. I thought you knew.'

'Really? OK. Then let's call it an exchange of ... background material. You've worked – to my knowledge – with vice as much as violent crime over the last few years. I gave you a name: Svanhild Olsvik. My understanding is that you haven't got anything on her?'

'By vice you're thinking...?'

'Prostitution perhaps.'

'Nothing.'

'She could've done it from home.'

'Of course she could. In which case, she might easily have passed under our radar. We've got a pretty good overview of street prostitution. The prostitutes who advertise on the net, very often under 'massage', we know about too, we think, even if our attempts to prove it have met with varying success. We have to carry out raids and catch them in the act. And then there are all those who go to hotel rooms and advertise beforehand, via mobile phone numbers. But they're constantly on the move and are hard to stop. As I said, however, the name you mentioned isn't in our files.'

'In the autumn she moved in with a man convicted of child pornography offences: Mikael Midtbø, who died in December as a result of what your colleagues defined as suicide. Now she lives alone with her daughter. Social services received a number of expressions of concern regarding her while she lived in Flaktveit. I saw her daughter myself a couple of days ago. She didn't look very happy.'

'OK. But we can't take any action because you've seen a little girl who doesn't look happy.' She took a sip of coffee. 'Was that what you wanted to tip me off about?'

'No, there's another woman. The daughter of another sex offender, also dead now. A drowning incident. Per Haugen.'

'Was he charged with you?'

'The charge against me was dropped.'

'Yeah, I know. But he was involved in the same case.'

I leaned forwards. 'It's shocking what goes on behind closed doors, Annemette. And now with the net as a portal to…' I stretched out my arms to the window overlooking Strømgaten '…the whole world.'

She had turned serious. 'I know, and we're working on the case. I can tell you in confidence that if we'd had a more generous budget, we would've formed a unit to specialise in this. And there's an understanding of this at the highest echelons, so maybe in a few years. We need officers experienced in IT, in network building and, not least, in the shady byways of the internet, to get to the bottom of this activity. The case you were involved in was a foretaste. Those boys weren't so smart. They left too many tell-tale signs after them. But we can already see how the villains have discovered new methods and are always several steps ahead of us. But they shouldn't feel too confident – we're on their trail, if not on the scale we'd hoped for. Yet.'

She drained her cup of coffee and looked towards the door. 'This daughter of … who did you say? … Per Haugen.'

'Yes. She's on drugs. An obvious result of what she was subjected to as a child. Now she's run up a substantial debt and her life's being threatened by debt collectors.'

'I see. Any names?'

'Laila Bratteli.'

'Address?'

I gave it to her.

'And who does she owe money to?'

'I don't know.'

'Sure?'

'But the heavy's name is Bjørn Hårkløv and he drives around in a black Audi.'

'Tell me something new. Registration number?'

'I … Oh, yes, a young security guard at Sletten took a snap of it earlier today.'

'And this guard's name is?'

'Kalle Blomkvist.'

'No kidding?'

'No. And he can confirm what I've told you. He was on duty this morning. It can't be that difficult to get hold of him.'

She looked at me despairingly. 'Varg – since it appears we're on first-name terms now – if you saw our schedule you'd know I can't set up a big initiative without having something more concrete to go on than this.'

'You can find Hårkløv's address on the net. If he's ever in his office, that is. And one more thing. The last time I had anything to do with him he was a henchman in the employ of a certain Bruno Karsten, a German Mr Big with his own branch in Bergen. Organised crime with a wide catchment area.' I repeated my refrain: 'Drugs, prostitution and cybercrime.'

She studied me pensively, took out a notebook and jotted down the few details I had given her. Then she slapped the book shut and put it in the smart little shoulder bag she had with her. 'Great. I'll pass this on to the department, then those higher up than me will have to take the decision.' With an acidic smile she added: 'But when they find out who tipped us off, well...'

She didn't say any more, but I took the point. With a quick nod she got up and left. I was left sitting next to an empty coffee cup. Now I had a choice. Another cup or the car? I followed Winnie the Pooh's example and chose both. I ordered another cup and sat, notepad in hand, deep in thought. Were there any more leads I could follow in these rather loosely connected cases?

I should confront Bjarne Bratteli with what Laila had told me. Perhaps talk to her brother again as well. And as Magne Molstad was the only priest in the case, perhaps I should make some discreet enquiries about him. It might also be interesting to have a chat with the neighbour who owned the wooden bat, Carl Fredrik Stiansen. The challenge was probably to find a connection between Per Haugen and Mikael Midtbø beyond the patently obvious. In that regard it would be interesting to talk to Karl Slåtthaug, even if it seemed it would involve a trip to Tønsberg at my own expense.

I walked to my car. From the roof of Bygarasjen I had a panoramic view of Bergen in all directions. The mountains here were close together: Ulriken to the south, Løvstakken to the west and Fløyen to the east. In the north the sky towered over the island of Askøy, bluish-green with a final streak of red where the sunset had splashed blood. From here everything looked harmonious and peaceful – if you ignored the traffic and the cars buzzing like angry wasps all around me – but I knew from bitter experience that behind the façades it could all be anything but. There, the most incomprehensible abuse could take place and, indoors, we were regularly in a state of confusion, often with long-lasting consequences – for ourselves, too; for the way we regarded our fellow human beings.

How many such incidents could a single individual endure? How many tragedies did we have the strength to digest? Was the time perhaps ripe for me to clock off as well and leave people of those inclinations to get on with their dirty lives on their own without being disturbed by what they called 'none of my business'?

An immense protest rose within me. Priests have a calling, they say, so why couldn't a poor social worker-cum-private investigator have the same? My calling was to delve into misery and see what I could find. If just one small child had a better life because of me, it was worthwhile. The thought of all those who'd had their lives destroyed was hard to bear. My job was given to me, if not by a heavenly power, then by fate. But it didn't pay cash up front. It barely paid after delivery, unless you rang an appropriate debt collector and asked him to sort things out for you.

But I hadn't got that far. Not yet.

21

I drove to the multi-storey car park in Markeveien and walked down to my office. There was no one waiting for me by the hotel reception desk. No one clawing at my door to get in. I unlocked, switched on the light, turned on the kettle to brew myself another cup of coffee and booted up the computer.

My first search was for Bjørn Hårkløv. The address of Hårkløv Kreditt was in Sandsli, which was a short distance from Flesland Airport, if he had any jobs out of town. I didn't discount the possibility that he had. Standard practice in his line of business was often to send debt collectors from Bergen to Oslo and vice versa. Some believed doing that left fewer traces, but the authorities had been aware of this *modus operandi* for a long time. On the other hand, perhaps the collectors weren't as easily recognised on the streets of the other town, so there was some advantage. If he was still Bruno Karsten's extended arm in the Bergen district Hårkløv would probably have to travel to Germany as well, to update his lord and master on the state of affairs in the old Hansa town.

The private address was the same as the one he had when I last had to deal with him. It was in Dag Hammarskjølds vei, a low block of flats not so far from where Svanhild Olsvik lived. Was he perhaps one of those who had promised her robust assistance if she needed it?

A general search of the net revealed only that Hårkløv Kreditt appeared on several web pages, with a telephone number and an address and a short description: 'credit investigation etc'. What lay behind 'etc' was probably the most important part of their activities, which I had seen demonstrated in Sletten a few hours earlier.

I tried a new search, this time for Carl Fredrik Stiansen. A private address in Frekhaug came up. In addition, I discovered he was on the prize list for various regattas in the vicinity, Round Askøy and others; he was rarely the winner, but definitely in the top tier. In a photo published by the local Nordhordland newspaper he stood beaming on the deck of a boat called *Alice* and, sure enough, another search informed me that Alice Stiansen lived at the same address in Frekhaug, his wife from what I could see. Carl Fredrik Stiansen looked like a well-built man who could handle a bat if necessary. Under profession it stated he was a civil engineer, but omitted to say where.

The last person whose telephone number I found was Hans Storebø in the Sund district, Per Haugen's brother-in-law and uncle of the children. This was something I could take up with him: the relationship between the two siblings, Laila and Knut.

I dialled the number without any luck. Thirty seconds later he rang back. From what I could hear he was outdoors. 'Who is it?'

'This is Veum. We met yesterday, at your sister's.'

'Oh, yes. I remember.'

'Since then I've met Knut and Laila, your two – your sister's children.'

'Well, that's more than I've done for many a year. That ship sailed a long time ago.'

'So I gathered.'

'How are they?'

'Laila got the short straw. She has a difficult life. Divorced, on pills, debts in a murky market – in brief, tough.' He listened to what I had to say without commenting. 'The brother seemed to be coping better. Good job, wife and children, as you told me. Slightly aggressive attitude maybe, but I suppose that's understandable when this subject comes up.' He still didn't comment. 'But Laila seemed bitter, towards her mother too.'

'Oh, yes?'

'She felt betrayed by her. She said she'd told her mother what her father had been doing while it was all happening. To no avail. And when they both testified in court the mother said she'd never noticed anything of the kind. She simply didn't believe anything the daughter said.'

'Yes, I was in court too. Of course, that hurt. But I've never confronted Tora with this. It would be too difficult.'

'Laila must've felt totally alone in the world. Let down by everyone. Her father, her mother, and later her husband.'

'Her husband?'

'She ... Well, that's another matter. But there's every reason to suppose he may've been involved in something as well.'

'That's terrible. Most of this is news to me, Veum. As I told you yesterday, I haven't had any contact with Laila or Knut since they were very small. But Tora knowing as well, and Laila going to her and saying ... That's almost incomprehensible. But as I also said yesterday, Tora's a slightly naïve soul, and after what we experienced during the war she's shied away from anything that might draw attention.' He sighed aloud. 'She didn't exactly get her wishes fulfilled when all this business with Per Haugen blew up.'

There was a short silence. Then he said: 'Well, I've promised to accompany her to her medical examination on Friday. Tora, that is. I don't think I'll discuss with her what Laila said. I'm frightened she's on her way into the mists, and something like this will only confuse her. And she's confused enough as she is.'

'I'm sure you're right. It's too late to do anything about the guilt she must be feeling anyway.'

'Yes. Was there anything else you had on your mind?'

'No, not at the moment. Thank you for your time.'

'Oh, I have plenty of that. Time's far from the biggest problem you have at my age.'

We concluded the conversation with a couple more platitudes. His last words rang in my ears. Time was a moot concept. Some people had too much on their hands, others too little. One person had to accompany his sister to the doctor; the other had to pay a debt the following day to stop it growing. I knew whose shoes I would prefer to be in. I was equally clear about who I had most sympathy for.

I looked at my watch. I wondered when the kindergarten where Bjarne Bratteli was employed closed for the day and if he went straight home. I'd give him an hour or two. This time I wasn't going to warn him of my arrival. Not until I was standing at his door.

22

I parked by the kerb and rang the doorbell of B. Bratteli. Shortly afterwards his voice came over the loudspeaker: 'Yes? Who is it?'

'Veum. Something new's come up.'

'Something new? About Laila?'

'Yes.'

'This isn't such a convenient time.'

'I'm afraid I have to insist. It won't take long.'

I heard him talking to another person, away from the microphone,
so that I couldn't catch what he was saying. Then he was back. 'Right.'
The lock buzzed and I pushed the door open.

He was standing in the doorway, waiting for me. He didn't invite me
in. 'What was it you had to say?'

'We-ell.' I motioned towards his door. 'Can we go in?'

He sent me a resigned look. 'I thought you said it wouldn't take long.'

'But it will take *some* time.'

He sighed, giving me a displeased expression, which might have
worked wonders in the kindergarten, but cut no ice with me. Then he
shrugged his shoulders, pushed the door wide open and went into the
flat ahead of me.

He wasn't alone. Knut Haugen was sitting in the chair where I had
sat the previous evening. He half stood when I entered, as if to show
that he possessed a certain degree of politeness, nodded a greeting
and sat down again. He was wearing the same dark suit as he had in
his office, but he had changed his tie, not that it had any impact at all.
Above his head hung the photograph of his sister in much better days.
Even now, having met her, I had trouble recognising in her the cheery
elegance of those days.

There were two mugs of coffee on the table where they had been sitting. Bratteli moved a dining-room chair, which looked like an heirloom and stood out from the rest of the furniture, into the middle of the floor. He motioned for me to sit there. He sat down in the other one and made no move to offer me any coffee.

'You've already met my brother-in-law, I understand,' he said.

'I have.'

'We're both worried about Laila.'

Knut Haugen nodded in agreement.

'With good reason,' I said and told them briefly about the incident with Bjørn Hårløv that morning.

'A debt collector?' Haugen said. 'Working for whom?'

'A few years ago he represented a German by the name of Bruno Karsten. Does that name mean anything to you?'

They looked at each other and shook their heads in unison, like twins.

'Organised crime. Drugs, prostitution and cybercrime.' I paused, but there was no reaction. 'His name's Bjørn Hårkløv. Hårkløv Kreditt, if you should need him.'

Bratteli mumbled, 'Drug debts.' He looked at his brother-in-law. 'That's what I said.'

'If not drugs, pills at any rate,' I said.

Haugen narrowed his eyes, but whether it was because he was shortsighted or because he was trying to appear dangerous was hard to say. 'I'll contact him. This has to be cleared up.'

'You can try,' Bratteli said. 'But I wouldn't be too optimistic if I were you. At least not on Laila's behalf.'

I looked at Haugen. 'You might remember … she had a friend when she was small. A girl called Marthe.'

Haugen nodded slowly. 'Yes, I remember her.'

'She took her own life a while back.'

He blinked, several times in a row. 'What are you saying? Little Marthe who … ? Well, of course she wasn't so little any more.'

'Do you remember her surname?'

'Mmmm,' he answered. 'Something beginning with M. Moll, Moll ... Molstad!'

I studied him. 'Molstad?'

He nodded.

'Do you remember if she had a brother called Magne?'

'Ye-es. She had a brother who was a few years older, but I don't recall his name. Could've been Magne, for all I know.'

'And he became a priest?'

'I don't know anything about that,' he said, stressing the final word.

'But she and Laila spent a lot of time together?'

'Yes, I do remember that. They were what you would call best friends, I suppose. It was terrible to hear she'd ... How did she do it   take her own life?'

'She jumped off Askøy Bridge.'

'Oh, my God.'

'You can say that again. According to Laila, it was a direct conse- quence of also being ... Of your father abusing her.'

He looked at me with sombre eyes and shook his head ruefully. 'Now it's coming out.'

I shifted my gaze to Bratteli. 'This kind of thing can have long-term consequences. Your whole life's marked by early experiences.'

He met my gaze and nodded slowly. 'Yes. It ...'

Haugen made a show of looking at his watch, a Rolex costing half my annual income. Only if it was a good year, mind you. 'I must go. Din- ner's at half past six today. We've talked about what was on our minds, you and I, Bjarne.'

'We have more to talk about, you and I, Haugen,' I said.

'Really? But not now. It'll have to be ... later.'

'I'll be in touch.'

'OK.' This didn't appear to be something he was looking forward to. 'You'll have to ring the office and make an appointment with the secretary.'

'The young lady I greeted the other day?'

'Yes.'

Haugen got to his feet. Bratteli did the same, eyeing me as he did so – a barely concealed instruction to follow suit. As I made no attempt to comply, he said: 'Was there anything else?'

'Yes.'

'I thought you came here to tell me about the debt collector and Laila?'

'There's another matter now that your brother-in-law's going.'

'OK, OK.' He sighed loudly.

Knut Haugen nodded goodbye and went into the hall, where he put on his coat and went out of the door.

Bratteli returned quickly. 'Right. What was it you had to say?' He stood in the middle of the floor to make it clear that he didn't have much time for me.

'Your ex-wife told me this morning why she was precisely that: your ex. And why she ended the marriage.'

'I'm not with you.'

'No?'

'It was a break-up that arose from the circumstances. Primarily her pill consumption and her uncontrollable drinking.'

'She said she'd caught you watching child porn on the computer.'

'Child—?'

'Images of young children in a variety of situations. Not exactly something you'd want to present at a parents' meeting. Or to talk about at home, either. Images of an exceedingly gross nature.'

'And she said this after only a few short seconds?'

'Short seconds?'

He looked away. 'Not that this is any business of yours, Veum.'

'Well, we're probably talking here about a duty to society, which each and every one of us should respect.'

'You don't understand. In this job I have …' He paused. I waited, and after a little while he continued: 'We have to familiarise ourselves with this material … to a certain extent.'

'Really? To what end?'

'To prevent this sort of thing going on.'

I ran my hand down the back of my head and neck. 'And you have to study it in detail to prevent it spreading?'

'Detail? I was looking … I had only just clicked on it when Laila came in, saw what was on the screen and kicked up one hell of a fuss.' He raised his voice. 'But I understood her reaction. With her background. Perhaps I would've reacted in the same way myself. Believe me … I'm not like that.'

'And you expect me to believe you when your wife didn't?'

'Listen to what I'm telling you. With her background it's not surprising she was suspicious. She was damaged as a result of her childhood.'

'Exactly. And so the least you could do was take precisely that into account.'

'Naturally enough, I didn't think she would … turn up like that.'

'And she obviously saw them for longer than the short seconds you talk about. She gave a pretty detailed description.'

He looked down. 'She demanded I show her the images again. I didn't feel I could deny her that.'

'No? She also said you might've taken some of the photos yourself. At the kindergarten.'

He flushed. 'You mustn't believe that! I could never have done that to … That would be a total betrayal of … What do you imagine the parents would've said? The children? No, no, no. That's impossible. I admit I was looking at the pictures. To see what they were. But that's all. I'm not like that.'

'You've just said that. What do you mean by … "like that"?'

'A paedophile. Like her father. Like so many others. I was just … curious.'

'It has a lot of names.'

'And you? Are you so pure? Have you never opened a page like that on the net?'

I got up from the chair. 'No, Bratteli. In fact I haven't. Not even for study purposes.' I pointed to his shelving unit. 'But the last time I was here I noticed that you had a lot of photo equipment and a film camera.'

'It's my hobby. Is that banned too now? You and all the others are so self-righteous.'

'Not all of us, unfortunately.' I gestured towards the door. 'Your brother-in-law, Knut – does he know about this?'

'About what? Laila's allegations?'

'Yes.'

'Well, he hasn't mentioned them. Do you think he would've come here to talk about what we could do to help her if he'd … If she'd told him?'

'Probably not.'

I walked towards the door. He made a move to grab my arm. 'What are you going to do now, Veum? You're not taking this any further!'

I turned to him. 'You can give it some thought this evening and over the next few days. What do you reckon?'

'Don't you bloody dare! If you do…'

'If I do…?'

'I won't answer for the consequences.'

'For me or for…?'

'For you, yes.'

'Shall I take that as a threat?'

'Take it as whatever you bloody want.'

We stood sizing each other up. Physically, he didn't frighten me. But you never knew what a desperate person might resort to. For all I knew, he had access to a VW Golf or other murder weapons.

'Let me put it like this, Bratteli: right now I have other matters to puzzle over. But with regards to your job … I would keep away from anything connected with such activities, whether on the net or in reality. I'm going to make some enquiries and if I have the slightest suspicion that you've violated the law, then … And you can take *that* as a threat, so now we're even.'

He put on a slightly tougher face, but I noticed to my satisfaction that he looked away first. Without saying another word, I left him hanging in the air, like a conjuror's rabbit, totally disorientated.

Back in my car, I found the number of Magne Molstad and rang him. He answered after a couple of rings. 'Yes, hello?'

'Veum here. We met yesterday.'

'Yes. How can I help?'

'Did you have a sister called Marthe?'

After a conspicuous silence, he replied: 'Yes.'

'She committed suicide.'

'Yes, she did unfortunately.'

'Could we meet and have a chat about this?'

'What has this to do … with all the other stuff?'

'I think you might know. However, if not, I can explain.'

'Really?'

'Face to face.'

'But … Alright then. We can meet tomorrow. At twelve.'

'Where?'

'There's a café in the middle of Knarvik Shopping Centre. Or better, we can meet in Åsane. The Åsane centre instead. The café's more or less in the middle. There's a bookshop right next to it. We can meet in front.'

'OK.'

Without further ado he rang off. I made a mental note that he wanted to meet a bit further away from home than Knarvik. Not that this was necessarily of any importance.

As I started the car I looked in my rear-view mirror. Fifty metres behind me a car pulled out without signalling. I reacted instantly. It was a Golf, of that I was fairly sure, and it was grey.

Nye Sandviksvei arched round towards Sverresborg Fortress, where I indicated to go left up Helgesens gate. I waited for an oncoming car to pass. The Golf re-appeared in the mirror, keeping the same distance as before. I turned up Helgesens gate with an eye on my mirror. The Golf continued towards the town centre.

For a moment I wondered whether I should turn round in the Stølen area and give chase. But I rejected the idea. It would be so far ahead of me by the time I had turned, and at Mariakirken I would have to decide which road to follow. I carried on up to Skansen and parked in Øvre Blekevei, as usual.

I felt a need to think about something else. But when I rang Sølvi it turned out she was busy with a friend and then looking after Helene. So it was going to be an evening alone in Telthussmuget instead, with a very basic meal: salami, beetroot and potatoes, a beer with the food and then whatever was left in my bottle of aquavit. It gave me everything it had, until it was empty. That was more than enough for me. When I went to bed I slept like a log through the night, so much so that I could barely get out of bed when the alarm clock rang; and I had what felt like the onset of a physical depression.

These days cases like the present one could do this to me. It was, I observed, the surest sign that I was getting old. That, and what I saw when I looked in the mirror. On a morning like this I refrained from doing that.

23

There was an email from Inspector Bjarne Solheim waiting for me when I reached the office. I opened the attachment and found a long list of the previous year's VW Golfs registered in Bergen and Hordaland.

I quickly scrolled down through the list without finding any names I immediately recognised, except for a couple of highly peripheral acquaintances I could in no way suspect of having tried to run me down one winter's evening by Lagunen. I printed the list and went through it again, car by car. The only thing I noticed was that twelve of them were registered to four car rental companies. I doubted very much I would be given the names of people who had rented the cars if I rang around. The police, on the other hand, would.

I called Solheim and, speaking in my nicest voice, I said: 'Hi Bjarne. Varg here. Thank you very much for the list.'

'Veum,' he stated, in a much more measured tone. 'Did you recognise any of the names?'

'Unfortunately not. No one I could suspect of this crime anyway. But … the ones registered to car rental companies…'

'Yes, we noticed them.'

'Would it be at all possible for you to get the names of the people who used the cars?'

'Mmm. I would think so. Might have to confer with the legal department, but I'd assume so.'

I coughed. 'When you've got a list, could you let me see it, too?'

'Yes. We could probably consider that. This case doesn't exactly have top priority, but…' Before I could interrupt him, he added quickly: 'Of course we'll check it. You'll hear from me when I have the list. Bye.' And he rang off.

I put down the phone and went through the piece of paper in front of me again. I could of course search through the listed names on the net to see if any priests turned up. But for the moment I would have to make do with the man I was meeting at twelve.

Cognisant of the time it usually took to find a parking spot there, I got into my car and drove to Åsane at eleven. Magne Molstad appeared on the stroke of twelve, even if no church bells rang to announce his morning service this time. I had taken up a position outside the bookshop and so had enough time to familiarise myself with the covers of several Christmas bestsellers still displayed in the windows. I hadn't received any of them for Christmas; I could count on three fingers the presents I had received: one from Sølvi, one from Helene and one from little Jakob in Oslo, doubtless chosen by his parents, Thomas and Mari. Useful presents though, all of them.

Molstad appeared like a genie from a lamp. This time, too, he made a strikingly grey impression, reinforced by his colourless clothes: dark-grey trousers, grey clerical shirt and a winter coat that was a composition in grey. His hair, eyebrows, everything was grey on grey. I put him in his mid-forties, but I wouldn't have been surprised if he was ten years older.

We headed for the café and decided on a table. I treated myself to a round of waffles and a cup of coffee. He followed my example, hardly unknown fare for someone with long experience of parish meetings.

'You didn't want my card last time we met, but here we are again anyway,' I said when we had both sat down.

'I couldn't see that we had anything else to discuss,' he said, looking at me expectantly.

'OK, but at that time I didn't know you had a sister called Marthe. Who took her own life a while back.'

'I just don't understand the link between that and what you wanted to talk to Haldis about.'

'We can come back to that. Tell me a little about your sister.'

He seemed fairly happy and his gaze wandered down the long atrium of the shopping centre before he said anything. 'Well, what is there to say about Marthe? Life took a wrong turn and she ended up on drugs, became addicted and in the end she committed suicide. I officiated at her funeral; the turnout was sparse.' He sent me a dejected look. 'A wasted life.'

'And what was the cause, do you think?'

'Well, what can I say? Everything went fine for me. There was nothing at home that could've caused this.'

'Your dialect suggests you moved here.'

'Yes, we came from Ålesund when I was ten and Marthe four. I kept my dialect, I suppose, at least most of it, while she switched to the Bergen dialect and never spoke anything else.'

'She had a friend called Laila.'

'Yes, I think she did, in Helleveien. They lived in one of those high-rises, didn't they?'

'In Brunestykket, yes. Does the name Per Haugen mean anything to you?'

'Per Haugen. No, can't say it does.'

'Sure?'

'Veum, as a priest you meet so many people in the most varied of contexts, but I definitely can't remember that name from any such occasions. Who is it?'

'Laila's father.'

'Oh, yes?' His face took on a pensive expression. 'Well, I have to admit I don't remember many grown-ups from there, except the parents of the children I became friends with, and there was no one called Haugen among them.'

'She had a brother called Knut. How old are you?'

'Me? Forty-three.'

'Then he was probably a bit younger than you.'

'I see. Well, I don't remember anyone called Knut anyway.'

We sat in silence for a while. I ate a couple of waffles and took a swig of coffee.

He broke the silence. 'I still don't understand the connection here. Can you explain?'

'Yes.' I put down my cup. 'This is how it is. Laila Haugen, whose name is Bratteli now, is in the same situation as your sister was. I'm thinking … addicted.'

'Really? So?'

'This Per Haugen was arrested eighteen months ago along with … a few others, all on the same charge. One of them was Mikael Midtbø.'

He hesitated. 'You mean … he was someone who sexually abused children?'

'Yes.'

Slowly the mists began to lift. 'Are you saying … that's what happened to Marthe when she was small?' He had two angry lines in his forehead, between his eyebrows.

'According to Laila, yes.'

'So this … this father of Laila abused Marthe?' His face had gone a wan colour.

'And his own daughter. And in all likelihood many more.'

'But that's, that's … monstrous! Why wasn't he reported?'

'Well, you could ask that. But the two victims I'm aware of were small girls, five to six years old. They were scared to speak up. Which was his doing. Perhaps they didn't know how to express themselves, and would they have been believed, more than thirty years ago?'

'But … didn't she have a mother, this Laila? A sibling? Did no one see anything?'

'She had a brother, the Knut I mentioned, a couple of years older than her. But he … well.' I shrugged. 'And yes, she had a mother. Laila told me she'd even said something to her, at a later point, but she didn't react. What's a small child supposed to do in that case?'

'This is terrible to hear. Now I understand … Well, why you're making connections with Haldis … with Mikael Midtbø. But, this mother, has she never been called to account?'

'I suppose you're one of those who believe in a higher court?'

'What?' He seemed confused. 'Yes, yes I am … but judgement is mine, saith the Lord, and we can only pray that we're treated with mercy when our day comes.'

'Then I can tell you that this woman, Tora Haugen, is passing into the darkness of senility and can hardly be confronted with anything at all any more. When the case came to court she denied everything and protected her husband, who accordingly was given the same mild sentence as ... Mikael Midtbø.'

He sat shaking his head, still distressed by what I had told him. 'But why have you come to me with this, Veum?'

'Because you're one of the links.'

'One of the ... What are you talking about?'

I thought carefully. 'To me it looks as though some people have had a lethal dose of fate here.'

'By which you mean what?'

'Your sister's dead. She took her own life. Mikael Midtbø's dead. He – apparently – took his own life. Per Haugen's dead.'

'What? Him, too?'

'He drowned. An accident maybe or ... well...'

'But for goodness' sake I'm not a link.'

'You're linked to Per Haugen through your sister. Her tragic life and ultimate fate are almost certainly a result of what she experienced as a child. You're linked to Mikael Midtbø through your relationship with his wife.'

'Relationship?! We didn't have a relationship, not until ... afterwards.'

'After what?'

'After they separated. We talked about this the day before yesterday. There's no link.'

'But Mikael Midtbø was expecting a visit from a priest on the day he died. At any rate, someone he called a pastor. You denied it was you the other day, but now I'm thinking it could still have been you.'

'And to what purpose?'

I opened my palms. 'What do I know about how priests think? To extend a placatory hand? To make him regret his actions, to pray to God for forgiveness? Or maybe you appeared as an avenging angel, on God's behalf?'

He looked furious. 'I appeared as neither! I've never met him. I don't know where he lived in Fyllingsdalen. And this Per Haugen I knew nothing of until you told me just now.'

'But you'd have liked a chat with him?'

'Had I known ... Had I ever guessed what lay behind what happened to Marthe ... Believe me, I did what I could to help her out of her mess. I contacted my friends in the Church City Mission, the Inner Mission and the Salvation Army. You must know that there are many Christian organisations that work for people whose lives have been turned upside down.'

'Absolutely. I do know.'

'But it was no use. And she never told me what was bothering her. If she had done, then ... maybe it would've helped. It does, Veum. Talking things over.'

'Yes, I believe you. We social workers do the same.'

'You're a social worker?'

'Yes, or I was.'

'I see,' he said, although I wasn't entirely sure he did. Then he continued: 'I made her go to a rehabilitation clinic, at least twice, but she relapsed. In the end, I suppose I gave up. I entrusted her into the Lord's hands.'

'And that led nowhere.'

'Yes, if that's how you see it, I suppose it did.' He stared sombrely into the distance. I couldn't help but feel for him. It wasn't his fault his sister had been subjected to a man like Per Haugen when she was small. A neighbour he couldn't even remember. One of life's many shadowy beasts, lying in wait for prey, and when one day a victim appears, they set upon her with lust in their hearts.

Per Haugen. Mikael Midtbø. Karl Slåtthaug. Was Bjarne Bratteli another? How many of them were out there? Was it possible to shine a light on them, one by one, to force them out of the shadows, into the light, so that we could all see them and protect ourselves? I was hardly alone in wishing this. Somewhere out there another person was perhaps on a mission, a lone wolf exacting vengeance, not even on God's behalf. Or was that precisely what he was doing, and, if so, who was he?

I sat looking at Magne Molstad. He was still a potential candidate, but I wasn't at all sure. No smoke was coming from the Vatican chimney while I was watching him. I would have to search elsewhere.

24

I was entering Eidsvåg Tunnel when my phone rang. As I didn't answer, it rang again before I was out. I turned down to the right into a supermarket car park and picked up my phone. It was an unfamiliar number. I rang back, and an excited voice said: 'Veum?'

'Yes.'

'This is Ghulam Mohammad. You must come. Someone's trying to get into Laila's again. He's banging on the door and won't stop.'

'Someone you've seen before?'

'Yes, it's him … her brother.'

'Knut Haugen? But he'll talk to you, won't he?'

'No. He doesn't listen to me. He calls me … horrible words. We should go back where we came from. That sort of thing.'

'I see. I'm on my way. Is Laila in?'

'Yes, but she won't open the door to him.'

'I'm coming.'

I rang off, reversed out of the parking bay and exceeded the speed limit down Helleveien for a few kilometres towards Fløyfell Tunnel. As this wasn't peak period, I cut through Danmarksplass like a summer mosquito heading for a sleeping sun worshipper, broke another couple of speed limits and was in Adolph Bergs vei in roughly ten minutes.

Getting out of the car, I heard angry voices coming from the house. Down on the pavement people had gathered and were staring with curiosity up at the gallery on the second floor. But no one made a move to do anything. This still might have been an everyday event in good old Chicago.

I took the stairs two steps at a time and ran along the gallery. Knut Haugen was standing, head bowed, shouting through her door at a volume that made the gallery – which was acting as a sounding board – vibrate. 'Laila! We have to talk. I'm not leaving until you open up. Do you hear me?'

When he saw me he pursed his lips. 'What the hell are you doing here?' He looked at Ghulam Mohammad, who had just appeared in his doorway. 'Right. I see. Darkie's blabbed.'

I was up close to him now. I fixed him with an icy stare and said: 'No one's blabbed and I don't see any darkies.'

'So what the fuck are you doing here?'

'I'm investigating a case.'

'Like fuck you are. All you're doing is snooping and sticking your snout in. That's what you're doing.'

'And what are *you* doing here?'

'I'm trying to talk to my sister, but it's fucking hard work.'

'Now you've used "fuck" three times and she still hasn't appeared.'

'That's none of your fucking business,' he shouted, as if to add defiance to his tirade. 'Didn't I tell you to leave my sister in peace?'

'Yes, but—'

'So why don't you leave her in peace?'

'Because there's something I want to ask her. Let me put my cards on the table, Haugen. I feel more and more certain your father didn't die a natural death.'

'So what. He deserved it.'

'Deserved what?'

'To die.'

'In that way?'

'In the worst possible way imaginable.'

His face was red with anger. Ghulam Mohammad followed our conversation as if it were a performance we were putting on especially for him.

Knut Haugen vented his annoyance on him. 'And what the fuck are you standing there and gaping for? You can just bloody go back to where you came from!'

Ghulam Muhammad pulled himself up to his full height. 'We've lived in Norway for more than twenty years. This is where we belong now.'

'His language is better than yours anyway,' I muttered.

Then something happened. The door behind us opened a fraction, on the safety chain. From above it Laila glowered at us. Her face was crimson. She fixed her eyes on her brother. 'I'll never talk to you again. You're just like our father – and Bjarne: a pig.'

I looked from her to Knut. His face had contorted with anger. 'What are you saying, you little bitch?'

'Don't you think I saw them? The photos you sent Bjarne – of your own children, of Toril and Elisabeth.'

He opened and shut his mouth.

'You're a pig.' She shifted her gaze to me. 'You're filthy pigs, all of you.' Then she looked at Ghulam Mohammad. 'And you're no bloody better, Ghulam.'

His jaw fell.

I tried to catch her attention, but her eyes were flitting wildly from one of us to the other. 'Laila, listen … If you have something specific to say, then…'

'Specific?' Next to me, Knut snorted. 'You can hear she's lost it. The bitch's out of her tiny mind.'

'Aaargghh!' she shrieked, spat at us from above the safety chain and slammed the door so hard the concrete walls around us sang.

For a moment we were stunned, all three of us, found guilty on account of our gender, clearly, as far as I could judge. We looked at each other. Ghulam threw up his arms, rolled his eyes, withdrew into his flat and slammed the door behind him. Not as hard as Laila, but hard enough to signal what he thought of us two, the ethnic Norwegians.

I eyed Knut. 'Well?'

'Stark, raving bonkers.'

I held his gaze. 'But what she said about the photos you sent to Bjarne…'

'She's lying through her teeth. You could see that for yourself. She needs sectioning. I'll bloody make sure she is. Sandviken next stop, no doubt about it.'

'She's lying?'

I held his gaze. He stared back. Then his eyes wandered to the side. And he focused on me again. Now it was his turn to throw up his arms. 'I'm simply not putting up with this, Veum. I'm off.'

He left. I watched him. I had been lied to before, many times. But life had taught me one thing. The person who lies rarely manages to hide it, not completely. And that was the feeling I was left with now.

Someone was lying to me, and one thing was sure: in such cases as this I seldom gave up until I found out who it was. And why.

25

When he was out of the building I turned back to Laila's door. I rang the bell. I knocked. I put my mouth against the door crack and called her name in as friendly a tone as possible. Nothing. She definitely didn't want to talk, neither to me, nor anyone else right now.

I walked to Ghulam Mohammad's flat and rang his bell. He opened the door warily, as though afraid I would kick it in. When he saw Haugen had gone, relief swept across his face. He looked at me with a serious expression, without speaking.

'He's gone,' I said, somewhat redundantly.

He nodded.

'I wonder if … Laila doesn't want to talk to anyone just now. Fatima seems to have the best relationship with her. Could you ask her to put in a word for me? She talked with me the last time I was here, so she knows I'm on her side. I can perhaps even help her with her debts. There'll be people other than her brother here, again and again, until they have what they want or something more serious happens.'

He listened with the same expression on his face as before, but he nodded a few times along the way. In the end he stroked one cheek. 'I'll tell Fatima.'

'You've got my phone number. Don't be frightened to call me. Even if a situation like today happens again. But first of all try to talk her round.'

'I'll do my best. This must end. The poor woman can't carry on like this.'

'No. We'll have to see what we can do.'

We exchanged a few final courteous looks. He closed the door as warily as he had opened it. I went down to my car.

The high-rise in the Landåstorget district was the oldest in Bergen, completed in 1957. I drove up, parked at the rear, walked to the library on the first floor of the annexe and gained access to a computer. I ran a search on Knut Haugen again and found confirmation that his address was in Nystuveien. I then ran another search, on the address this time, to see if there were any other occupants. There were. Vibeke Haugen lived at the same address. Her name didn't produce any hits, except for on the tax list, where it transpired her assets were greater than her taxable income. However, I assumed they corresponded to half of the marital home.

I thanked the librarian for letting me use a computer and received a friendly smile in return. Back in my car, I reflected for a moment, then made up my mind.

Nystuveien winds its way between Ole Irgens vei and Starefoss-veien, apparently named after Starefossen, when it was a little rural area with the overspill from Jølster and other places in the districts around Bergen. The house where I was going had a basement of whitewashed brick and a shiny front door. On the floor above there were large pano-ramic windows with views of Bergensdalen valley. The space behind them was well illuminated. In addition, there were bright Christmas stars hanging against the glass, an indication that the residents hadn't finished their Yuletide celebrations. On the way up to the house I passed a thawing snowman bent at the hip, an arthritic terpsichorean.

From the nameplate I could see I was at the right address and pressed the doorbell. After a while the loudspeaker above the button crackled. A woman's voice said: 'Yes? Who is it?'

'My name's Veum. Varg Veum. Is that Vibeke Haugen?'

'What was your name again?'

'Varg Veum.'

'I have nothing to say. My husband's warned me.'

'Warned you about what?'

'You. He said if someone turns up with your name, I'm not to open the door or listen to what you say. If you don't accept that, I'm to … call the police.'

'That's what I'd call a clear message.'

'So, goodbye, herr Veum.'

'Don't you have an opinion of your own?'

'Just go.'

'I'll have another chat with your husband then.'

'Goodbye.'

She sounded so sure of herself that I didn't see any point in arguing any further. I could of course have hung around to see if she would actually call the police. In which case, I would have the opportunity to tell them something that was unlikely to please her husband. The loudspeaker crackled again: 'I'll give you one more chance. Otherwise I'm calling the police.'

I took some steps back from the house and looked up. She was in the window, directly under one of the Christmas stars, a St Lucia's Day princess who had arrived too late for the procession. She was wearing a loose white blouse, which reinforced this impression. Her hair was tidy and attractive. She definitely wouldn't disgrace herself or her husband if she was introduced at a dinner party. But so far only I was present, and the look she was sending me was so cool I could have been a snowman in the process of crumbling myself, standing next to the other one. In her hand she had a mobile phone, which she held up in my direction, as a threat. *Mene, mene, tekel, upharsin.* I had been weighed and found wanting.

I arched my eyebrows, nodded to confirm I understood what she meant, and left. In the street, I turned round again. She was standing in the window, watching me. I raised a hand to wave goodbye. She didn't reciprocate.

Vibeke Haugen, I said to myself. *Why so distant, why so cool? Have you also got something to hide? Something you don't wish to know more about? You too?*

26

I parked in Markeveien and chose the shortest route to my office. Once inside, I took out my notepad. There was another loose end to tie up, a person I hadn't yet questioned. I found the number of the neighbour in Frekhaug, the man with the bat: Carl Fredrik Stiansen.

When he answered I introduced myself and explained: 'I'm investigating what happened to your former neighbour, Mikael Midtbø.'

'Oh, yes?'

'You know he's dead?'

'I saw mention of his death in the paper, yes. We cracked open a bottle of champers to celebrate the event.'

'Right. Is it convenient to have a chat about the case?'

'About what happened when the bastard abused our daughter?'

'That, too.'

'What did you say you were? A private investigator?'

'Yes.'

'A bit more effective than the cops, I hope.'

'Well...'

'Fine. I'm in my office in Kanalveien and can give you fifteen minutes. Shall we say in half an hour?'

'Good. Where in Kanalveien?'

He gave me the number and name of the firm: Brokonsult AS.

My loyal Toyota Corolla didn't have much of a chance to catch its breath in Markeveien. I found a gap in front of a furniture shop in Kanalveien, parked and saw the entrance to the bridge consultancy firm at the given address. There wasn't a canal in Kanalveien any more, but bridges were sprouting up everywhere. In that sense, the firm was located at a symbolic address.

A rare sight greeted me – a male vestibule attendant, a youth in a casual outfit: a suit jacket over jeans and an open-necked shirt. He would have been given the boot at an estate agent's. In this office-scape, he fitted in perfectly. On the walls around him there were large photographs of several completed construction projects. I recognised the newly built bridge over Brennøy Sound in one of them. I had myself been there when the previous one was blown up.

Behind him, the staff's work stations were in bays, their heads protruding like small underground trolls. He accompanied me to one of the bays. 'Carl, you have a visitor.'

Carl Fredrik Stiansen looked up, nodded and got to his feet. 'Veum?'

'Yep.'

'Let's find ourselves a conference room.'

Without bothering to shake hands, he walked right past me and strode ahead, across the large room, opened a door and led me into a room with a view of Mount Ulriken. We each sat down on a hard chair around a conference table. You had to speak quickly and efficiently here, it seemed. No one could sit for long on these chairs.

Carl Fredrik Stiansen sported the same outfit as the receptionist, and it struck me this might be a form of uniform as well, a combination of masculine efficiency and elegance. As far as I had seen, there was only one woman on the floor, and she'd had her hair cut short so as not to stand out from the others. Stiansen's hair was shaven down to his scalp, which gave him a military look. He looked pretty fit, too. If he was swinging a wooden bat, you would keep a safe distance.

He took the initiative. 'I don't quite understand what you're after, Veum. There was never any doubt what that bastard was up to.'

'No? Could you give me your version?'

'Mine…? I wasn't there, was I. All the things we found out … Well, I'll tell you my version. Being rung up by the police came as quite a shock. They told us they'd been given our names by our neighbour's wife, fru Midtbø, and they wanted to talk about our daughter, Trine. We had no idea what was going on, but we were summoned to Bergen Central Police Station, where we met an officer called Solheim.'

'I know him.'

'You can imagine how we felt when he said what the case was about. They'd found pictures on Midtbø's computer that had been spread all over – not only Norway, but the whole world. And then he showed us some of the photos, and Trine was in two of them. She was lying…' he gasped for breath and his voice was strangled with pent-up fury as he continued '…on a bed, almost naked, with her pyjama bottoms pulled down, and … Well, you can imagine. Partly on her side, but nevertheless! I can feel myself boiling with rage at the mere thought of it.'

I nodded sympathetically, without speaking.

'Have you got children?'

'A grown-up son and a grandchild.'

'Then you can perhaps understand. We didn't know where the photos had been taken because Trine had slept over many times at Anne's house. That's their daughter. We trusted them, after all. Who could believe this sort of thing about your own neighbours? It's not written in capital letters outside their house what sort of people they are. They aren't monsters. They look just like you and me. For all we knew, he could've been touching her, fondling her, doing terrible things to her.'

'Did the police examine her?'

'Yes, they did. She was sent to a doctor – a female – who carried out a discreet check-up. At any rate she established that Trine hadn't been "penetrated" – the doctor's word. But what else he might've done…' He bared his palms. Then he leaned over the table. 'Do you know what I mean, Veum? People like him deserve the death sentence.'

'That might be a bit—'

'Then he should be castrated! At the very least.'

'Now…'

'They're released again! And they can move to a new town and just carry on with the same activities. How long was Midtbø sentenced to exactly? If it had been up to me there would've been posters of him put up wherever he settled. "Watch out! A paedophile's moved into the neighbourhood." Like they do in the States.'

'I've heard about that. In some places.'

'Then you know where they are and you can keep an eye on them. But in Norway? Here they're patted on the head – "There, there. Now don't do that again! Promise me you'll be a good boy and we'll let you out tomorrow." Do you understand?'

'Yes, I do.' I did.

'But they're not the bloody victims here. What about the children whose lives they've ruined? Maybe forever?'

'Yes. Have you noticed anything about … Trine?'

He looked at me intently. 'No, luckily we haven't. She's still as trusting. Fortunately I don't think she was fully aware of what was going on. Of course there was a lot of gossip among the neighbours and probably at school. But as there was no evidence of a serious assault, then … well, we'll have to see. I've heard things can come to light many years later.'

'That was probably why he was set free so soon. They couldn't find anything else – apart from the photos.'

His lips tightened. 'You should've seen them.'

'I can understand why you were angry. Haldis Midtbø said you appeared at their door brandishing a bat.'

He looked down for a moment. Then he fixed me with a stare. 'Yes, well … I have to admit … That was the evening the police rang us. I was so angry. I hit the roof. Alice tried to hold me back, but … I grabbed the bat and strode off to the neighbour's. If he'd been at home I would've bloody smashed…' He paused. 'I would've beaten him up so badly he wouldn't have been able to stand upright for several days.'

'Would that have helped, do you think?'

'Helped? It would've taught him a lesson.'

'And you had a bat to hand?'

He glared at me. 'Doesn't every well-equipped home have one?'

'Mine doesn't.'

'At any rate, I had one. But unfortunately he'd already been arrested, so it was never used.'

'Not that night.'

'No.' Suddenly he reacted. 'Not that...? What do you mean by that?'

'I was just thinking. As you had a bat, you must've used it for some-thing. In this country it's mostly used as a weapon. In criminal circles.'

'I studied in England. We played cricket there. I brought a cricket bat back as a souvenir.'

'Mhm?'

'Mhm, yes. You don't need to look so sceptical. It's true! But ... a weapon in the house can always come in handy.'

'I can see. But ... you were aware Midtbø had been released.'

'Yes, and?'

'How did you know?'

He shrugged. 'I must've heard, I imagine.'

'In Norway, they let them out, you said.'

'Yes, but I meant in general.'

'He didn't come back to Frekhaug then?'

Again I could see the rage building in him. 'No, that would've been all I needed. If I'd met him in the street...'

'You would've gone indoors for your cricket bat?'

His face darkened. 'He would've definitely got the benefit of my opinion.'

'Do you know where he moved to?'

With wary eyes, he replied: 'No. Where?'

'Or how he died?'

'What are you babbling on about? No, I don't know where he moved to or how he died!' He took out his phone, flipped the lid and checked the time. 'That's more or less the quarter of an hour I promised you. In fact, it's more.'

'He moved to Fyllingsdalen. He fell from the tenth storey of a high-rise and died.'

'Fell?'

'Yes.'

'Well, it's an efficient way of disposing of rubbish.'

'Throwing it off the balcony?'

He gave an involuntary grin. 'Yes? I didn't see an obituary anywhere, a word about how much he was missed or what a good father and husband he had been. All I saw was news of his death.'

'And you took note?'

'As I said, we cracked open a bottle of champagne. Seriously.' He stood up as a sign the audience was over. 'In fact, now I have to do what they pay me for here.'

'And that is … to build bridges?'

He nodded, clearly unwilling to expand.

'Per Haugen. Does that name mean anything to you?' I said, getting up.

'Eh? Per Haugen? Who's that?'

'Karl Slåtthaug?'

'Never heard of him. What are you trying to say?'

'Consider it a test. Neither of these names means anything to you?'

'Not at all. Have we finished the kiddies' games now?'

'We have.'

'You still haven't said what you're actually investigating.'

'Well, it's the circumstances surrounding the death of Mikael Midtbø … and one other person.'

'Another person?'

'Yes.'

'For Christ's sake, you don't think I would … sacrifice the rest of my life for a sack of shit like Midtbø, do you?'

'You weren't that angry?'

'I was angry, yes, but not that much.'

'One last question: what make of car do you drive?'

'Car? A Volvo estate. Why do you ask?'

'Curiosity, that's all. A form of statistics … you might say.'

He looked at me, puzzled. Then he shook his head. Without saying much more he accompanied me to the young man in reception. He was working in front of a computer. For all I knew, he was designing a bridge, too.

I walked back down to my car. In my head I had no problem seeing Carl Fredrik Stiansen swinging a bat and chasing Mikael Midtbø onto the balcony in Fyllingsdalen, then dropping the bat and tipping Midtbø over the railing to his death.

I could identify with his anger. To protect our children we might well do something we normally considered impossible, even killing another person. But most people would suppress these emotions and let the mills of justice grind, however slowly. As for myself, I had grown up as an only child and never experienced home as anything but the safe haven it was supposed to be. As a father to my son I had been away a lot because of my job, but when I had been at home I had been present and later – as a divorced father – I had grasped every opportunity I had to be there for him. For me, as for fathers like Carl Fredrik Stiansen, it was incomprehensible that anyone could commit such crimes on their own children – or anyone else's.

But the case didn't stop there. There was another trail I hadn't followed far enough yet. I would have to ring Foyn to find out whether he had discovered anything about Karl Slåtthaug. And I would have to continue looking both ways – twice – before I crossed the road.

27

I was still in the car when Sølvi rang to see if I wanted to join Helene and her for dinner. I said yes at once. This was exactly what I needed after all the misery. A harmonious meal in Saudalskleivane. I didn't even drive home; I went straight there.

Sølvi welcomed me in the hallway. I put my arms around her, ran my hand down her spine to where she became rounder. I patted her backside and she kissed me on the cheek. Did that make me an old pig? Hardly. She was no more than ten years younger than me and a grown woman. I confined myself to a friendly stroke of Helene's hair – an appropriate way for adults to greet children they like.

In the dining room the table was set, and there was a lovely aroma of beef stroganoff or something similar wafting in from the kitchen. While Sølvi was finishing there, Helene was sat curled up on the sofa with a girls' magazine, and it struck me: in a year and a half she would be a teen-ager and on her way into a stage of her life when she would be subject to attention from not only boys of her age but also males older than her – and perhaps some much too old. There was something innocent and pure and beautiful about her sitting there – blonde hair, slightly untidy curls and a little smile playing around her mouth as she read. She was wearing casual clothes: dark-red trousers and a striped jumper. Her hair was gathered together with a light-blue ribbon and there was still something childish about her face – she wore no make-up. She would make an attractive woman, as her mother was, and hopefully just as sensible, even when she was confronted by difficult situations.

If you delved into filth, as I did, however, it was hard not to think about the other possibility: that someone might subject her to awful acts, against which she had no protection. Nevertheless, judging by all the outward signs, Helene had had a secure childhood. The worst that had happened to her was that she had lost her father prematurely and in a very dramatic way. The reflective and perhaps grieving expressions that occasionally flitted across her face were undoubtedly signs of the impact this had had.

And I thought: most children are like that. Most children live safe, protected lives with parents who love them. But some – indeed, not only some, but all too many – experienced the contrary, what should not happen; what ought to be a guarantee of security turning into something else, a safe haven becoming a spewing volcano, a Vesuvius speedily laying waste to Pompeii and leaving no more than stiffened figures, drawn in ash, fossilised in their own fates.

Sølvi came in from the kitchen with the food. My sense of smell hadn't been quite accurate. At close range it turned out to be a meat stew, not too distant from *boeuf bourguignon*, served with sparkling water for Helene and a glass of red wine for each of the adults. Neither of us complained about the service, neither the old man nor the young girl.

Eating together like this, I flashed back more than thirty years, to the time when another trio – Beate, Thomas and I – sat around a similar dinner table, probably with cheaper food than Sølvi served, but in the same format: two adults and a child. The child had been a boy and younger than Helene was now; the two adults had been younger than Sølvi and I. But there was still a kind of harmony and symmetry to the image, which filled my body with a strange peace, a break from the dark circles I had been moving in over the last few days.

Sølvi served us second helpings and poured herself another glass of red wine. I still wasn't halfway through my first. After the meal we moved over to the sofa. Helene was asked to make us some coffee, which she did without protest.

We behaved like a small family. Helene still had some homework to finish; Sølvi and I each immersed ourselves in our own pile of newspapers. Eventually we watched the news and the following TV programme.

Then my phone rang. I looked at the display. It was the same message as once before: *Unknown number*. I stood up and went towards the hall. Away from Sølvi and Helene, I responded to the call, but didn't speak. Nor did my interlocutor. This time there were no sounds of traffic in the background; there was only a heavy, ominous silence. Then the connection ended. I made an annoyed gesture with the phone as if I wanted to shake the caller's name out, not that it helped much.

I went back to the others. Sølvi looked up at me quizzically, but I just shook my head. 'Nothing important.'

However, I couldn't draw a line under it. This was the second time in a couple of days that someone had rung me and I had been met with silence, a veiled threat it wasn't hard to imagine was connected with at least one of two matters: the hit-and-run attempt up by Lagunen, and the investigation I was carrying out on my own initiative following the incident. Or – if they were connected, as I feared – both. But whoever he or she was, they weren't going to intimidate me. This just made me even more determined to get to the bottom of what was going on.

At ten Helene went to bed. Sølvi had opened another bottle of red wine and was now onto her fourth or fifth glass, but I was a few glasses behind. If it had been aquavit, then perhaps…

She peered at me over her wine glass with a dark glow in her eyes. 'How's the case you're working on going? Have you got any further?'

'Not really, I'm afraid.'

'I can see that in your face. There's something bothering you.'

I hadn't told her about the incident on Sunday, when I was almost run over near Lagunen. I had only briefly mentioned the articles about the two deaths I had noticed and that I was investigating the circumstances around them off my own bat. This was probably because of the backdrop to the deaths. We had never talked about what happened in the dramatic weeks that autumn about a year and a half ago, when she had herself broken the law by hiding me from the police. And not only that; she'd had some days when perhaps she hadn't been one hundred percent sure how innocent I was in that matter.

I hesitated. 'I'm swimming in pretty murky waters. There are men who commit sexual crimes against children in a way that suggests it's both systematic and – to some extent – organised.'

'Like … last time?'

'Yes. In fact, some of the same characters are involved. Ones who'd been released.'

Her jaw fell. 'What! They're out again? Already?'

'Yes.'

'But you said … "who'd been released".'

'Two of them are dead.'

'Dead? You surely don't mean … someone killed them?'

'That's exactly what I'm trying to find out.'

She compressed her lips. Then she said: 'And why? Does anyone mourn their passing?'

'Mm. A spouse in one case. Probably the second man's partner as well.'

'Yes, but … no one asked you to do this. Why…?' Suddenly a light came on in her eyes. 'You're frightened something similar might happen to you?'

'The charge against me was dropped, but … well, there was a minor incident on Sunday. It might've been a coincidence, but … I was almost run over, in a dark side street, up by Lagunen.'

'Run over? But … what were you doing there?'

'I was on a job. Something completely different. A car loomed up out of nowhere and … well, I had to throw myself to the side to avoid being hit.'

'Out of nowhere?' She expressed her amazement with the whole of her body. 'I assume you've reported this to the police?'

'Of course. But you know how efficient they are.' I grinned.

'Oh, Varg.' All of a sudden she was around my neck. 'You have to watch out. I don't want anything to happen to you, too.'

I wrapped my arms around her and squeezed her tight. In a much calmer voice than I felt inside, I said: 'Nothing'll happen, Sølvi. First of all, I was innocent, as innocent as I could be. They weren't. And, secondly, I'm on my guard. They probably weren't.'

She straightened up, keeping her arms around my neck. But she moved away a little, as if to see me properly. 'I can well understand someone doing something like that.'

'By which you mean…?'

'I can understand someone taking the law into their own hands, with animals like those men out on the street again, less than a year since they were sentenced. It's just absolutely terrible.'

'It's all tied up with the law. The burden of proof. That kind of thing.'

'Law. Burden of proof. I'm telling you, Varg, that if anything like this had happened to Helena…' a sudden savagery distorted her features '…I would've killed them with my bare hands. I wouldn't have hesitated. I'd have been like a lioness. And I think that's how most women would react.'

I looked at her. Women constituted only a tiny percentage of the murder statistics in Norway. Not as victims, sadly, but as the guilty party. But what she said took root in me, like a moment of inspiration. On the occasions women committed a murder it was often a reaction to something exactly like this, a crime perpetrated against them, against a sister or their children. These murders were personal, directed against the perpetrator. Perhaps it was just the short lapse of time between these two deaths that had made me react. Perhaps there was no connection other than the fact that both men had committed the same type of crime. Perhaps there wasn't a hypothetical pastor I should be looking for, but two women: one for each fatal incident, if they did indeed turn out to be murders.

She stretched out a hand, took her wine glass, drained it, set it back on the table, kissed me with her lips apart, wet with wine, and mumbled: 'Let's not talk about this. Let's. I want…'

There was no doubt about what she wanted. Not long afterwards, we were in her bed, two rooms further along, and for a passionate hour I forgot all about eyebrow-raising fatalities and any other context except the love-making of two people embroiled in a mixture of red-wine-induced euphoria and rhythmical gymnastics.

Afterwards we lay, slowly getting our breath back. My phone rang.

She sent me a wry, provocative look: *Are you going to answer it or let it ring?*

I let it ring, but picked it up to see if it was anyone I knew. I hadn't entered his name in my phone yet, but I recognised the number. It was Foyn from Tønsberg.

I sent her an apologetic expression. 'I think I'll have to answer this one.'

She shrugged. Then started kissing my chest and working her way downwards, like a further provocation: *Now or in a while?*

So in a while it was. I tapped in his number at almost midnight. He hadn't gone to bed, but his voice sounded a little slurred too.

'Veum? Foyn here.'

'Yes, I saw. I wasn't able to ring back until now.'

'That's okay. The guy you asked me to check out, Karl Slåtthaug?'

'Yes. Did you find anything?'

'Any chance you can come over to Tønsberg tomorrow?'

'I can try. What—?'

'The police would like to talk to you.'

'The police? But—'

'Thing is, this Slåtthaug … has gone missing.'

'Has he now?!'

Sølvi heard from the intonation that something had happened and gave me an enquiring glance. I caressed her hair and she lowered her head again.

'He'd told his office he was meeting a priest.'

I sat up in bed so abruptly Sølvi fell off. 'What! A priest?'

'Yes.'

'Let me just … I'll go and check for flights straightaway. I'll be on the first one tomorrow morning.'

'I can pick you up from Torp.'

'Deal.'

Sølvi looked at me. 'Another death?'

'Hard to say, but…'

She wriggled back up and kissed me on the mouth this time. 'Do you have to go home then?'

'I'll have to check the flights first, but I'm hoping I can drive to Flesland straight from here.'

She smiled gently. 'Mmmmm. Sounds good.'

On my return from looking for flights, she was asleep. I lay pondering for several hours before I fell asleep. *Karl Slåtthaug. The next for the chop*?

28

From the air I could already see that there was a great deal more snow in Vestfold than in the lowlands around Bergen. We landed to the north and, after turning, taxied towards what was called Torp Airport, Sandefjord, but which wasn't very far from Tønsberg, either.

Foyn, the lawyer, was waiting for me in the arrivals hall. We hadn't met face to face before, but his forensic gaze examining the small crowd of passengers arriving from Bergen gave him away. When our eyes met, we nodded to each other as though we were old acquaintances. We shook hands.

'Svend F-Foyn.'

'Varg Veum.'

'Th-th-thanks for your help, I should say.'

'And the same to you. That case was a result too, wasn't it?'

'I think so.'

He was over one metre ninety tall, well built with a well-tended, reddish beard and longish hair. He was wearing a three quarter length jacket over dark-brown cord trousers and solid winter boots.

He nodded towards the carousel. 'Any luggage?'

'Just this.' I showed him my light walking rucksack, which held little more than the toiletries I kept at the Saudalskleivane branch of my business.

He motioned towards the exit. 'My car's outside.'

I followed him out. In Bergen it had been eight or nine degrees when I left. Here, the temperature hovered above zero and you could feel it. There were great banks of snow along the edges of the car park and the ground underfoot was slippery. A high, icy-blue sky towered over Torp, like a frozen dome in space.

The car Foyn was leading me towards was a red Jaguar. The characteristically long bonnet reminded me of an elegant beast of prey, perfectly fitting its name. It was considerably wider than my Toyota Corolla, but would also be easier to recognise in traffic. I would have chosen a different car for tailing jobs. 'Wow! It's a long time since I've seen one of these. Does it go too?'

'Like a bell.'

He unlocked the passenger's door. A slightly odd smell met my nostrils, and when I looked over the back of the seat I saw a large, sleeping St Bernard. It opened one eye a fraction to welcome me. 'And you've brought a guard with you?'

'This is Hulda. As meek as a lamb.'

'No barrel around her neck though.'

'No, we'll have to wait until later for some brandy.'

We got in. Before he could start up, I asked: 'Any news on Slåtthaug?'

'Nothing. My man in the Tønsberg police force, Wilhelm M-Mørk, told me to take you there.'

'To the police station?'

'Yes.'

'You said last night that Slåtthaug had some arrangement with a priest. What did you mean by that?'

He glanced in my direction. 'What I said. It was the last thing he'd uttered when he went home on Wednesday. He was meeting a priest. Since then no one's seen him.'

'No more details?'

'I think we'll have to talk to the person I got this from: his colleague, Anne Kristine Kaldnes.'

'Can we do that before going to the police?'

'Of course we can. I didn't fix a time with Mørk.'

'Great.'

On the way into Tønsberg we passed several copses of beech trees – bare now in January – and large fields, which reminded me that we were in an area where agriculture still played an important role. During the drive Foyn reported back on the research he had already done. He had made enquiries about the refugee reception centre in question. No one had said anything of significance about the director, Karl Slåtthaug, but the police had noticed that two refugee children had disappeared from the centre just before Christmas and had not reappeared. It was assumed they had escaped together because the date for a new assessment of their application for residence permits was approaching. Earlier that autumn there had been a couple of similar disappearances as well. 'Entirely normal, according to the police,' Foyn said.

'The same happened in other institutions that had employed Slåtthaug.'

'Really?' He smiled wryly. 'That's why he was meeting a priest, you see. To confess his sins.'

'Or to be led to perdition.'

'Is that what priests do then?'

'Some of them.'

We were approaching Tønsberg, where Slottsfjellet Tower rose above us – a landmark, visible from a long distance. Then, as far as I could judge, Foyn crossed the town to the north of Slottsfjellet and drove west.

The refugee reception centre was situated on top of a hill, surrounded by open fields. It was a large, yellow building with three floors, the first constructed with brick. A sign by the driveway said, *Children's Reception Centre, Tønsberg.* Two tall trees towered over the car park. Opposite the main house there was a red farm building. Above the front door it said: *ANNO 1933.*

He turned in towards this building and parked beside the main entrance. We got out and closed the doors behind us, me much more carefully than Foyn, afraid to damage this beautiful car. Hulda showed no signs of wanting to get out and went on snoozing serenely on the back seat.

'Former domestic-science school,' Foyn said. 'Up until last year an upper secondary school. Classes were orientated towards agriculture, so they had cows and pigs here, at least when the domestic-science school was in use. They still grow potatoes, I'm sure, but the animals have gone.'

The woman who came out onto the front step I recognised from the webpage I had found. She came down and addressed Foyn directly. 'Any news?'

'No, I'm afraid not. Not from your side either, I gather.'

'No.'

He introduced her to me and we shook hands briefly. She was wearing a big grey-and-white jumper and light-blue dungarees. Across her forehead and down to the back of her neck she wore a broad, red headband to keep her blonde hair together in a kind of ponytail.

'Veum knows Slåtthaug from Bergen.'

'Mhm.' She looked at me enquiringly.

'Actually,' I said, 'I'm afraid something may have happened to him.'

'Happened?' She made a move towards the house. 'Let's go inside. It's much too cold to stand out here.'

We followed her into the building. A staircase led up to another floor. Two doors went off in different directions. It was remarkably quiet.

'The children have classes now,' Anne Kristine said. 'Generally they take place on the first floor.' To me she said: 'We're trying to prepare them in such a way that they can integrate into the country. Those of them who are allowed to stay.'

'And how many is that?'

'Unfortunately it's not us who decides. Some will be allowed to stay. Others will have to go.'

'And how do they react?'

'In different ways, understandably enough. Many are terribly upset. Some get panic attacks. Most have experienced things children in Norway cannot even begin to imagine: war, abuse, perilous escape routes; parents murdered or simply missing. I'm still shocked by what some of the children tell me. But then…' she held a hand in the air and flicked her fingers silently '…at the stroke of a Foreign Office pen they're sent out of the country, and if they refuse to go, the police come for them. Like in their home countries, where the police can be a lot more brutal than they are here, but they don't know that. All they see is uniforms. We've witnessed some heart-breaking scenes here, even though we're a new institution, barely six months old.'

'But some children escape?'

'Yes, they do. Let's go into the lounge. Would you like a cup of coffee?'

'Please.'

She led us through the door to the right. What she called a lounge was a large room with several seated areas, a billiard table in one corner, a bookcase with a selection of children's books and reference works, and in the opposite corner a shelving unit with a combined radio and CD player, amplifier and speakers. The flowers on the low tables were artificial and covered with a layer of dust.

I walked over to the windows on one side of the building. They looked out onto the back garden, which was surrounded by bushes, and a dip in the terrain and the outlying fields and, then, further away, a broad woodland area.

Anne Kristina Kaldnes came up alongside me. 'All of this is going to be developed. Soon we'll have rows of houses around us.'

'Town planners call that in-fill.'

'Yes.' She shrugged. 'Well … I'll get the coffee.'

I turned to Foyn. 'Enormous building.'

He nodded. 'I remember all too well when it was a domestic-science school,' he said with a little smile, without going any deeper. 'Tell me though. How well did you know this Slåtthaug?'

'He wasn't a close friend, if I can put it like that. We were both trained child-welfare workers, but he joined twenty years after me. He had to stop because there was some suspicion that he'd been too intimate with the girls in one institution, and I was tangentially involved in the matter. We met later once and I realised he bore me a grudge because of it. Then we ended up in the clink together, but that's a longer story, which I'll tell you some other time. And definitely not here.'

I cast an explanatory glance at the door as Anne Kristine came in.

She set down a tray bearing a pot of coffee, three cups and a small carton of cream onto a low table and motioned for us to sit there. We helped ourselves to coffee; she was the only one to take cream.

For a while we sat quietly sipping. Eventually I broke the silence. 'I've been told that there have been a few escapes.'

She sighed deeply. 'Yes, I'm afraid so. Four, to be precise. Two in October and there were two just before Christmas. The latter two were siblings waiting for a decision from the Foreign Office, but it was on an appeal – as they'd been turned down before; so it was easy enough to understand why they made off.'

'And the ones in October?'

'That was two separate incidents. One at the beginning of the month, one fairly late.'

'Boys or girls?'

'The two in October were girls. The others were siblings, as I said. A boy and a girl. He was seventeen; she was sixteen.'

'I assume you informed the police?'

'Of course. But … to no avail. If you knew how many missing cases there are from refugee centres up and down the country. These are not exactly priority cases, to put it mildly.'

'I know.'

'But why are you so interested in this?'

I took a sip of coffee while considering how to phrase an answer. 'Let me ask you a question. When you appointed Karl Slåtthaug … didn't you ask the police for a background check?'

'A background check? Would that … ?' She paused. 'It wasn't me who appointed him. The management board did, so you'll have to ask them.'

I dredged up a name from my memory. 'Pål Vassbotn?'

'He's one of them. The chairman anyway.'

'Was Slåtthaug in any way – how shall I put this? – around, when these children disappeared?'

She blushed. 'Around? What do you mean?' After a short pause she added: 'I'll have to look at the duty roster, but right back to October … that'll take a bit of time.'

'So you don't remember? I would've thought the police would question anyone who was around when the children went missing.'

She snorted. 'Not necessarily. There was one officer who popped by the first time … Jespersen, I think his name was. But he went through what happened extremely superficially and examined her room to see if there was anything there. Obviously there wasn't, because we never heard another thing, even though we reminded them.'

'Your faith in the local police is clearly not what it should be.'

'In the police full stop. I can promise you that. I have many years' experience in this kind of work, and I've banged my head against a wall so many times that the little faith I once had disappeared long ago.'

'Back to Karl Slåtthaug.'

'Yes?' She sent me a somewhat hostile glance. 'You still haven't told me what you think may've happened.'

'There's some evidence to suggest he may be in danger. When Foyn rang me yesterday to say he'd gone missing I came over as fast as I could.'

'Really?' She looked at me expectantly.

'Foyn told me you'd said something about a priest?'

She glanced at Foyn, who confirmed with a nod.

'Slåtthaug said he was meeting a priest?' I said.

'Yes, that's correct. When he went home on Wednesday he grinned and said he was meeting someone that evening. A priest.'

'Meeting someone? Did he mention anything else? A name or where he knew this priest from?'

'No. I didn't have the impression he knew him. He said they were meeting in town and would have a glass together. "Something stronger than altar wine, I hope", he said.'

'In town? Did he mention where?'

'No.'

'And when did he go missing?'

'That was the day after. When he didn't turn up for work on Thursday and there'd been no contact, we were worried. I called his mobile, but there was no answer. Then we were even more worried. So I went there.'

'There? To where he lived?'

'Yes.'

'Where's that?'

'Guttegata, as we call it. Hertug Guttorms gata.'

'Just under Slottsfjellet,' Foyn added.

'I rang the bell, but there was no answer, so then … I let myself in.'

'You had a key?'

'Yes, but … the flat was empty.'

'Empty?'

'Yes, I mean he wasn't there.'

'So what did you do?'

'I tried calling him again. When he didn't answer this time either, I rang the police.'

There was another silence.

Foyn cleared his throat. 'The fact that you had a key … Does that mean you were in a relationship with Slåtthaug?'

'No, we … Yes, maybe.'

I refrained from commenting. Karl Slåtthaug wasn't someone I would have had a relationship with, but then I wasn't a woman. I said: 'Did he tell you anything about his background?'

'He said he had the same background as me: social worker. He'd worked in child welfare and later he'd been an active member of organisations helping street children, in Europe and other parts of the world.'

'And did he say he'd been to prison?'

She blanched. 'Prison? No. What for?'

They were both staring at me now. 'He was involved in the dissemination of child porn material on the net. He and several others were convicted and did time.'

'How long?' Foyn asked.

'Not long enough, if you ask me. But you're the lawyer, so you know yourself how important proof is.'

Anne Kristine Kaldnes appeared to be stunned by this information. In a low voice she said: 'Child pornography?'

'Yes. That's why I asked about the background check. In my opinion, people like Karl Slåtthaug shouldn't be allowed to work in places like this after the sentence he was given.'

'No, I can understand that.'

'We social workers ought to be agreed on that.'

'We?'

'I'm also a trained social worker.'

She looked at me, lost for words.

Foyn took over. 'Do you think there could be a connection between the conviction and his disappearance, Veum?'

I nodded slowly. 'This sort of thing's happened before, hasn't it?'

'It has. If the worst has happened, there's an obvious place to search for motives here.'

I shifted my gaze back to Anne Kristine. 'The key to his flat – have you still got it?'

Foyn sent me an admonitory look. 'Veum … we have to meet Mørk after leaving here.'

'Yes? Have you never…?'

'Yes, I probably have, but…'

She interrupted us. 'I haven't got it any more.'

We turned our attention back to her. 'You haven't?'

'The police took it. Inspector Hole.'

Foyn rolled his eyes. 'The holy Inspector Hole…'

'A priestly sort as well?'

'As righteous as a traffic warden.'

'Even to Jaguar drivers?'

'Especially to us.'

Anne Kristine looked from Foyn to me and back again. 'What are you two talking about?'

I caught her eye. 'Back to Karl Slåtthaug's meeting. Is there anyone else here, apart from you, he might've spoken to in more detail?'

Her face tautened. 'I doubt it.'

'When you were together…' Her face, if possible, became even tauter. 'Did he ever mention anything that might indicate he knew some priests?' She shook her head. 'Magne Molstad. Does that name mean anything to you?'

'Never heard of him. That I can remember, anyway. We ... He didn't say any more about ... the past. He was a bit secretive. Perhaps that was why I ...' She didn't complete the sentence.

'... was attracted to him?'

She shrugged.

'Well ... these children who disappeared: you said that the siblings were sixteen and seventeen. What about the two who disappeared in October?'

'Moira was ... They were both sixteen. Amina's probably sixteen now.'

'Both are over the age of consent.'

'Yes?' Again she looked at me defiantly, as if I had provoked her in some way.

'Nationality?'

'They were from Afghanistan.'

'And the siblings?'

'Isaac and Hirute. Originally from Eritrea.'

'And you haven't heard a word from any of them since they left?'

She shook her head and symbolically chewed her lower lip.

I made a note of all the names in case I came to need them. Then I gave her my card. 'If you remember anything else, you have my address here. Or if Karl Slåtthaug should turn up. In which case, he should contact me at once.'

She glanced at my card and nodded. We finished our coffee and she accompanied us out. We got back into the Jaguar. Before Foyn turned out of the drive, he braked and half turned to me. 'Why have I got the feeling there's something you haven't told me, Veum?'

'Well ...' I hesitated.

'Because I'm right, aren't I? Why do you think Slåtthaug's in danger? Because of the conviction you were talking about in there?'

'Yes. There were four men arrested on the same charge. Three of them were convicted and sentenced. Two of them are dead as a result of what have been described as fatal accidents. The third person on the list is Karl Slåtthaug.'

'And the fourth?'

'Is me.' I hastened to add: 'But the charge against me was dropped.'

He opened and shut his mouth. 'Tell me more.'

'A brandy's waiting for us later in the day, didn't you say?'

'A Bache-Gabrielsen's waiting for you when the day's work is done. Is there anyone else you'd like to visit before we see Mørk?'

'Yes,' I said, and I didn't need to tell him who.

29

Nøtterø Savings Bank had its head office in Teie, which is on the island of Nøtterø. We passed Kanal bridge and it wasn't long before we were there.

There wasn't much going on at Teie Market this Friday in January. We parked right in front of the red-brick bank. In a yellow timber building on the opposite side of the market was a bakery, to the west of us a modern church, also in red brick. Once inside the bank, we were told that Pål Vassbotn was busy and wasn't receiving anyone.

That gave Foyn a chance to bristle his feathers. 'Tell herr Vassbotn that Svend Foyn is here on behalf of a client, and we need to talk to him now.'

For some reason, that helped. I assumed it was the distinguished family name that gave him the extra authority in Tønsberg and district. The statue of the great Svend Foyn, the founder of modern industrial whaling, was firmly located in front of the cathedral in town, the workers' houses he had built were still in use, and Svend Foyns gate cut through the centre of town on the other side of the strait between the island of Notterøy and Tønsberg. Svend Foyn was the human equivalent of Slottsfjellet Tower, putting Tønsberg on the map for perpetuity.

Vassbotn came out in person to meet us. He was dressed as I remembered him from the webpage: grey suit, white shirt and a tie. Regular features with a determined chin, bright blue eyes and a short, blond fringe. He was the type you had to meet a lot of times before you recognised him in the street.

He appeared to know Foyn. 'What's this all about? Who's the client you're representing?'

Foyn nodded towards me and I flashed my most amiable smile. 'Veum,' I said.

He shook his head as if to say that the name was completely unknown to him.

'This is about the refugee reception centre in Olsrød.'

'Right?'

'Can we speak in a more private place?'

He sized me up for a couple of seconds. Then he looked demonstratively at his watch, a Rolex as far as I could discern, which I had been told was the finance world's self-promoting character reference. 'Five minutes.'

He spun on his heel and led us briskly into a side office with open windows facing the customer-service area. Inside, he turned to us and remained on his feet – a clear signal that this was not going to take long.

I took the hint and went for a quick, efficient approach too. 'You know of course that some children have gone missing from the centre over the time it's been in existence: Moira, Amina, Isaac and Hirute.'

'Yes. I don't remember any of these names myself, but…'

'When you employed Karl Slåtthaug as the director, did you check his criminal record?'

'Slåtthaug? He came with the best references from the organisations where he'd worked.'

'Volunteer organisations?'

'Yes … I suppose they were.'

'Not from the police?'

He blinked. 'Should we have done?'

'Yes. He's been in prison for downloading and disseminating images of child abuse. There's also some suspicion that children may've gone missing from institutions where he's been employed before.'

He was in shock. 'What are you saying? I had no idea. But then … I'll summon him to a meeting as soon as I have … time.' He glanced up at the wall clock in the customer area.

'For the moment that's not possible.'

'And why not?

'Because he's gone missing.'

'Gone missing! Slåtthaug? Since when?'

'Since a couple of days ago.'

'A couple … I suppose the police are looking for him?' He shifted his gaze to Foyn. 'Why are you here, Foyn? I presume the police are taking care of the matter.'

Foyn smiled genially. 'Maybe not very quickly. He might be in hiding.'

'Oh, yes? Well, I can ring him anyway.'

'He's not picking up,' I said.

He eyed me with irritation, and I carried on: 'So I assume you didn't check his criminal record.'

'No. We may not have done. I regret that. We're a private foundation. There's a lot to think about.'

'These children who have gone missing – hasn't that worried you?'

'Of course it's worried me! Us. But we reported the disappearances to the police, didn't we.'

'Yes, you did. But when nothing happened, did you follow the matter up?'

'Well, we … Actually that wasn't my sphere of responsibility. I assumed…' He paused, and in a slightly weaker voice added: '…Slåtthaug had done that.'

I met his eyes. 'Well … I hope you've learned a lesson for when you appoint his successor.'

'Successor? He hasn't resigned.'

'No?'

'Not yet…'

'It'll be a union case anyway,' I said, turning to Foyn. 'Anything you'd like to ask herr Vassbotn?'

Vassbotn got agitated again. 'Who is this client of yours actually, Foyn?'

'Client?'

'You can have my card in case you remember any more details,' I said, taking a business card from my wallet and passing it to him.

He looked at it as though it were something he had picked up from the gutter. He pulled a grimace to show he would definitely not be taking any notice of it. 'Private investigator?'

I nodded.

'From Bergen?'

'Right on both counts.'

'We don't have any of them in Tønsberg. Fortunately.'

'Don't you?' After a short pause, I added: 'But then you have Foyn.'

On our way out to the car, Foyn said: 'I like your style, Veum. You gave him short shrift. Impressive, I must say. More than a touch of "Gimme a B. Gimme an R. Gimme an A. FC Brann" about it.'

'Yes, shame FC Eik-Tønsberg doesn't have the same touch at the moment.'

'Not at the moment, no.'

We sat in the Jaguar, and once again I felt like a king visiting the town. 'What do we do now? Lay a wreath at the statue of Svend Foyn?'

'Pay a call on Mørk at the police station, I think.'

But when we arrived, Mørk wasn't there. He had been called away, we were told. When Foyn asked what the call was, it obviously helped to be the person he was. A body had been found in the strait between the islands, the desk officer said.

'Where?' Foyn asked.

'By Ollebukta Bay,' came the answer.

30

Foyn turned down towards the strait between the island of Nøtterøy and the mainland. 'Byfjord,' he said, pointing west. 'The strait we call Kanalen,' he said, nodding down towards the sea as he parked.

This time Hulda came with us. Foyn attached a chain to the dog's collar and let her down from the back seat. She tagged along with us good-naturedly, down to the quay beside the sea, obviously happy to be active at last.

A thin film of ice lay over the water, like a covering of greyish-white plastic. We walked down to what was clearly a marina. Several piers led out into the sea and there were moorings in the sea and on the piers. Some big cabin cruisers were scattered around in the water, but most of the berths were empty.

'Doesn't this water freeze over when it's really cold?' I asked.

'They've got de-icing machines to keep the marina open,' Foyn said. 'I keep my dinghy here in the summer, but in winter I bring it ashore.'

By a small red house at the foot of one pier a crowd of people had gathered, facing the sea. An ambulance and a number of police vehicles were parked nearby, and uniformed officers were putting up a cordon to keep rubberneckers at a distance. Two men in wetsuits were tying straps around something in the water. On the quay, paramedics in orange gear were holding a stretcher at the ready.

Foyn said: 'Let's go over.'

We headed in their direction. We were stopped at the cordon by a female officer with dark hair in a ponytail. She refused to let us under the cordon.

Foyn shouted over her shoulder: 'Mørk!'

A man as tall and well built as himself turned in our direction. He mouthed: *Foyn?*

'We have some information. A possible ID.'

Alright.

Mørk motioned to the officer to let us in. She lifted the cordon, looking doubtfully at Hulda, and we bent down to crawl underneath, Hulda at Foyn's side, as if she wasn't sure the permission applied to her as well.

On the wall of the red house a sign said it belonged to Tønsberg Boat Club. 'There are nightwatchmen here in the summer,' Foyn said. 'Not now though, as there are hardly any boats.'

He led the way to the policeman. Mørk was bare-headed, with hair that matched his surname – dark; he wore a loose grey coat over the brown suit and white shirt, open at the neck with a casually knotted tie with red and blue stripes, like a kind of medal ribbon under his collar. When we were close up I noticed his dark-brown, sensitive eyes, in sharp contrast to the otherwise masculine impression he gave.

He looked at me with raised eyebrows.

'Varg Veum. Private investigator.'

'From Bergen,' Foyn added.

'I can hear that,' the policeman said, eyeing me sceptically. 'Private investigator?'

'Yes.'

'Well.' He extended a hand. 'Wilhelm Mørk. Inspector.' He turned back to Foyn. 'What did you say about an ID? Do you know the deceased?'

'We may do,' Foyn said.

'We … I have a suspicion,' I said. 'The reason I'm here is that the person I wanted to talk to has been reported missing. And … I can explain the details later, but … in the last six months there have been two other deaths of a similar nature to this one, from the same milieu, so to speak.'

'All we know is that a body has been found in the sea. Obviously dead, but we don't know what happened, what the cause of death might be, whether it was an accident or … something else. In short, I have to say you're a step ahead of us if you already suspect you know who it is. Impressively so. Conspicuously so, too, I might add.'

Foyn nodded to me. 'It's Veum you need to talk to, Mørk.'

'The person we're looking for is called Karl Slåtthaug. He's the director of the child refugee reception centre in Olsrød.'

'Really? Is he someone you would recognise?'

'If he isn't in too bad a state. I've met him many times.'

Mørk nodded and turned to the crowd behind him. 'He's on his way up from the water now, so let's…' He motioned to Foyn and me to follow him to the edge of the quay.

Foyn tightened the lead on Hulda and held her close. Two uniformed fire officers pulled carefully at the straps their colleagues in the sea had attached to the body. They hoisted it up to the edge of the quay while one of the men in wetsuits clambered up a ladder beside them. He held one hand underneath the body, which hung in what looked like a long hammock. With a firm grip the two on the quay grabbed one end of the broad canvas and turned the head of the dead man shorewards. Two more officers came over, and the four of them lifted the body onto land and the waiting stretcher. They folded the canvas to the side, so that the water could run off him, and beckoned to the paramedics in the ambulance.

'Just a moment,' Mørk said in an authoritative voice. He held my arm and led me to the stretcher.

It came as no surprise or shock. Despite having been in the water for what I judged was a day or two, he was easy to recognise. If there were any courts of law in the hereafter, this was where Slåtthaug was heading now. He had been released from earth forever.

31

After a formal interview at the police station, we agreed, at Foyn's suggestion, to meet for a glass or two at the Grand at nine that evening, Mørk, Foyn and I. The close relationship between Foyn and Mørk impressed me. I had never experienced anything of the sort in Bergen, not even with Vegard Vadheim while he had been alive.

As the last plane was therefore out of the question, I checked in at the Grand Hotel, which was in the same block as the police station, and went with Foyn to a part of the town called Fjerdingen, where he lived in Reidar Sendemanns gate. It was a side street off Hertug Guttorms gate, where Karl Slåtthaug had lived, and from the crossing between the streets we were able to see straight up the hill to Slottsfjellet Tower. We rounded the corner and Foyn pointed to the house number Anne Kristine Kaldnes had given him, a building with white laminate sheets on the front and green doors and window mouldings.

'I'd like to have a dekko in there,' I said, looking up at the house front.

'You'll have to make do with my humble abode,' Foyn said.

He had a nice flat in a red timbered house which, to judge by the architecture, was more than a hundred years old. Hulda soon found her regular spot in a large basket in the corner. As for me, I got to taste his best cognac, a Bache-Gabrielsen XO, which, according to the label was *très vieux*. As old as the house, for all I knew.

We had a bite to eat at a local pizzeria by the market place. At nine o'clock we were waiting in the bar at the Grand. From a window in the corner we could see down Øvre Langgate and straight into the floodlit old fire station with the characteristic tower that had given a name to the pub on the first floor: Big Ben. We each had a beer and another brandy while waiting for Mørk. He arrived at closer to half past nine than nine, cast a quick glance at what we were drinking and ordered the same.

Mørk had tightened his tie since we met on the quay, and the brown suit was considerably more elegant than I was used to among his colleagues in Bergen. I noticed a couple of women in the room watching him as he passed, but they stopped when they saw him join male company and immediately started chatting.

'Private investigator? Can you live off that?'

'Barely.'

'And what do the police say when you turn up unbidden at crime scenes?'

'I'm already on their blacklist, so they don't say much now. Besides, I don't usually.'

'Oh, yes? I had a quick chat with one of my colleagues in Bergen, and he said the opposite. "Veum? A body as well, was there?" he said.'

'Hamre?'

He grinned. 'You're old friends?'

'Soon be thirty years.'

'But he was right. We had a body and you appeared. With our local celeb.'

He glanced at Foyn, who raised his glass and toasted us. 'To friends, old and new,' he said.

'OK, Veum. Slåtthaug had a bank card and a driving licence in his inside pocket, so we've confirmed your identification. We also spoke to a colleague of his at the refugee centre, and she said he hadn't turned up for work as usual. She'd been to his flat and it had been empty. Obviously a close collegial relationship,' he said with an eloquent wink and glanced from Foyn to me as though to hear if we had any comments.

'Obviously,' Foyn said, and I nodded in assent.

'Seemed so, yes,' I said. 'What also worries me is the children missing from the centre.'

'You're thinking about the teenagers who went missing?'

'Yes. Child refugees are a very vulnerable group, and without the control parents or similar can give, they can easily end up on the skids.'

'Most go to Oslo,' Foyn added. 'The drugs community soon picks them up. The boys are forced into various types of criminality and the girls are quickly pressed into prostitution. And what do the authorities do? Little to nothing.'

'It's a manpower problem, not least in the capital,' Mørk said.

'Manpower or priorities, if you ask me,' Foyn said.

'Did you investigate these cases properly?' I interjected. 'Slåtthaug's fallen under suspicion in several similar cases in Vestland.'

'Well, no one asked us to check his records,' Mørk said.

'No. Can you take that up with the management committee at the centre? The chairman is one Pål Vassbotn.'

'We'd better have a look at the case. Right now we have to concentrate on what happened to Slåtthaug. You explained the link between these two other deaths during the interview at the station, but there was one detail you forgot, which Hamre told me about.'

'I can imagine. Yes, initially I was suspected of committing the same offence, but the charge was dropped. Someone had planted images on my computer and in fact this was proved by the police's own experts.'

'Yes, he told me that. But it means you have a very personal commitment to this matter. So personal that I'm afraid I'll have to ask you the routine question: where were you on Wednesday evening?'

'Wednesday? I was definitely in Bergen.' I thought back quickly. 'Late that afternoon I visited a few people connected with one of the other deaths. If asked, they'll confirm that. Afterwards, I was alone with a bottle of aquavit, but I don't think planes fly to Torp from Bergen that late in the day.'

'Aquavit?' Foyn repeated sardonically and raised his glass of brandy in tacit comment.

'We'll check the passenger lists on flights between Bergen and Torp on the relevant days. This priest you were talking about…'

I opened my palms. 'Well, I know nothing except that the term pastor was used about someone who could've been involved in one of the other deaths. That's all. But it's also why I reacted at once when Foyn mentioned that Slåtthaug was meeting a priest on Wednesday evening.'

'That's what his colleague, Anne Kristine Kaldnes, told me anyway,' Foyn added.

'And has since confirmed,' I said.

'Exactly,' Mørk said. 'And when we spoke at the station earlier today, you mentioned another priest, didn't you?'

'Yes, I did. Magne Molstad. He's married to the ex-wife of one of the deceased. And his sister was a victim of the second man to die. A clear revenge motive in the latter case. As for the former … well, I can't say any more. But there's definitely the shadow of a motive there too, although not so strong as the other one.'

'We're checking the numbers Slåtthaug called on his mobile phone during the relevant days and slightly further back. No Magne Molstad has appeared yet. But there are a few calls from an unusual number this week, on Monday, Tuesday and Wednesday.'

'Unusual in what way?'

'They're from the phone box at Bergen railway station.'

I nodded. 'Yes, in fact there are still some telephone boxes.'

'So we'll have to get some help from our Bergen colleagues to establish whether anyone has noticed a person using the phone box several days in a row.'

'It's in the entrance, as far as I remember. The staff working at the café might've seen someone.'

'I'll make a note of that. And then there's a German number, registered to a Norwegian.'

'Oh, yes?'

'Frøken Kaldnes drew our attention to it, and when we were searching back through his phone conversations it appeared regularly until about three weeks ago. Since then there's been nothing. When we checked with the German phone company they said the account had been closed, but they gave us the name and address of a Norwegian living in Hamburg. The name's Stein Sløvåg.' He focused on me. 'Does that ring any bells?'

'Sløvåg's a ferry terminal north of Bergen. Otherwise, no bells.'

'We checked the address, but it turned out to be a kind of boarding house, and the person in question moved out almost precisely three weeks ago, in mid-December, and he didn't leave any forwarding address.'

'Stein Sløvåg.' I took out my notepad and jotted down the name and the Hamburg address.

'We can't find anyone registered under that name in Norway. That suggests it's false.'

'I see. That alone is suspicious enough, isn't it?'

'Of course. So we have a little lead to work on there. We don't have a cause of death yet, and until it's confirmed that this really is murder and not an accident we can't throw all our weight behind it.'

'What about the link with the other deaths?'

'I asked Hamre about that, and the Bergen police haven't defined either of them as murder.'

'I know. But when you told him about Slåtthaug?'

'Well, he did react, I'll admit that, and he promised he would get out the other two case files now.'

'That's something then.'

'But let me add that Karl Slåtthaug isn't the first body we've fished out of Ollebukta. There are several watering holes nearby and if someone's walking home and needs a pee it's easy to go down to the sea and accidentally fall in. In winter, especially, this can have catastrophic consequences.'

'I understand that, but it's now the third death among a very small circle of people. That doesn't exactly smack of chance.'

'No, it doesn't.' He took a swig of beer, set the glass down and tasted the brandy, then said in a knowing tone: 'So there's only you left, Veum, isn't there?'

I looked at him solemnly. 'I'm afraid so, yes.'

32

There were a few more rounds of brandy before we each went our separate ways on this Friday evening. I agreed with Mørk and Foyn that we should keep in touch in case anything else of interest cropped up. I doubted Mørk would stay true to his word, but was confident Foyn would keep me posted.

On Saturday morning I flew back to Bergen, from two degrees below zero and a clear sky in Torp to six degrees above and discreet cloud cover in Flesland. I sat on the airport bus planning what I was going to do next.

The investigation in Tønsberg would have to take its own course. And I would have to try and pick up the threads again in Bergen. There were two questions I wanted answered: who was this anonymous priest who had appeared in both Tønsberg and Bergen? And was it possible to find out who was hiding behind the name of Stein Sløvåg?

As for the second question, there was a vague trail leading to Hamburg. Not only did a bell ring; alarm bells clanged. The 2002 case had involved a Mr Big from Hamburg who had also been in Bergen whenever his presence was required. He was responsible for the organisation of drugs sales, prostitution and cybercrime. In addition, he had been directly involved in precisely such cases as those that had occurred in Tønsberg: children going missing from the refugee centre. I had mentioned him when I talked to Annemette Bergesen. His name was Bruno Karsten. Like most big-time operators he was skilled at covering his traces – so skilled that the Bergen police had never managed to pin anything on him. I had no idea if he was on the German police's radar.

Playing some role or other, Karl Slåtthaug had been tied to Karsten's network in Bergen, although at the time I had been unable to establish precisely how. If it was possible to connect this Stein Sløvåg with Karsten it would, at any rate, explain the link between Sløvåg and Slåtthaug.

I got off the airport bus at the market place and walked straight to my office, where I switched on the computer and took out my phone. Actually I should have gone to Hamburg myself, but I hadn't been there since the year I went to sea, which was in the early 1960s. Besides, my paymaster – me, that was – didn't allow such financial indulgence at the moment. There was one other possibility, however.

I sat down at the keyboard and searched for 'Detektivbüros Hamburg'. I soon had a long list. Most looked like detective agencies of a size that didn't exist in Norway. Deciding who to contact would definitely be a shot in the dark. Most seemed well organised and punctilious, with office hours at any time of the day or night, the possibility of making an appointment via the net, maps showing directions to their offices and information about public transport to get there. It made me feel like the chairman of a tiny Norwegian football club trying to agree a training match with Bayern München.

I scrolled down the list to see if I could find something like my own business – a single investigator with a corresponding set of ambitions. The name *Aktivsucher* appealed to me. An actively searching detective was how I often felt. Under this term appeared one Thomas Lang. Further down the list I found what was probably a married couple, or siblings: Hanne u. Bernhard Schultz.

I tried the active searcher first, but he was obviously out, living up to his name. At any rate, he didn't answer the phone. When I tried Hanne u. Bernhard Schultz, my call was answered by a woman. She apologised for her poor English, the language I had chosen to communicate with her in, as my German was pretty nonexistent, and she put me through to '*mein Mann*', Herr Schultz, whose English was excellent and who listened with interest to what I had to say. In fact, it sounded as if he thought it fun to be called up by a colleague from Norway, a country he and his wife had visited many times as tourists, he said. When he heard I was ringing from Bergen he was even more effusive, and I sent a silent message of thanks to the local tourism director and his staff for ensuring that the town was flooded with German tourists from March to October, thus preparing the ground for cordial interaction between the two nations.

Herr Schultz noted down my questions, as well as the names of Bruno Karsten and Stein Sløvåg. We agreed he would make some enquiries in exchange for what he called 'a nice price' if I were willing to give them some assistance, should they need a similar service in Bergen. We shook hands on this, symbolically speaking, and he promised to ring as soon as he had anything.

I leaned back in my chair, fairly satisfied with my progress. As for the priest, I was stuck in a rut for the time being. I could of course get hold of a list of all the priests in Bergen and district, and then work through it. But it would be lengthy and pretty impossible to sift through as priests in the Free Church parishes also used the term pastor.

I considered all the people I had spoken to during the last week. Was there anyone else apart from the deceased Mikael Midtbø and Karl Slåtthaug who had met this priest? What about the third man, Per Haugen? Neither his bereaved wife, nor his brother-in-law, Hans Storebø, was aware of any pastor turning up in his flat. That didn't mean there hadn't been one. Haugen could have met this person in the street. He (or she) could have walked with him down to the sea. The same *modus operandi* as in Tønsberg maybe?

Moreover, there was the idea I'd had after seeing Sølvi's reaction when we talked about the cases. Were there any lionesses out there? Had some of the women I had spoken to taken action, out of pure rancour, as the parish priest in Biskopshavn had suggested. Had a woman I'd not met done this?

Once again I flipped through my notes. Once again, the name Stein Sløvåg brought me to a halt. There was something about this connection with Hamburg – and, possibly, Bruno Karsten – that quickened my blood. And there was yet another link: Bjørn Hårkløv. All the evidence suggested I should pay a call on him now, with all the risks that entailed. But it was Saturday morning and he was unlikely to be in the office. I didn't fancy visiting him at home, either.

My line of thought was interrupted by a phone call. It wasn't a number I had entered, but I recognised it from a few days before. I recognised the voice too: 'I apologise for disturbing you on a Saturday, Veum. This is Hans Storebø.'

'No worries. I'm just sitting here thinking.'

'You see ... I went with my sister to the doctor's yesterday. I might've mentioned this appointment when we last spoke.'

'Yes, you did. How did it go?'

'The doctor was very specific. She can no longer live alone and was put on an emergency list for a place in a home. I signed on behalf of the family. From what he said, there might be a move as soon as next week.'

'That's quick.'

'But...' He coughed. 'There was something I'd like to tell you as you're investigating this case.'

'OK. Do you want to meet?'

'That's not necessary. We can talk now if that's alright with you.'

'Fine.'

'The doctor informed me that she showed obvious signs of dementia. But that doesn't mean she doesn't have moments of lucidity in between. When we came back from the doctor's yesterday she had one such moment. And what she said worried me.'

'Oh, yes? And that was ...?'

'She was talking about a woman. A young woman, she said, but in her mind *young* can mean anything from fifty downwards. A woman had rung them the day before Per died. "The day before!" she emphasised and looked me straight in the eye with such clarity it was like ... well, how she used to be. Later the same day she'd been shopping, to buy a few things. When she came back and was about to take the lift, the door opened and the woman who emerged was so agitated that she almost knocked my sister down in her hurry. Upstairs in the flat, my sister could see from the way Per looked that something had happened. He was much more restless than usual. He kept going to the window and looking down, as though he were keeping an eye on something. A couple of times he went onto the balcony and looked down, too. That same evening, so late that night was falling, he went for a walk, which was very unusual for him. He said he needed some fresh air. She didn't remember how long he was gone, but when he came back, he seemed to have calmed down. The following day he got up as usual and went fishing. And that was the day he didn't return.'

'She remembered all this quite clearly? But ... didn't she tell the police at the time of the accident?'

He sighed. 'I asked her that. But she answered: "Tell the police? Tell them what?" And I said: "About this woman." And she just looked at me in surprise and asked: "What woman?" Suddenly she was back in the mists. As I told you, there was a moment of lucidity, and then it was gone. But ... the way she told me, that clarity of hers ... made me nervous, very nervous. What if it was true? Someone had a score to settle with Per. She visited him at home, perhaps met him that evening – what do I know? – and then either arranged to meet him or, equally possible, met him the following morning, down in Frøviken.'

I nodded to myself. Sølvi had used the word 'lioness'. A furious mother? Or perhaps a victim herself? 'I think you should tell the police this, Storebø.'

'And what do you think they'll do? This was in October, three months ago. An unknown woman, no description, and a death they'd decided ages ago was an accident. And the only witness is a partially senile woman. That's why I'm ringing you, Veum.'

'I'm a one-man band. So I can't set up door-to-door enquiries. I have no machinery I can swing into action. The police can. And, as you say, there's nothing really tangible. She – your sister – she didn't give you any form of description of this woman, except that she was – your res-ervations accepted – young?'

'No. I think I've quoted her almost verbatim. But I've wondered about Laila's testimony in court. That was sexual abuse. Perhaps he didn't stop at her. Perhaps there were others – girls in the neighbour-hood, girls Laila was friends with; what do I know?'

'I know about one at any rate, but she's dead. Killed herself.' And she had no sisters; only a brother, and he was a priest.

'There you are. I've heard that in such cases the first abuse opens the sluice gates. Later it happens again and again. Even though he was only my brother-in-law, I'm ashamed to be related to him. I'm not unaware that the condition Tora's in now could've been accelerated by what she experienced at home and, as you said last time we spoke, she denied it. Denied it ever happened. The doctor suggested as much. One of the causes of dementia at such an early age, as in Tora's case, is trauma – the kind she must be carrying, and which she has repressed because she refuses to assimilate it, to accept it's happened, and so she shuts out the rest of the world too.'

'That doesn't sound unlikely. In which case, we're talking about her as another victim, even though in a way she was an accessory and prepared the ground for her own fate.'

'I wouldn't call her an accessory, Veum, more a dumb witness. That's as far as I can go. Perhaps it was the knowledge she took from our experiences as children, in Televåg, and the German reprisals afterwards. There was no point protesting. They were a lot stronger than we were; they burned our farms, killed our men, as Inger Hagerup wrote so grippingly about in one of her poems. The confrontation with pure evil.'

Pure evil. These were the same words Hamre had used when we discussed this earlier in the week. And it wasn't so hard to understand. What I had been confronted with over recent years had made such a strong impression on me that I had to ask myself the question: was this what it all boiled down to? Was this what we were talking about? Pure evil?

'Do you think there would be any point my visiting your sister again, Storebø?'

'To tell the truth, I don't know. Even if you were lucky enough to encounter a moment of lucidity I doubt you'd get a description of this woman out of her.'

'What if I showed her some photos of various women, as the police often do in similar situations?'

'Photos of whom, for example?'

'Yes, that's a point.' I couldn't answer his question because I didn't know. 'Well, thank you for calling me. I'll give this a bit more thought. If you should find out anything else, get in touch again. But I still think you should tell the police.'

'Point taken, Veum. I might have to eat humble pie, even though I don't really like crawling to those in authority.'

'Are you at your sister's now?'

'No, I'm at home. But I'll be in Bergen tomorrow and over the weekend. After all, she's managed on her own up till now. I don't see her everyday situation as that dramatic.'

'If she has any more moments of lucidity, see if you can get some more details out of her. If nothing else, the clothes this woman was wearing. That's the kind of thing women notice and that could be useful for the police or anyone else conducting an investigation.'

With that we rang off.

I sat looking through the window. It was past three and darkness was falling. On the other side of Vågen bay was the building where Knut Haugen had his office. Further up, in the Fjellsiden district, was Telthussmuget, where I lived. Above it I saw the profile of Mount Fløyen. Between the trees I could glimpse white patches of snow right up to Fjellveien. It was as though I could feel a tingling in my calves. Head up there, put on my skis, set off into virgin nature, without a thought about all the humanity below, about something so foul some called it pure evil.

The phone rang again. This time I could see on the display it was Sølvi. I answered the call, but before I could say a word I heard her voice, loud and shrill: 'Varg!'

'Yes, what is it?'

'It's Sølvi!'

'I can see that.'

'We were out walking, Helene and I, and someone tried to run us down.'

I almost jumped out of the chair. 'What?!' I got up. 'How…? Are you alright? Both of you?'

'Yes, we …' She let out a long sob. 'We're at home now.'

'Where did this happen?'

'Up the hill here.'

'At home?'

'Yes.'

'Did you see the car?'

'Yes, it was grey, but I have no idea what make it was.'

'The reg?'

'I got some letters and numbers. I've rung the police and reported it.'

'Well done. I'll be over at once.'

'Thank you,' she said, wearily, and hung up.

33

Sølvi opened the door only after she had checked through the kitchen window that it was me outside. She let me in, locked the door and then turned to me. I wrapped my arms around her and held her tight. Her body was trembling. After a few seconds she freed herself from my embrace, took a tissue from a packet she kept in her pocket and dried her eyes. The look she sent me was cautious and contained something I hadn't seen there before: anxiety, maybe fear.

When we went into the sitting room Helene was sitting in her usual place on the sofa. She, too, met me with a look I hadn't seen before, as though this were my fault. In her hand she held an unopened magazine; it didn't look as if she had been reading it. There was a wan, dispirited air about her, and I could see she had been crying.

'Hi Helene,' I said.

She just nodded mutely back, her mouth pinched shut.

I turned back to Sølvi and looked at her enquiringly. *Tell me what happened.* 'Have you heard from the police?'

'No, but they were supposed to be coming here to talk to us. But first they wanted to identify who owned the car and perhaps collar the person in question.'

'Was it grey?'

She nodded.

'Could it have been a Volkswagen Golf?'

'I haven't a clue. But it reminded me of...' She glanced towards Helene and lowered her voice. 'What you said ... what happened to you a few days ago.'

'Yes.' I hesitated, then said: 'There's every possibility this is linked.'

She nodded solemnly. 'That's what I was afraid of. Let's...' She glanced at Helene again. 'Let's go to the kitchen and make some coffee. You just relax, Helene. Nothing else is going to happen. Varg's here, and soon the police will be here to talk to us as well.'

Helene nodded slowly, without looking particularly convinced.

Sølvi beckoned to me and led the way to the kitchen. There, she turned to me again. 'I don't know what we're going to do. We can't live like this.'

'No, I'm really sorry, Sølvi. Just tell me … exactly what happened.'

She glanced towards the window. It was pitch-black outside now. Only the street lights and the illuminated windows further up Saudalskleivane showed us where we were. 'We … we'd just been for a walk up … not quite as far as Mount Geitanuken, we turned back before, because of the snow that was still on the ground. When we were back on the road … We were almost home.' She pointed through the window. 'I heard a car behind us, racing down the hill, and I thought: *What's going on? It must be going far too fast.* I grabbed Helene and dragged her to the edge of the road, then I half turned and the car seemed to be coming straight at us. I pushed her to the side and threw myself after her.' She looked at me, eyes open wide. 'I felt the draught as the car passed, Varg! I think it even touched my jacket. It's amazing it didn't hit me.'

I could feel the anger rising in me. I recognised the situation. It was identical to my own experience. With tensed vocal cords, I said: 'Did you see anyone behind the wheel?'

She shook her head. 'It happened too fast.'

'But you said … you saw the registration plate?'

'Yes, I did. He had to brake before the bend here.' She motioned with her head to the window. 'I looked up and tried to focus. I'm fairly sure the letters were S, T, and the first number was seven, the second either an eight or a three.'

I opened the envelope I had taken from the office. In it was the list of all the registered VW Golfs, last year's model, in Bergen and Hordaland. I unfolded the sheets and quickly ran my finger down.

'What's that?' Sølvi asked.

I explained, and my finger stopped at a number. 'The closest I can get to it is this. In which case, it's a three. It's registered to a car-rental firm.'

'But is it possible to find out who's rented it?'

'For the police it is.'

She looked at her watch. 'What do you think they're doing?'

'They've probably radioed all the patrol cars to keep an eye out for the car. You gave them the reg as well, I take it?'

She nodded.

'Who did you talk to?'

'Just the emergency number. I wasn't given a name.'

'But you were expecting to hear from them?'

'They said they would send someone round to talk to us, yes.'

I stood with the list of registration numbers in my hand. 'Of course I could give them a ring myself.'

'The police?'

'The car-rental people.'

She waggled her head and shrugged. Then she turned to the worktop. 'I'll put some coffee on and then I have to … I've got a chocolate cake in the freezer. I'll get it out.' With a glint in her eyes, she added: 'We have to celebrate, don't we. Surviving, I mean.'

I smiled wanly. Then I held my phone in the air. 'In the meantime I'm going to try this. Can I use your office?'

She nodded.

I found the number of the car-rental company and rang. A youthful male voice answered.

'Hello. My name's Veum. I'm ringing about a car registered to your firm.' I read out the full number starting with ST-73. 'It's been involved in a near collision.'

'I see.'

'Can you give me the name of the person who rented it?'

'No, I'm afraid we can't. We can't give this information to just anyone.'

'We aren't just anyone. My … partner was almost knocked down.'

'I see. I'm afraid we have to stick to our principles on this. I assume you've reported this to the police?'

'Yes, but—'

'Then there's no more I can say except … Good luck.'

With that, he rang off, and I stared at the phone, none the wiser.

I went back to the kitchen. There was already an aroma of chocolate cake issuing from the oven. Sølvi was keeping an eye on it through the glass panel and looked up as I entered the room.

'They wouldn't give me a name,' I said.

She didn't answer.

Three-quarters of an hour later we were sitting in the living room, eating cake in oppressive silence, when a policeman came to the door. Sølvi went out and opened up. It was Arne Melvær. He was an officer in his early thirties, with auburn hair, a Bulandet dialect and a slightly shy demeanour. I had encountered him many times professionally, but had never managed to get to know him any better.

When he spotted me, he arched his eyebrows in surprise, but he caught himself and greeted me in a measured tone, without any visible enthusiasm. 'Veum? What are you doing here?'

'Sølvi is … a friend of mine. We suspect this case has more ramifications than there seem to be at first sight.'

He blinked, apparently confused. 'Erm, really?' Then he pulled himself together and took out a notebook. 'First and foremost though…' He looked down at his pad. 'I've been instructed to speak to fru Hegge.' He looked at Helene, then Sølvi. 'Have you got a room where we can speak in peace and quiet?'

'I have a little office. We can go there.'

His glance at me as he followed Sølvi into the hall spoke volumes. I was left with Helene. On the other side of the room, the TV was on: a children's programme with the sound so low it was clear neither of us was interested.

I looked at her. 'This will sort itself out, Helene. It was probably just someone who'd had a glass too many and trod on the accelerator instead of the brake.' At the same time it struck me that perhaps I ought to tell her the truth. But how honest can you be with an eleven-year-old? How much detail should you give when explaining the background to the incident? Was this just as difficult as it was for a young girl to talk about inexplicable sexual abuse committed against her by an adult, perhaps a father or a close relative?

She stared at me with the same gravity she had shown all afternoon. But she said nothing, just shrugged her shoulders in a way that reminded me of her mother. Then she grabbed the magazine lying beside her, opened it and pretended to read, if for no other reason than to make it clear she had nothing to say to me. Not now.

I sat staring into space.

There was an eerie pattern in this. The deaths of the other three – Karl Slåtthaug the latest. The attempt to run me over a few days ago, and now Sølvi and Helene – even more serious. Now this was dirty. It was no longer an understandable vendetta against three convicted child abusers. This was an act of revenge against me personally, using people who were close to me.

At the back of my mind an idea was beginning to germinate, one with unsuspected consequences, and not only for me.

My thoughts were interrupted by Melvær asking if I could join him. I did as he said, with a final glance at Helene, who deliberately ignored me.

We stood in the hall. 'Fru Hegge has told me what happened. She also said that you'd been the victim of a similar incident earlier this week.'

'Last Sunday. A grey Golf. But both Hamre and Solheim know about this.'

'I see. I haven't been able to confer with them yet. So you think there's a connection between these two events?'

'I don't just think it. It's obvious, surely. She gave you what she saw of the car reg, didn't she?'

'Yes, to the emergency switchboard.'

'Have you followed it up?'

'Patrol cars were radioed that they should look for a car with the numbers and letters she identified. And a car was sent here, with no result.'

'One car?'

'Yes. We have a manpower problem. On Saturday afternoons and evenings we concentrate mainly on the town centre.'

'Right. So an attempt to run down a woman and her daughter is not a priority?'

He seemed indignant, on behalf of the police force. 'Of course they are. Why do you think I'm here? We'll follow this up, you can be sure of that.'

'Then I think the first thing you can do is ring the car-rental firm in question and ask for the name of the person who rented this car.' I held up the list of numbers in front of him and pointed to the relevant number.

'Where did you get this list?'

'Solheim sent it to me.'

'I see. Well … I doubt I'll get an answer over the phone. We'll have to pay them a call, perhaps get them to ring the station directly. I'll take care of this once I'm back.'

Sølvi appeared in the office doorway. 'Well? What's the next step? Are there any more questions to answer?'

Melvær turned to her again. 'No, I don't think so. We'll try and find out who was driving the car and take it from there.'

'Good luck,' Sølvi said, with biting irony.

I had nothing to add.

34

Melvær had barely got out of the door when Sølvi grabbed my lapels and glared at me. 'If anything happens to Helene, I'll never forgive you, Varg.'

'Nothing will happen, neither to Helene, nor to you. I'll take care of this.'

She wasn't so sure of that, judging by her taut mouth and the look she sent me. 'And what can you do that the police … ?' She didn't complete the sentence.

'I can focus on this and this alone until I've found the person who's threatening us.'

'Have you got any suspicions?'

'Not yet, but … I have a few leads to follow.'

'Right now?' She eyed me anxiously. 'I don't know if I can be on my own here, just me and Helene for the whole weekend.'

'Well, I can't get much done until Monday anyway. Shall we simply take this evening off and try to relax?'

Her face softened and she met my eyes with a tenderness I interpreted as a thank-you for the suggestion. 'I'll find us a pizza. You join Helene in the meantime.'

'She doesn't seem to be as keen on me as she used to be.'

Sølvi nodded slowly. 'Well … it'll get better. It was a scary experience for her, too.'

'I know.'

I followed her advice and joined Helene. She sat immersed in a book while I watched the news without taking in a fraction of the content. I had an idea about who might be behind these two attempts to strike at me personally and I couldn't get it out of my head. It lay there smouldering for the rest of the weekend.

Together with Helene we watched the rest of the evening's TV without much enthusiasm on any of our parts. Sølvi and I shared a bottle of red wine. We drew the line at one on this night. When Helene had gone to bed, without a goodnight hug for me, Sølvi wanted to hear how I thought we should take 'precautions' – making air quotes and with a sceptical grimace.

I had already given this some thought and I had a few options prepared. Sølvi could take a few days off work and stay at home, but Helene had to go to school and it was probably important for her to maintain as normal an everyday routine as possible. We could also send her away, if there was someone in the family who would step up, but Sølvi rejected this idea out of hand, without any further explanation. She looked very unhappy. 'I don't like this situation at all, Varg.'

'You're not alone in that. Perhaps you should simply take Helene with you to the office for a couple of days, until we've got to the bottom of this matter?'

'We?'

'Yes, me. And the police.'

'Well, that's a possibility of course. But then I'll have to take her out of school.'

We agreed that this was perhaps how it would have to be. Later we went to bed, but neither of us was in the mood for a reprise of the previous evening. However, it looked as if I fell asleep before her – judging by the drawn expression on her face in the morning, anyway.

The mood on this Sunday wasn't good. We stayed indoors all morning. My phone was as quiet as a sepulchre. No one rang on a Sunday unless something terrible had happened. Sølvi made lunch while I flicked through Saturday's newspapers, which were turning more and more into overgrown weeklies. Helene finished her book and started another. In the background the radio alternated between schmooze, tittle-tattle and last year's pop songs: nothing worth listening to with more than half an ear.

I sat philosophising over why the music sounded so much more homogeneous in the 2000s than it had done in most of the previous decades, both the ones I could remember myself and most of those before. Much of modern pop music sounded as if it had been written by robots and performed by lovesick young girls. Not that the young men who performed were any better. And robots had written their songs, too. The drummers and pianists were replaced by synthesisers, and the vocalists' voices were so similar it was hard to tell them apart. Where was the next Ella Fitzgerald, where the next Frank Sinatra, Elvis Presley or Bob Dylan? Weren't people born with such voices any more? Were they rejected at birth?

As bedtime approached I floated a suggestion that I might go home, but Sølvi insisted I had to stay, although there was no entertainment on offer this evening, either. On Monday morning we each got into our own car. She took Helene with her to the office. I drove home to change my clothes and then to my office, opposite hers across Vågen.

35

I sat down at the desk and took out my notepad. I had what Hans Storebø had told me on Saturday at the back of my mind. I opened my notepad and jotted down a list of the women I had met in the last week.

The ones who in some way could be linked directly with Per Haugen, apart from Tora, were his daughter Laila and daughter-in-law, Vibeke. I had hardly spoken to Vibeke. And Laila? She was emotionally unstable, with good reason, and was vulnerable in every way. But the mother would surely have recognised her own daughter, even if she was well on her way into dementia? The daughter-in-law, on the other hand. Perhaps Tora had never met her? But still: Did she have a real motive, beyond the absolutely obvious?

Svanhild Olsvik was an explosive enough woman for her to be a potential candidate. But did she have any connection with Per Haugen, apart from him and her partner, Mikael Midtbø, being convicted of the same kind of crime? Unless Per Haugen had been one of her customers in Flaktveit. Of course, that was a possibility.

The same applied to Haldis Midtbø. After that, there were no more women on my list. I hadn't registered a female partner for the third dead man, Karl Slåtthaug. There was Anne Kristine Kaldnes, of course, but from her to Haugen and Midtbø there was a distance of so many miles it was futile imagining any connection.

So I was back to reality and blank sheets of paper. But, as Hans Storebø had said, in cases like this there could be many unknown factors. An in-depth investigation would mean examining the relations between Per Haugen and his neighbours over many years and perhaps not only as an adult. In short, it was an insuperable task for one investigator of my calibre. I just had to admit it.

And what about the driver of the grey Golf? Neither Sølvi nor I had seen who it was. For all we knew, it could have been a woman behind the wheel.

I rang the police station and asked for Melvær. He was out on a job, I was told. 'What about Solheim then?' He was there.

'Veum?'

'Have you heard that my partner was almost run over by a grey Golf on Saturday?'

'We have the details.'

'And do you remember it was a grey Golf that tried to run me down as well, last weekend? One of the rental cars on the list you gave me has the same first two letters and numbers as the car Sølvi saw. Melvær took down this information from us on Saturday evening.'

'We're on the case, Veum. There are some legal niceties here, but we reckon we'll have a name within the day.'

'Will you ring me, if so?'

He paused before answering. 'If we have any questions to ask you, we'll ring. If not … We don't want any interference in this investigation from – what shall we say? – freelancers.'

'But—'

'And that's all I have to say on the matter. Have a nice day, Veum.' He put down the phone, as forthright as always.

The next person I called was Foyn. He hadn't heard from Mørk yet, but promised he would try to contact him in the course of the day. 'The death's mentioned in *Tønsbergs Blad* today,' he said. 'But it's referred to as a drowning accident. Or "most probably a drowning accident", to quote them correctly.'

The next on the list was Ghulam Mohammad. I asked him if his wife had enquired whether Laila would talk to me again. 'What?' he answered, in a somewhat distracted tone. 'No, I don't think so. She hasn't said anything to me, anyway.'

'Could you ask her to do so? It's important I talk to Laila. You want her to get some help, don't you?'

'Yes, I do. I'll pass on the message to Fatima.'

'And then tell me when we can talk.'

'And then I'll tell you,' he said and hung up.

The third phone call was to Germany. Frau Schultz answered. She told me her husband was out on a job at that moment and they hadn't found anything yet about what I had asked them to investigate. 'We ring back as soon as we have something,' she said in her somewhat halting English.

I had no intention of warning the last person on the list of my imminent arrival. Bjørn Hårkløv had his office in Sandsli. I had some difficulty finding the correct address. It turned out that Hårkløv had his so-called office in a building more reminiscent of a workmen's hut, not so far from where SH Data had their offices – a company I had visited a few times before and had every intention of returning to once I was finished with Hårkløv.

The hut was at the end of a small side street. The closest neighbour was a car dealership. I parked there and walked the short distance to the hut. A little sign on the wall said that *Hårkløv Kreditt* resided here. In front of the hut was the black Audi. I took this as a sign that he was at home. This impression was confirmed when I peered through the window I had to pass to reach the white front door. Bjørn Hårkløv stared at me with an expression he had borrowed from a catfish, and when he got up from his chair he didn't appear to be in a mood to welcome me with open arms. It was more the old bouncer that had come to life in him, rough and brutal. Or were we talking pure evil here, too?

Before I had reached the door, it opened with a bang. Bjørn Hårkløv came out, slammed the door behind him and marched towards me. Ten centimetres away he stopped. 'What the fuck do you want here, Veum?'

'To have a few words with you.'

'You can have a few words with the fucking man on the moon, you can. If you stick your nose in my business, I'll…'

'You'll what? Ring the police?'

'You just keep the cops away from my business. I have my own methods.'

'Yes, I remember. But it didn't go very well then, either, did it.'

'I won't make the same mistake again.' He towered over me and swelled like a rutting capercaillie.

'You still work for Karsten, I understand.'

'Do I?'

'Same old shit, new packaging.'

'Yer what?'

'Let me tell you something. You're going to drop the demands all of you are making on Laila Bratteli.'

'Says who?'

'Says me. I've reported the matter to the police. They've noted down your name. Of course, they already had it, but now they've got it for this case too. If anything at all happens to her, you're the one they'll haul in, you can be sure of that.'

He glowered at me. 'Oh yeah? Are you going to pay her debts then? You know that won't happen, Veum. Someone wants that money, whatever it costs.'

'And this someone is … ?'

He pursed his lips and puffed himself up even further. If he went on like this there was a good chance he would burst. I saw him clench his fists, and I prepared to beat a hasty retreat if he made good this threat.

'How long is it since you've spoken to Stein Sløvåg, Hårkløv?'

'Eh? I don't know any … Sløvåg.'

'No? You use his real name, do you?'

This time he came for me, but not at top speed, more like a large rock rolling down a hill and slowly picking up pace. I quickly stepped to the side, so as not to be flattened in the fall.

'I'm going to crush you.' He glanced over at the car showroom, where a man stood outside smoking and looking in our direction. Then he lowered his arms. 'But not here. You're skating on thin ice now. Make no mistake about it, I'll get Laila Bratteli's money. There are people waiting for it. And these people you go round asking questions about … You're a flea in all of this. Make no mistake about that. A flea!' He lifted his right hand and demonstrated how little it would take to crush me between his thumb and first finger.

I searched for something stinging that might linger in the air after my departure, a contribution to the series of Famous Last Words. All I could think of was: 'Yeah, but watch out for flea bites!' I doubted this would bother him. But it didn't matter.

36

I strolled back to the car without letting him out of my sight. He watched me until I had got into my car, started the engine and pulled out from where I had parked. Only then did he go back into his hut. 'Hårkløv Kreditt,' I mumbled to myself. 'Creditworthy? Hardly.'

But I didn't leave Sandsli at once. I had another job to do while I was there.

I had been in the big office block before. I found a vacant bay, parked and crossed over to the main entrance. Inside the enormous atrium I nodded to the security guard sitting on display in his glass box with what I hoped passed for nonchalance and then headed straight for the staircase leading up into the building. SH Data was on the third floor; just like the last time, I got no further than the solid glass door. Through it I could see into the bright company rooms, where most of the staff sat at their places, while a few moved from one area to another on who-knows-what errands.

I didn't recognise the woman in reception with the short, dark hair, but I addressed her via the intercom at the side of the door. She spoke into a microphone mounted on a headset in front of her mouth like a lollipop while staring straight at me through the glass door.

'Ruth Olsen. Is she about?'

'Have you got an appointment?'

'No.'

'And what was the name?'

'Veum. Varg Veum.'

'I'll ask.'

Ruth Olsen was the ex-wife of Sigurd Svendsbø, who vanished into Bjørnafjord that dramatic autumn evening a year and a half earlier. One of Svendsbø's daughters had been in many of the photos he had put on the net. Unfortunately I had been in some of them, too. As if that weren't enough, the self-same Ruth Olsen had been in a relationship with one of the others in the network, as far as I knew, although I was unclear about the background. This man was still in prison. If anyone had a reason to be furious about what had happened, it was her. Perhaps her anger was so great, she'd felt the need to take her revenge on the men who had been convicted along with her ex-husband? The list had been short and snappy. It comprised Per Haugen, Mikael Midtbø, Karl Slåtthaug and – until the contrary had been proved – myself.

The receptionist nodded to me and said: 'She's on her way.'

I waited for her to open the door, but she didn't. I stood there until Ruth Olsen appeared. She sent me a fierce glare, exchanged a few words with the receptionist and came to the door herself.

I had no difficulty recognising her. She was a small, compact woman, elegantly dressed in black trousers and an ice-blue blouse that was in sharp contrast with the deep blue of her glasses. She walked in a jerky, aggressive way that did not invite any form of intimacy.

She pressed a button on the inside and the door slid open. She came out and waited until the door had closed behind her. Then she locked her eyes onto mine. 'What on earth are you doing here, Veum? Do you think I want anything to do with you?'

I made a gesture with my hands, as if to signal my sympathy. 'I understand that you might not be thrilled to see me, but I was acquitted of any involvement with what went on and the photos you were exposed to … I've explained all this before. At the time I was in fact unconscious.'

'That didn't make it any better,' she said with a slight tremor in her voice.

'No, but it was actually your husband – your ex-husband who took the photos.'

'They're still in my brain,' she exclaimed in a burst of emotion. 'Sometimes I wake up in the night and can see them, and then I can't get back to sleep for ages.'

'I can understand that.'

'So why have you come here, raking up the past now, when all of us who were involuntarily dragged into this business are doing our best to forget it?'

'Because it's resurfaced.' I looked around. 'Is there anywhere we can talk?'

'We can talk here.' She gestured. 'This way.'

I followed her along the internal balcony. Above us arched a high glass ceiling. From where she was standing we could see down four storeys into the atrium. We could wave to the security monkey in the cage or we could swing over the railing and down if we felt the need.

She still had the fierce expression on her face. 'What do you mean the case has resurfaced?'

'Some of the men who were convicted have died. I seem to remember you followed the trials. I saw you in court.'

Her eyes narrowed. 'I had to hear what the bastards had to say for themselves – their excuses.'

'Per Haugen died in October. Mikael Midtbø died in December. Karl Slåtthaug died in January.'

'I see. Not worth a damn, the lot of them, if you ask me.'

'But … that's not why I wanted to talk to you.'

'Right.' She gazed at me with measured interest.

It struck me there was something resigned and distant about the way she regarded me. The woman standing here with me was indisputably one of the victims in this case. One of her daughters was in the images presented to the court – with me, to my mortification. Her ex-husband was revealed to be someone she had probably never remotely considered criminal. The man she had established a new relationship with had turned out to be involved in developing the computer program that had circulated the images and, in addition, a murderer. What right did I have to come here and create even more uncertainty in her life? I was unable to do anything else. Because the growing suspicions I nurtured were too strong.

'Your ex-husband, Sigurd Svendsbø. Have you ever heard from him again?'

She blanched, visibly. Then her eyes widened and she instinctively took a few steps backwards. She stared at me as if she had seen a ghost, and in a way that was probably exactly what I was evoking by asking such questions. In a voice so weak I had to lean forwards to catch what she was saying, she said: 'Siggen! What are you talking about? He drowned, didn't he? You witnessed it yourself. Have you lost your mind or what?'

'It's just that … no body was ever found, as you know. And now someone from Germany has turned up with a very different name, but the initials are the same, as though, in searching for a new name, he couldn't quite let go of the old one.'

'What? Now I don't understand what you're saying. I can't follow you.'

'The name Stein Sløvåg, does that mean anything to you?'

'Stein Sløvåg? No. Is it meant to be—?'

I held up my hands. 'I don't know, Ruth. That's why I've come to see you. I thought he might try to contact you. That he might be hoping to see his daughters again.'

'See Herdis and Bente again?' Her voice was stronger now. 'In his dreams! If so, it will be over my dead body. He has no right…' She raised her voice a notch. 'Absolutely no right! To anything. He should just keep well away.'

'This is only an idea off the top of my head. It might be completely wrong. Your ex-husband might be at the bottom of the sea, crab fodder, but I had to ask you the question.'

'Do you know what, Veum? You've really rattled me now. There hasn't been a day since I saw the photos that I haven't thought, *This will never happen again. I'll protect my daughters with everything I possess. An animal like him will never get close to them.* Eugh!'

At once tears sprang from her eyes, not meek, sad tears, but ones that burst forth like projectiles from a hidden launch pad, a sign of an anger that knew no bounds. I couldn't get the word Sølvi had used a few days ago out of my brain: a lioness, ready to protect her offspring, even at the risk of losing her own life.

'He hasn't contacted you then?'

She came towards me, so close that I could feel the heat of her body, the smell of the strong perfume she used, a lavender scent. Her face flushed, she cried: 'He has not. I can promise you that.'

I took out my wallet, gave her my card and said: 'If you should hear from him, would you mind getting in touch?'

She looked down at the card with contempt. 'You? If he contacts me in any way whatsoever, I'll call the police! You can be damn sure I will.'

'Good. Just do that. But … I'd still like to know.'

'Fine.' She shrugged and took the card in one hand. Then she said: 'I don't promise anything. But … thank you for letting me know. I'm never going to forget this case now. Not until they fish the bastard up from the deep and show him to me. Only then will I get a decent night's sleep again. Though I'm not at all sure that a good night's sleep exists for people who have experienced what I have. Can you understand that?'

'Yes, in fact I can.'

'So take this as a final farewell. And I hope I never see you again. Understand?'

'I understand that, too.'

We gazed at each other for a few seconds. Then she looked away, stepped to the side, walked past me and back to the glass door. She beckoned to the receptionist inside and the door opened like magic, let her in and closed behind her.

As for me, I had to find my way out without any help. No one had asked me to come here, either. I was used to that. Only very rarely was I a welcome guest. And where I was going later today I was hardly likely to be welcome, either.

37

The phone rang before I had a chance to get into my car. It was Ghulam Mohammad. 'Fatima says Laila can talk to you, if you're still interested.'

'I am. I'm on my way.'

I got in, started up and drove the quickest route to Sletten. I parked a short distance from the house, then walked back and up to the second floor.

Mohammad was standing in the doorway as I appeared. 'She said you should call by phone before you came so that she could hear it was you.'

I nodded, took out my phone and dialled her number. Her voicemail came on. I answered it. 'Hi, Laila. This is Veum. I'm outside your front door.'

Thirty seconds later she opened the door, still with the security chain on. She peered out, as though to ensure I was alone. Then she closed the door, released the chain and reopened.

I nodded to Muhammad and followed Laila into the flat. From the hallway she led me into the sitting room. It was very simply furnished: a tired-looking coffee table, three chairs around it, an old-fashioned TV set in the opposite corner and that was it. The TV was on, with no sound, and was showing some soap opera from the 1980s, judging by the clothes the actors were wearing. The only picture on the wall was one of the prints they give you when you buy something from IKEA, happy to be rid of them. This one didn't even hang straight, but had a pronounced slant to the left.

On the table lay a well-thumbed weekly magazine open at a page showing new fashions, plus some scrunched-up sweet papers and a tin of throat pastilles. In the chair where presumably she had been sitting I saw white pill bottles that had been pushed down into a corner behind a cushion; easily accessible if she should need them. She made a beeline for the chair, plumped down, turned her phone round so that she could read the display and then raised her eyes to me.

She nodded briefly towards one of the two other chairs. 'You can sit there.'

'Thank you for agreeing to speak to me.'

She grimaced and tossed her head, without saying a word.

'Let me start with what's probably of most concern to you. I have informed the police that you're having problems with Bjørn Hårkløv.'

Her eyes widened, and her face took on a horrified expression. 'What?' she said in a hoarse voice. 'The police? But…'

'In addition, I've spoken to him.'

'Him?'

'Bjørn Hårkløv. You might know him as only Bønni. I said they should forget the debt.'

She stared at me in disbelief. 'And you think they will? Then you don't know those people.'

'Who is there apart from Hårkløv?'

She shrugged. 'Drug dealers. Lots of them. But the people behind them are the same, of course.'

'And who's that?'

'I don't know! It's Bønni who collects the money. He's done it for years.'

I sighed. 'Yes, I know actually. It's just odd that they can never get anything on him.'

'The cops? They don't give a shit about his sort. It's us they're after. It's us they like to torment.'

'Surely that can't be right.'

'Isn't it? Ask all the others on the street. Take a trip round the park and listen. Everyone will say the same.'

'I suppose you talk about where your stuff comes from, too?'

'We know where it comes from. Abroad, of course. More often than not via Oslo, but sometimes direct. How much do you think comes from Copenhagen, either by plane or ferry? Or by car over the Swedish border and straight over the Hardanger Plain. You can only speculate.'

'Well…' I opened my palms. 'At least they're warned now.'

'Hah! Warned.' She didn't believe me for a second, and in a way I was afraid she was right.

'The other thing I wanted to talk to you about—'

Her phone vibrated. She took it, checked the display, grimaced again and placed it on the table in front of her, face down.

'Are you still on drugs?'

'And where would I get them? Don't you think the word has spread?'

'Aren't there others trying to get in with their offers? Always cheap at the start, isn't it.'

'Always cheap at the start,' she imitated. 'You sound like a bloody social worker.'

'Mm.'

'But does it give me peace? Eh? Does it?'

'What I wanted to talk to you about…'

'So it wasn't that?' She was brimming with a mixture of sarcasm and despair.

'Well, when your brother and I were outside here on Tuesday you made some fairly strong allegations against him.'

'Yes?' She glared at me defiantly. 'So?'

'What—?'

'They weren't allegations. It was true.'

'That you'd seen some photos of Knut's children that he'd sent to your ex-husband, Bjarne?'

'Yes! I saw them.' She looked round the room, as though there was something there that might help her to explain what she was talking about. She gasped for breath. 'It was as terrible as … as when my father…' She stared hard at me. 'They were photos of his girls, Toril and Elisabeth, and they looked as if they were asleep, but … they were completely naked and beside them stood … I couldn't see who it was because you couldn't see the head, but it was a man and he stood there…' She made some explicit hand gestures. 'With no clothes on.'

Then the air seemed to go out of her. She slumped even deeper into the chair and bent forwards as though she were looking for the foetal position she had been in before birth. It was as though I could hear the voice of singer Jan Eggum in my head: *Mum, I want to go back*...

She whispered to herself: 'It's so terrible. I can barely talk about it.'

Convulsive tremors racked her body. I felt like extending a hand, stroking her shoulder comfortingly, but something inside me held me back. The best thing was to let her get it out. I leaned back in my chair and breathed slowly in and out. There was no question that this was having an effect on me, too.

'Poor Knut,' she said in a low voice.

'Knut?' I said gently.

She straightened up and regarded me with tears in her eyes. 'Don't you understand? He was abused, too.'

'Yes, you mentioned that last time we met, but ... By your father, from what you said.'

She gave an almost imperceptible nod. 'I remember ... We were in the same room. I remember being woken by him crying in bed. When I sat up my father was there and said ... I should just go back to sleep. Knut was only ... a little sad.' She seemed to be having difficulty breathing. 'When I asked him the day afterwards – when I asked Knut, he just turned his face to the wall and refused to answer.' There was something stony and ugly about her as she continued: 'What he did to me – and Marthe – happened during the day, at the weekend, when he was alone with us. What he did to Knut was always at night, when it was dark, as though he ... As though it was something he wouldn't admit, that it made no difference to him ... whether it was girls or boys he abused.'

When she paused, I said: 'Apparently it's not unusual for abused children to become abusers themselves.'

'Yes, so I've heard.' She had begun to unwind from the foetal position. 'But someone must stop the devilry, mustn't they. Surely it can't be original sin, can it?'

'Preferably not.'

'Perhaps my father was abused as a child himself. Does that excuse what he himself did later in life, when he was an adult? Does it excuse what Knut's been doing?'

'But ... Do you know any more about it, other than the photos you saw with your husband? Have you confronted him about it?'

She stared into the distance and answered as if she hadn't heard my question. 'Once when we were ... I was maybe twelve, he was fourteen. We talked about it and we shook hands ... We swore to each other that as soon as we were grown up enough, we would leave home and never return. And we did! When I was eighteen I moved out and I never saw my mother and father again until ... the courtroom, sixteen or seventeen years later. Knut did the same.'

I repeated my question. 'But when you saw the photos Knut had sent to your husband, did you confront him?'

She looked at me as if I was just a stupid social worker who understood nothing of what she was up against. 'Confront him? I spewed. I lay in bed throwing up for a day afterwards. And then I left that home, too. I never went back to Bjarne and I couldn't bear even the thought of talking to Knut. When he was here on Thursday and wanted to come in ... I became desperate. I couldn't control myself. I've lost my faith in all men. And that applies to you too! Don't think you can come here and help with anything. As soon as you've gone, the bloody debt collectors will be at the door again, and if I can't pay them in the end they'll kill me.' She tossed her head, like a fish caught in a net. 'And perhaps that's the best when it comes down to it. Just have done with the whole shit, like Marthe did.'

'You've got a sister-in-law – Vibeke. The mother of Toril and Elisabeth. You could contact her.'

She looked at me vacantly. 'Vibeke? She pretended she hadn't seen anything, either. Mothers!' She almost spat the word out. 'Bitches! We're the ones who suffered. The children.'

'Yes.'

I could visualise the distant woman in the window in Nystuveien, hear her unsympathetic voice in the intercom by the door. A bitch, as Laila called her, or a lioness?

I felt unwell and ill at ease. With every conversation I had in this case, which barely deserved the term 'investigation', it was as though I was moving further and further into a dark web of evil crimes, unmentionable acts, lives built on an insecure childhood, in which fathers rose like monstrous shadows over their children, mothers closed their eyes, and childhood memories became traumas and nightmares that led to breakdowns, dependence on medication and drugs, and rootless existence.

Laila had talked about stopping the devilry, as she called it. She wasn't the only person who thought like this. Was there, somewhere out in the darkness, an invisible avenger, an angel who had come down to earth from God, sword of fire in hand, to separate the pure from the impure, the guilty from the innocent? But if that were so, how clear-thinking was the angel? Could they distinguish between wolves and sheep? It was a question that remained unanswered. It was a question that had consequences for me personally.

38

Before I drove any further I rang Sølvi to ask how things were going.

'Fine, but Helene's bored of course. She'd rather be at school.'

'I've spoken to the police. They're working on the case.'

'I really hope they are. Talk later.'

'OK. Take care.'

'Take care.'

She rang off, and I sat with the phone in my hand. What now? I had a gut instinct there was someone I should talk more to: Bjarne Bratteli. He was still at work. In a kindergarten. I could of course pay him a call there, but if I was going to get anything out of him it would be simpler if I could visit him at home. And who did I meet the last time I was there? Knut Haugen. I should talk to him anyway, after the conversation with his sister. I could see him at work, if I could get past his receptionist-cum-guard, that is.

I drove back to town, parked the car in Markeveien and popped into the office to check that there were no other emails for me apart from an offer to inherit a million dollars in Nigeria. Apparently there was a distant relative of mine there whose name I had never come across, but who had left this sum to me personally. Now he had died in a car accident and the sum could be transferred, against a tiny commission of sixty percent. I saved the offer for a rainy day when I needed cheering up.

Then I crossed the market square. It was deserted on this Monday in January. Not so much as a delayed tourist from Transylvania to be seen. When I arrived at BI-IT I was met by the same young lady in reception. She even appeared to recognise me.

'Knut Haugen,' I said. 'You can tell him it's Veum this time as well.'

She nodded, turned aside and spoke into the phone with her back to me. I had seen worse backs, and far worse above and below. She turned to me and met my wandering eyes with silence. You are unlikely to see anything more withering on a Monday. 'Knut said you'd better come in, otherwise there'd only be trouble.'

'Trouble? Me?' I grinned and passed close enough to her to smell the fragrance of ice roses or whatever perfume it was she liked to wear.

Knut Haugen received me in the corridor with a sullen face, held open the door to his office and then closed it firmly behind me. He nodded to the chair that had a view of Vågen and sat down behind his desk, so that the light fell on me. But it wasn't so bright that I couldn't see the beads of sweat on his brow beneath the short fringe.

'What is it this time, Veum?' he said, then changed the topic. 'By the way, I heard you were outside my wife's door before the weekend. If that happens again, we'll call the police.'

'To tell them what exactly?'

'That you're harassing us. My wife has nothing to do with any of this.'

'And by "this" you're referring to … your father?'

'Vibeke never met my father. I'm referring to Laila. All the commotion there. However, I can inform you I've solved that case myself now.'

'Solved … which case?'

'I made a call to this herr Hårkløv and was told what she owed them. I've transferred the outstanding amount.'

'Really? When did you do that?'

He looked at his watch; the same expensive Rolex. 'An hour ago.'

'I spoke to herr Hårkløv myself two hours ago and he wasn't remotely relaxed then.'

'As I said, you can drop that case now.'

I observed him. 'Really? So you think I should drop all the other stuff in the case too, do you?'

He automatically tensed his mouth before answering. 'Yes, everything. Just drop all of it.'

'All the abuse Laila hurled at you when we were there on Thursday and which she's elaborated on this morning?'

'This…? Have you been talking to Laila today?'

'I've just come from hers now. And she hadn't been informed that you'd paid her debt.'

'Well, no bloody surprise there. She doesn't answer the phone, does she.'

'No, perhaps you'll have to go via the neighbour as well then.'

'The neighbour? That…?'

'Save the swear words for a more appropriate occasion. Yes, I'm talking about Ghulam Mohammad and his wife, Fatima. The only people who seem to have bothered about Laila recently. But we shouldn't be talking about them now. We should be talking about…' I leaned forwards slightly to emphasise that what I said was confidential. 'I know you had a difficult childhood, both Laila and you. She wasn't alone in being abused. The same happened to you. Your father had catholic tastes, if I can put it like that.'

His face turned waxen in front of me. It was as though a mask had been pulled down over his head, a faithful copy of himself, but with all his facial features distorted and askew, like a grotesque caricature of himself, a reflection of a pain so bitter and sad that he was unable to hide it.

He moistened his lips, looked to the side and searched for the right words. When he did finally say something it was in a voice that had become hoarse from the tension that had arisen in his larynx. 'This is … history, Veum. We've put it behind us, at least I have. And it wasn't that serious. It didn't happen that often.'

'No? But the experience of it was definitely so intense that you and Laila shook hands and swore to each other you would leave home as soon as you were old enough; and you did too, from what I've been told.'

He nodded. 'Yes.'

'But then we come to the next chapter.'

He looked at me with despondent eyes. He shook his head, as though already denying what I was going to say.

'On Wednesday evening I visited your brother-in-law, Bjarne

Bratteli. You were there. If I'm to believe Laila, you two had mutual interests, and ... There's a bit of birds of a feather in all this, isn't there? You shared the titbits. You got something from him. He got something from you. Where did he get the photos from? The kindergarten? And you ... Well, actually Laila saw them with her own eyes. From your own home. Your own daughters, Toril and Elisabeth.'

He watched me, his face grey now. There was no resistance left in him. He didn't deny anything. It was as though I was talking to a wax figure, an abandoned display dummy in a closed-down gentleman's outfitters.

'Does your wife know about these photos, Haugen? Does she know who you are, behind the façade?'

He gave a start, as though I had stirred him from a dream. 'What? Vibeke! Of course not. What do you take me for?'

'What I think or don't think is of no significance. We're talking about what you've done here.'

Again his body slumped. He held his trembling hands in front of him, opening them and looking down at his palms, which were moist with sweat. He was speaking in such a low voice that I had to lean closer to catch his words. 'My sort, we don't have a right to live. We should be erased from the face of the earth. As my father, and the other man, were. We carry all the sins of the world upon our shoulders, although we can't help it!' He raised his head and looked at me, his eyes shiny. 'I shouldn't be like this, either. He made me what I am; and I couldn't resist, I couldn't refrain.'

No. I could have been brutal and said: *You've always had a choice, Knut. You're a free man, you make your own decisions, and in the end it is you and you alone who has to stand to account for the decisions you took.* But I didn't. I said: 'I have to repeat my question. Does your wife know about your tendencies – what you're like?'

He shook his head. 'No one knows!'

'Yes, they do. Your brother-in-law knows. Your sister knows. Now I know. Have you ever tried to get some help? To resist. Professional help.'

Large tears were running down his cheeks. I felt suddenly ill at ease, as though I had put him under too much pressure. What if one of his colleagues walked in on us?

'It started … I noticed it early on. Long before I met Vibeke. I used to … I used to hang around outside nurseries, schools, not to do anything, just to catch a glimpse of them – the small children.' He gasped for breath. 'When I got to know Vibeke and … fell in love … I hoped she would liberate me from this – these obsessive thoughts. And she did. She did! For a while. We had some good years together, at the beginning. But then, when we had our own children, and I no longer needed to go to nurseries and schools, but had them inside our own walls, then …' Again his voice sank so low that I had difficulty hearing. 'Then it came back. Then …' He gestured helplessly, half turned and looked at the sky over Askøy, as though there were some form of consolation to be found there. But that was unlikely. The sky never gave an answer; I knew that from my own experience.

'How did you find out that your brother-in-law had the same leanings?'

He raised his voice a notch. 'Bjarne? He … No comment. You'll have to speak to him yourself.'

'But you admit you exchanged photos?'

He repeated: 'You'd better talk to him about that. I have no comment to make.'

'Back to you then. At least you admit you were attracted by … your own daughters?'

He gazed down, without answering.

'What about actual abuse?'

He rose halfway out of his chair, once again with despair in his eyes. 'It's never happened! Not in my home at any rate.'

I waited.

'It hasn't!'

'Laila told me about a photo she'd seen on Bjarne's computer screen. She recognised both Toril and Elisabeth. They looked as if they were asleep, actually, but above them stood a naked man and he …' I made the same unambiguous gestures with my right hand that Laila had done when she told me.

'They were asleep! I didn't touch them! Ever.'

I sat watching him. 'A lot depends on how this case develops, but it's very likely that it'll reach a point where a doctor will have to examine your children.'

'Why? You mustn't … Vibeke must never know about this.'

'No?'

'She'd go wild. She'd kill me!'

'You said a little while ago that your sort doesn't have a right to live, that they should be erased from the face of the earth.'

'Yes, but … not me. I didn't mean it like that. It would ruin our lives, the girls', Vibeke's…'

We stared at each other. I didn't have any more questions and in a way I felt for him. He was himself a damaged child and perhaps not the worst of his kind.

I said: 'How do you think Laila felt? When she discovered the pictures on Bjarne's screen? When she saw herself surrounded by sex offenders? Her father, brother and husband. Is it any wonder she broke down? Starting drinking? Going onto stronger stuff?'

He didn't answer.

'It's fine that you've paid her debts, this time. However, that's peanuts compared with what you all owe her. Your late father, your brother-in-law and you yourself. And you shouldn't ignore the possibility that she'll need more help later – financial help, at any rate.'

'I can't help her if you go to the police with this.'

'Oh, you're in no danger of receiving a sentence of any length, judging by standard legal practices. But of course there might be someone standing outside the prison gates waiting for you when you get out.'

'Someone … Who?'

'Well, that's in the stars.'

I left it at that. He had more than enough to worry about with his previous life. And, truth to say, so did I.

39

I was halfway across the market square to my office when my phone rang. I studied the display. It was a number I hadn't saved.

'Yes?'

'Solheim here. Can you meet me in my office within the next half-hour?'

'I can be there in five minutes. Anything—?'

'See you here in five then.'

Without another word, he rang off. I changed course and headed for the police station. I didn't have much choice.

Melvær met me downstairs and accompanied me up to the third floor. When we reached the office, Solheim showed me to a chair on the other side of his desk, while Melvær posted himself in the doorway as though they wanted to make sure I didn't try to make a run for it.

I sat down. 'And how can I help you boys?'

Solheim met my gaze. 'It's more how we can help you, isn't it?'

'Well.' I shrugged. 'Earlier today you said I'd be called in if you had some questions. So I assume that's why I'm here.'

He eyed me pensively. 'Let's just say we've got a step further with the case. We've got a name from the car-rental company.'

'Let's hear it.'

'It's Stein Sløvåg.'

'Right!'

'Does it mean anything to you?'

'Yes and no. Did he give an address?'

'Kind of. He gave us two.'

'And they are…?'

'One is the Grand Hotel Terminus, in Bergen. The other's in

Germany. But we called Terminus and they had no registered guests under that name. The address in Germany is also temporary accommodation, but he checked out ages ago.'

'Yes, that's correct. I knew that.'

'So you know who he is?'

'No. It's a false name. There's no one with that name in the whole of Norway.'

He looked at me condescendingly. 'We found that out for ourselves. Have you anything else to offer?'

'Your colleagues in Tønsberg are working on this case. You can contact them. Inspector Mørk. See if he knows any more.'

'The Tønsberg police?'

'It was you yourself who told me that Karl Slåtthaug had settled in Tønsberg. When I went there to talk to him, we found him in the sea, drowned.'

'We?'

'Well, your colleagues. He'd been reported missing the day before.'

'And what had happened?'

'No one knows, like the two other deaths I told you about almost precisely a week ago. It's a remarkable coincidence, don't you think?'

He angled his head, then straightened it again. 'Yes...'

'Inspector Mørk informed me that Slåtthaug had been in telephone contact with this Stein Sløvåg.'

'Informed you?'

'Yes, when he asked me the same question you've just asked: did the name mean anything to me? But it didn't then, either.'

'Telephone contact ... So they've got his phone number?'

'Sort of. But it was a German number and the account had been closed. Didn't he have to leave a phone number at the car-rental place here?'

'Yes, he did. We've checked it. But it's not registered and the phone was obviously a pay-as-you-go.'

'As usual in criminal circles.'

He nodded. 'But...'

'When did he rent the car and for how long?'

'Three or four days ago. The advance payment covered two weeks and he still has the car. But that brings us back to your case, Veum.'

'Yes.'

'If we're to take you and your partner at your word – and there's no reason not to, is there?' He fixed his eyes on me questioningly for a second or two, but when I didn't answer, he carried on: 'Why would a man calling himself Stein Sløvåg attempt to run you down first, and then a week later your partner? What could his motive be?'

'Obviously to get at me. And, furthermore, the connection with Karl Slåtthaug indicates that it has something to do with the same case as the other two deaths. Not least because Slåtthaug also ended up a corpse.'

'What do the Tønsberg police think about the death?'

I looked at him wryly. 'If you believe what's in *Tønsbergs Blad* it was accidental drowning. But I think you should talk to Mørk yourself.'

'You can be sure I will. What about you? Do you have any ideas about who this Stein Sløvåg could be?'

I reflected for a moment. How far should I go? I decided to go the whole hog. 'Then I might have to stretch your perception of my credibility a touch further.'

'You've done that so many times. Once more will hardly make any difference.'

'When I spoke to Hamre and you a week ago we touched on a person who disappeared in Bjørna fjord one September day in 2002, when all the machinations against me were revealed. Are you with me?'

'I'm with you: your crown witness who went missing and never reappeared.'

'Not only a crown witness, but someone guilty of a murder as well – and quite probably a long series of sexual offences against children.'

'Well…' He still looked just as puzzled.

'What if he didn't die in Bjørna fjord, but somehow managed to reach land? He was part of Bruno Karsten's criminal network and could probably have got some help from him to leave the country and establish a new identity. He was a useful man for Karsten, with his computer know-how.'

'And this man's name is … ?'

'Sigurd Svendsbø. Two S's, as in Stein Sløvåg.'

'A man with a feel for alliteration, anyway?'

'Or perhaps he did it for sentimental reasons. What do I know?'

'Yes, what do you actually know … aside from making a wild stab in the dark?'

'At least it's something.' But to myself I had to admit that the reasoning behind this conjecture was weak. 'I contacted his ex-wife earlier today.'

'Oh, yes? Had she heard from him after he drowned?'

'No, but—'

'I think we'll shelve this hypothesis until we have something concrete. And the most concrete lead we have is the Golf and the registration number.' He looked at Melvær. 'Check the switchboard to see if there's anything new on that.'

'Will do.' Melvær nodded and went out.

Solheim leaned back in his chair. 'One thing you can be sure of, Veum. We're taking this case seriously.' He smirked. 'When he tried to run you down that was his business, but when he tried the same on your partner and her daughter, then it's all systems go. In our profession you have to be careful about offering any guarantees. But I promise you one thing: if he hasn't dumped the car in the sea we'll find it in a day or two, max. Patrols are out all over the country and in Sweden and Denmark too, so we'll find it. Whether Stein Sløvåg will still be behind the wheel is harder to guarantee.'

'Well, I'll do my best to find it, too.'

'You? You sit back and take it easy, Veum, and look twice before you cross the road. I advise you to look after your partner and her daughter, and leave the rest to us. Have you got the message?'

'Loud and clear,' I said. *Clear, but not loud enough*, I said to myself.

Melvær reappeared. 'No, nothing new yet,' he reported.

'OK. I've explained to Veum that we're well on top of this case now. I've promised him we'll find the car, so we just have to keep up the good work. Could you accompany Veum out so that he doesn't get lost in our corridors?'

Melvær did as he had been bidden. He accompanied me all the way out of the front door, where the January sun waited for me with a chilly gaze, so chilly that a chill ran down my spine. No comfort here, either. No comfort to be found anywhere, it seemed.

40

I walked back to the office, flipped open my notepad and embarked on a mental clear-out. I would leave tracking down Stein Sløvåg to the police for the moment. So what was I left with?

If Knut Haugen really had paid off Laila's debt, I could perhaps strike a line through Bjørn Hårkløv and the pressure he had exerted on her. But I still had him on the list of potential lines of communication to Bruno Karsten and Germany – and thus also 'Stein Sløvåg'. Was 'Sløvåg' working on behalf of Karsten perhaps? A remote-controlled operator in a VW Golf; a kind of tit for tat for all the problems I had also caused Karsten about a year and a half ago?

As for the three deaths in this case, I didn't have much to go on, either. Knut Haugen had said himself his sort didn't have any right to live. Could he have decided to attack others with the same leanings and started on his father and those accused with him? And what about the uncommunicative Vibeke? Could she be the unknown woman who had visited Per Haugen the day before he died? But was it likely that she had attacked Mikael Midtbø and Karl Slåtthaug afterwards? Hardly. There were still too many loose ends in these cases, and, when it came down to it, there might not be any connection at all. Perhaps they were just three random accidents that had a common multiple, turning the whole thing into an arithmetic calculation – for those of us with antennae for hidden interconnections, at least. And then there was this pastor. I hadn't made any progress on him or her either.

Knut Haugen had an extremely complicated relationship with his father. It made me think of the unopened envelope from the Public Health Institute I had in my desk drawer. The person I thought of as my biological father, tram conductor Anders Veum from Fjaler in Sunnfjord, had at least not been a sexual predator. I could barely remember him laying a finger on me. He went to work at the crack of dawn when he was on the early shift, and around lunchtime when he was on the evening shift. Accordingly he came home either for lunch or so late I had long gone to bed. Sometimes he came into my bedroom to see if I was asleep. If I was awake he would ask me a few questions about how school had been that day, whether I had got some tests back or if I had any new homework. The only thing that made his face light up was if I said we had some Norwegian history homework, preferably from saga times. Otherwise he maintained the distant and somewhat pensive expression he always wore. The clearest image I had of him was when he was sitting in the special chair by the tatty coffee table, immersed in a book about Norse mythology. If I asked him a question about it he would brighten up and suddenly be very chatty for a few minutes, then gradually become distant again, turn over a page and depart this world. I would withdraw into one of my comic magazines, about Batman, Superman or one of the other heroes.

Then one day, in 1956, when I was fourteen, his heart stopped beating. He was heading for Valhalla, which was what he wanted, I think. But whether tram conductors who died of a heart attack were allowed in, I had no idea. My mother and I stayed down here. Many years later I heard something that made me wonder whether he had been my father at all. Perhaps that was why he always looked at me with such a distant gaze, the way he would have regarded the child of another person – someone he might not even have met, such as a saxophonist called Leif Pedersen.

The answer to this question probably lay in the unopened envelope in my drawer. It was out of respect for the tram conductor, who perhaps had not been allowed to enter Valhalla, that even after so many months I hadn't opened it. And I wasn't going to today, either. But I had no unresolved issues with Anders Veum; nor for that matter with Leif Pedersen. But during the week I had worked on these cases there were enough father figures I wouldn't have given a rotten fig to get to know. Indeed, they were extremely unpleasant acquaintances, every single one of them.

Although Solheim had as good as banned me from continuing with my investigations, I found it difficult to stay inactive. I was still keen to know whether they had discovered anything in Tønsberg.

I dialled Foyn's number. He had clearly slotted me into his system because he answered cheerfully: 'Hi, Varg. Still imp-patient?'

'Well … I'm sitting here musing. I was wondering if you'd heard from Mørk.'

'I have, in fact. I was just about to give you a ring myself. It must be telepathy, eh?'

'Possibly. I'd be more interested to know what Mørk had to say.'

He chuckled. 'Alright, alright. I understand. I know myself how hard it is when you feel a case is stuck in a rut. Although I'm not sure I can help you much. I do have some information for you, though.'

'I'm all ears, as the bishop said to the actress.'

'Mørk's colleagues in Oslo have actually arrested the siblings who ran off from here: Isaac and Hirute. They told the police that Karl Slåtthaug had taken Hirute to one side and said he could get her an au pair job in Oslo, which would secure her Norwegian residence. This frightened them, because he'd promised the two girls, Moira and Amina, the same back in October. They'd never told anyone, but they'd received texts from Moira telling them it wasn't an au pair job at all – she was locked in a flat where men came and had sex with her for money. A few weeks later she wrote that Amina was there, too. If they protested they were beaten and if they'd managed to escape … well, Varg, they have absolutely no faith in the police, these young people.'

'But now the police know, surely they'll do something?'

'But they don't know where to look. This was in October. The last text came at the beginning of November. The police had no idea what had happened to them afterwards. And the person who might've given them an address, Slåtthaug, is dead.'

'Not without reason probably. This fits so well into the pattern I'm trying to establish, Svend. But of the three deaths I've investigated so far, Slåtthaug's is the one linked most closely to organised crime in this area, which his contact with Germany will probably bear out. There's a system behind this that's cynically exploiting young people in extreme distress. Child refugees or Norwegian children in vulnerable situations. I can hardly imagine anything more despicable. And what are the politicians doing about it? Generally speaking, sitting on the fence, and if you try to draw their attention to the issue, they turn their backs and pretend they can't hear. It's easy to understand why someone can become so desperate that they take the law into their own hands.'

'Indeed. I've come across cases like this, both as a lawyer and … well, in my capacity as a kind of freelance investigator.'

'Talking of which, do you know if Mørk and his colleagues have come to any conclusions regarding what happened to Slåtthaug?'

'The cause of death is in all probability drowning, as I told you earlier today. But the report says Slåtthaug had a very high level of alcohol in his blood. More than two point eight. At that level you'd actually be dead drunk.'

'Wow, he really knocked it back. But he might've been an old soak. I seem to remember he liked a tot when I met him.'

'They made enquiries at all the watering holes around Ollebukta and up towards the market square, but found nothing. The problem is, of course, that Slåtthaug was relatively new in town. He wasn't a known face in such places.'

'Mm, I can understand that.'

'But Mørk said he was going to contact you. They've got copies of the passenger lists of all the Widerøe flights between Bergen and Torp on the days before and after the Wednesday in question. He said he was going to send them to you, in case you recognised any of the names.'

'Sounds good. Did he say when?'

'Today some time.'

'I'll expect them then. Should anything new come up, give me a call.'

'At the moment I'm heavily involved in another case, Varg, but of course if I hear anything, I'll let you know.'

After the conversation I once again sat flicking through my notes. I was interrupted by the phone ringing, a long number with a German code.

'Veum here,' I said in English.

It was Schultz. 'Good afternoon Mr Veum,' he said, as formally as only Germans can be. Nevertheless, he got straight to the point. 'I have something for you.'

'Right. Go ahead.'

'I visited the address you gave me. It was a kind of boarding house. Herr Stein Sløvåg' – he pronounced the name 'Schtein Slövak' – 'he'd shown his passport and the landlady had taken a photocopy, as usual.' I could feel my interest growing. 'For a couple of hundred-euro notes she was willing to let me have a copy of the copy. I have it here in my hand, so if you give me your email address, Mr Veum, I can send it to you directly.'

'This is more than I'd hoped for. Thank you. Let me know how much you had to pay, and I'll transfer the sum with the fee.'

'Ja, ja. Thank you. Two hundred euros will cover everything. And we have a deal on possible co-operation if necessary.'

'You have my word, Bernhard.' Then I added 'Herr Schultz' to be on the safe side. '*Auf Wiedersehen.*'

'*Auf Wiedersehen*, Herr Veum.'

I clicked off the screensaver, opened my email account and sat waiting. Every so often I impatiently pressed Send/Receive and eventually an email from Hanne u. Bernhard Schultz arrived, with a paper-clip icon to say there was an attachment.

I quickly scanned his email. Schultz thanked me for the job and hoped we could continue to work together. He wished me luck with the rest of the investigation and hoped the attached photocopy of Mr Stein Sløvåg's passport might be of some help. It was as though I could hear the laborious way he expressed himself, but I hurriedly opened the attachment, clicked on the copy of the passport photo and magnified it as much as I could.

Actually it came as no surprise. My suspicions were confirmed. He had grown a beard and dyed his hair and beard a dark colour, but behind this disguise I recognised him. The last time I had seen him we were standing face to face on a slippery rock facing Bjørna fjord. Then he had disappeared, but not forever. Now he had returned from the dead, on a passport photo sent to me from Germany, under the melodious pseudonym he had chosen himself: Stein Sløvåg. There was no longer any doubt: Sigurd Svendsbø was staring at me from the screen like an old photo from police files. Wanted. Now more than ever.

41

I called Solheim.

He sighed aloud. 'What is it now?'

I quickly told him what I was looking at and offered to send him the copy of the passport. He adopted a much gentler tone as he accepted, then added: 'But this is still our case, Veum. You do nothing. Is that understood?' When I didn't answer at once, he repeated: 'Understood?'

'Yes, I've understood. Good luck.'

'Thank you.'

I had understood. But I still had a few loose ends to tidy up in the other cases, and the first person I was going to talk to was Bjarne Bratteli.

Before I did anything I checked the time: 16:45. Then I called Sølvi. She answered after two rings. 'Hi.'

'Hi. How's it going?'

'We've come home. Helene's bored and now she wants to visit a friend from her class, but I've said she has to stay here. She's not pleased. She's slamming doors and has locked herself in her room.'

'Mm. I'm sorry. But now the police know who rented the car. It's just a question of time before they find him. That's what they say anyway.'

'How long then?'

'A day or two, maximum, they told me.'

'I hope that's right. Keep me posted. Now I'd better make her something to eat or she'll be annoyed about that, too.'

'If anyone rings the doorbell, don't open unless you can see who it is.'

'And if it's someone I don't know, call you?'

'That sort of thing.'

'Very reassuring,' she said, and rang off with no further comment. I stared at the phone, then put it down carefully, afraid it might snap at me, too.

So what was the plan? Initially, Bjarne Bratteli. I had a swift bite to eat at Brasserie Lido, just around the corner: fried saithe with onions. At around half past six I drove to Nye Sandviksvei in the hope of catching him at home. Before I had found a parking spot I saw another car turn in and park in front of the entrance to the block where he lived. It wasn't a Golf; it looked more like a BMW. It was black and had such a long bonnet it reminded me of a cartoon version of a melancholy wolf. I had met the man who stepped out of the car before – and in the same place. It was Knut Haugen.

I drove on, pulled into the kerb on the east side of the street and parked. In front of me was the steep rock face up to Rothaugen School. To the right, the last line of houses in the street. To the left, the International Blue Cross building towered up with its sallow-brown cladding. When there were polls in *Bergensavisen* or *Bergens Tidende* for Bergen's ugliest building, the IBC always achieved a podium finish.

I switched off the engine and sat looking in the rear-view mirror at the entrance fifty metres behind me on the opposite side. Haugen spoke into the intercom and was buzzed in. OK, another meeting of the brothers-in-law? If so, they met more often than was usual in families where most of the members didn't talk to each other.

But this time it wasn't a long meeting. Five minutes later they both came out. Haugen opened the boot lid and Bratteli put in two leather bags – the kind you use to transport film and camera equipment. I sank even lower in the front seat, but neither of them looked in my direction. They got into the car and immediately afterwards passed me, heading north and around the bend by Rothaugen. I started the engine, pulled out and followed. *Follow the money*, they said in the States. *Cherchez la femme*, in France. My motto was much simpler: *Follow the car*.

The black BMW went down Sandviksveien and continued along the E16 towards Åsane. After passing the old ropewalk on the left, they turned off and into Fløyfjell Tunnel.

In recent decades, the mountains around Bergen had changed into overgrown Swiss cheeses with extensive holes in all directions. From Fløyfjell Tunnel Haugen drove on to Nygårds Tunnel, across Puddefjord Bridge, and then into another tunnel, Løvstakk, which actually dated all the way back to 1968. It led to Fyllingsdalen, and I could feel my excitement growing as they branched off to Dag Hammarskjølds vei, continued along it in a curve to the east, and then back west. It struck me that we were on the way to where Bjørn Hårkløv lived, but it turned out that they were going a little further. When the BMW turned in towards two high-rises, I couldn't go on. But I had kept several cars between us all the way, so I drove into the car park by one of the low blocks in the area and waited there, careful not to lose sight of the BMW.

Knut Haugen sat at the wheel while Bjarne Bratteli got out of the car, crossed the car park and went into the block where Svanhild Olsvik lived. I would have been a poor PI if I hadn't assumed that was where he was going. It wasn't much more than five minutes before he was out again. He wasn't alone this time though. With him came Svanhild Olsvik and her daughter, Astrid. The mother held her daughter's hand, but she still lagged behind, as though this was against her wishes. She glared at her mother and said something it was impossible to catch from this distance. The mother just shook her head firmly and said something back. Bratteli held the rear door open for them. Svanhild Olsvik lifted her daughter up and put her in the car, then followed her in. Bratteli closed the door behind them and sat at the front. Less than a minute later the car was off again.

To reach the main road they passed perilously close to where I was parked, and now I had sunk so low in my seat that it must have looked as if the car was empty. I heard the low whine of the passing car, waited a few seconds, sat up warily and turned to find them. They were at the end of Dag Hammarskjølds vei, waiting for a gap in the traffic. Then there was a quick blink to the right and the car headed for Oasen Shopping Centre. I sat upright, started the car and followed them. The excitement was still there, but now it was joined by another, even stronger, feeling: one of intense aversion.

My head was a seething mass of thoughts. During the drive from

Nye Sandviksvei to here, so far two of the cases had meshed together. The deaths of Mikael Midtbø and Per Haugen were both represented in the car ahead of me, and I had a strong feeling it wasn't going to stop there. The feeling grew with every kilometre we covered in our discreet procession. There was more traffic now, and I had to alternate between having a vehicle or two between us and keeping enough distance for them not to recognise me.

They left Fyllingsdalen and drove into Bjørgeveien, or Burmaveien as we used to call it on our teenage cycle trips in this area. It had received that name because its construction was started during the war and people in town compared it with the building of the strategically important road from Burma to China. We also used to whistle the theme from *The Bridge on the River Kwai* as we cycled through, although we had no idea why.

From here I followed the black BMW to Loddefjord and further along Lyderhornsveien before it headed towards Sotra Bridge and went over it. There was still quite a bit of traffic on the roads, and I was able to keep several cars between me and them.

A little way after the bridge they indicated left, stopped and waited for a couple of oncoming cars to pass and then raced down to the sea. I performed the same manoeuvre, but because of the distance I had kept, I was held up for a long time and lost sight of them. When I finally crossed the opposite lane and went down the side road to the south-east, there were thin veils of exhaust fumes in the air, showing where they had been. I followed cautiously. There were several turn-offs to bigger and smaller houses, but as I approached the sea there were fewer of them. To the north I could see a large industrial plant. Now I was descending to an area where there had been light sea-related industry, much of it abandoned now because the fish-processing sheds had been moved, and the oil industry required more room and deeper waters.

I looked to the right and left to see if I could locate the black car. On the seaward side I spotted a closed gate with a clear warning in the form of a sign saying: *No admittance to unauthorised personnel*. Down towards the sea I glimpsed a large, grey timber structure with a stone quay into the connecting strait, Kobbeleia. At the bottom of the drive, in front of the building, was the black BMW. It was empty. The occupants had gone, in all probability into the building.

I started up the car and drove five hundred metres further down, where the road terminated in a kind of turnaround. With a view to making a quick escape I doubled back so that the nose of the car pointed upwards, then parked on the far edge of the turnaround, up against some wintergreen juniper bushes. I took a torch from the glove compartment, stuffed it into my pocket, got out of the car and walked back up the road.

The darkness was in my favour. I opened the gate, closed it neatly behind me and ran the risk of being seen as I walked down the drive to the BMW. It was deathly quiet. The only sounds I could hear were a plane coming in to land at Flesland Airport to the east and the regular drone of a ship's engine in Kobbeleia – I could make out the stern of a passenger ferry heading south, probably no further than Denmark.

Once down by the BMW, I veered off the drive and onto the bare rock to the south, in order to get a better view of the building and the location. Even in the dark I could see signs of wear and tear in the wood-work, great light patches where the paint had peeled off. There was an entrance at the rear, and from one of the four windows facing me came some light, but the rolled-down blinds prevented me from seeing what was going on inside.

I felt an unease growing within me. I didn't like the idea that there was a little girl in the company of two adult males who had shown an unhealthy interest in children, and a mother with a dubious reputation. The connection between this bunch and two of the three suspicious deaths over the last six months didn't make me feel particularly com-fortable, either.

From where I stood, I could see two windows high up on the south wall. There were no blinds and a dim light seeped out from inside. But it was impossible to climb up without a ladder. Nevertheless I made my way down there and stood measuring the distance up to the two windows. I reckoned it was at least four or five metres. I looked around for something to stand on, but found nothing. Then I sidled along the wall to the corner facing the sea. The ground beneath me sloped away to the water, and the building rested on wide concrete pillars with open space underneath. And there I found exactly what I needed: a ladder.

Again I listened. All I could hear was the distant mumble of what could have been the waves lapping onto the bare rock below or else voices from inside the house. Then I heard a shrill girl's voice cut through the night: 'I don't want to, Mummy! I don't want to!'

Quickly I hauled up the ladder, carried it around the corner, found a secure position for it in a hollow in the ground and placed it against the wall. I looked around me. Then I shinned up, carefully raised my head to window height and peered inside.

42

It was a heart-breaking sight. The little girl, Astrid, was sitting fully clothed on a wide chair, as far as I could see, with her arms bound to the arms of the chair and her legs bound to the legs. The expression on her face was one of despair and her eyes were staring at her mother, who held a can of beer in one hand and her face partly averted, as if not wishing to look at her daughter. A man with dark hair and a trim beard held a roll of gaffer tape in front of Astrid's face, without moving, as though threatening her rather than doing anything in particular. It was Sigurd Svendsbø, or Stein Sløvåg, as his passport said now.

They were in a large hall with bare walls, illuminated only by some bright spotlights mounted on stands and directed towards the little girl in the chair. There was some other furniture – a sofa and a suite of chairs around a coffee table, placed carelessly against the rear wall.

Between five and ten metres away from the chair stood Bjarne Bratteli. He was rigging up a camera on top of a stand with the lens pointing at Astrid. The third man in the room, Knut Haugen, stood with his back to me, his shoulders stooped, as though waiting for what was going to happen.

I couldn't stand still and watch. I shinned back down the ladder. Too late I heard a car come screaming down the short section of road between the gate and the disused industrial building. The headlamps swept over the walls, and for a few seconds, just as I jumped off the ladder, I was bathed in light.

I flung myself back against the wall in the hope that I hadn't been seen, while grabbing the phone from my inside pocket. Then I heard heavy footsteps from around the corner and an imposing figure appeared.

'What the…? Veum!'

It was Bjørn Hårkløv, and I dropped my phone.

'What the fuck are you doing here?'

'Stretching my legs. And you?'

He didn't bother answering; he came straight for me. I looked around. If I was lucky I could run around him. In my younger days I might have succeeded. I was almost past him when he grabbed my arm and wrenched it so hard that I lost balance and fell headlong. At the same time he directed a well-aimed kick into my ribs and the air hissed out of me as if from a burst balloon. Then he lifted me up and banged me so hard against the wall, it felt as if he was planning to use me as a battering ram to get inside.

For a moment everything went black. When I came to with a start he was half carrying, half dragging me into the building. He kicked the front door shut behind him. I raised my head and studied my surroundings. We were in a room with wardrobe cabinets along one wall, most of them ajar, as abandoned as the rest of the building. Two closed doors in a short wall used classic pictograms to indicate they were toilets, one for women, one for men.

A door at the opposite end of the room burst open. Knut Haugen appeared in the doorway, closely followed by Sigurd Svendsbø.

'What the hell?' exclaimed Haugen.

'Veum,' Svendsbø said, and I didn't like his tone one bit. It was as if this was the moment he had been longing for.

'Look what I found, Siggen,' Hårkløv said, not even bothering to conceal the identity of his interlocutor. 'Keep a watch outside.'

'Do I need to?' Svendsbø answered. 'I've got you, haven't I. But…' He looked at his watch. 'Late, aren't you?'

'I was delayed. But it looks as if I came in the nick of time.'

'In time to be nicked. Now the wolf's at your door,' I mumbled, to remind them I was still present. 'I don't suppose you imagine I came without back-up, do you?'

'Oh, yes?' Hårkløv sneered in my direction. 'The cavalry? I didn't see any.'

'They're on their way.'

Svendsbø glanced enquiringly at Hårkløv, who shook his head firmly. 'He's bluffing.' He forced me forwards in a classic police half-nelson. 'I'll soon shut him up.'

Svendsbø nodded with an ominous expression, as though this were even more of what he had been looking forward to. Haugen stepped to the side to let us through. I was led, stooped, into the immense hall. As I passed Svendsbø, I turned my head towards him. 'Sold your soul to Poseidon, have you?'

He just arched his eyebrows by way of a response.

'Poseidon? What the fuck's he talking about?' Hårkløv said and led me into the hall.

Astrid looked at me in despair from where she was sitting, unable to move in the chair. Her mother was still standing there with a can of beer in her hand. She raised it to me in a kind of welcome.

Over by the camera Bjarne Bratteli was unable to hide his surprise when he saw who was on his way in. 'Veum?'

Svendsbø said: 'Veum's trying to be witty. The last time he saw me I was disappearing from sight into Bjørna fjord. Poseidon's the Greek god of the sea. Get it?'

Hårkløv still appeared puzzled, but shrugged his shoulders as though it didn't matter.

To me, Svendsbø said: 'Well, I've always been good at holding my breath under water. I reached one of the skerries past the diving platform, and as soon as you'd gone I made it to land.'

'Bruno Karsten helped you, I would guess. And he could use a man with your qualities in Hamburg, too.'

Hårkløv forced me down with one arm up my back and my face on the floor. He sat on me heavily. 'Gimme that tape.'

Svendsbø handed it to him, and Hårkløv wasted no time in taping my arms together, so tightly that I could barely move them. 'Here,' he said to Svendsbø, and passed him the roll. 'You do his ankles.'

Svendsbø bent down and did what he had been told. When he had finished, Hårkløv stood up, took hold of my arms, dragged me off and dumped me on the floor staring up at the ceiling, next to an old, worn-out armchair with an indefinable, nauseating stench, as though someone had once relieved themselves in it.

I raised my head. Astrid was sitting open-mouthed and wide-eyed. She was breathing heavily and great tears were running down her cheeks. By the coffee table Svanhild Olsvik was crushing the empty beer can with masculine force, then she took another from the table and opened it with a loud hiss. The look she sent me was stony and intransigent. Bjarne Bratteli stared mutely at me, one arm partly round his camera stand, as if to protect it from attack. Knut Haugen was moving up and down on the balls of his feet, still apparently waiting for something to happen. As though this wasn't enough. Carefully, I lowered my head and half turned to the side so that I could keep an eye on everyone in the room.

'What the hell do we do now?' Haugen said.

Svendsbø shrugged. 'We have to shut him up. For good.'

Hårkløv grinned. 'That's easy enough. The sea's right outside the door.'

Haugen said: 'You … You two are going to…?'

From the camera Bratteli said: 'Now listen here…'

I raised my head again and looked straight at Haugen. 'They're going to turn you into a murderer, Knut.' I shifted my gaze to Bratteli 'You, too.'

'Shut your mouth,' Hårkløv said, took a step forwards and kicked me hard in the ribs.

'Mummy,' Astrid whimpered. 'What are they talking about?'

'Don't take any notice. You just do as they say, like always.'

The girl scowled at her mother. Suddenly her eyes filled with tears, she sobbed aloud and her body twitched violently, then she forced her lips together so that not a sound would emerge, whatever punishment might ensue.

Svanhild Olsvik turned to the others. 'Aren't we going to do what we've come here for?' With pointless emphasis, she added: 'Don't forget she has to go to school at the usual time tomorrow.'

'With him there on the floor?' Bratteli said.

Hårkløv bent down, lifted me and sat me with my back against the nauseating armchair. 'Perhaps he'd like to watch?' he said with a grin. 'After all, you have a taste for that sort of thing, don't you, Veum?'

I started to say something, but his raised hand stopped me. 'And you just button it! One word from you and we'll tape your mouth so hard you won't even be able to breathe.'

'Why don't we get rid of him right now?' Svanhild Olsvik said.

'Don't you think we should torture him a bit first?' Hårkløv answered. 'Mentally, then ... physically.'

'We owe him that,' Svendsbø declared unemotionally. 'I lost my wife because of him.'

'Who hasn't?' Bratteli said. As they all turned to him, he added: 'Lost a wife, that is.'

'She died,' Svendsbø said.

'And Veum will, too,' Hårkløv rejoined.

Wisely, I held my own counsel.

'Why do you think I targeted your woman?' Svendsbø continued, fixing his eyes on mine. 'And her little daughter?' He seemed to be getting het up at the thought. 'You should fucking find out what it feels like, too! Losing the person you love. No longer being allowed to see your own children.'

'She isn't my...'

Hårkløv kicked me in the ribs. 'Shut your mouth, I said.'

'And you tried to kill me first.'

Hårkløv leaned over me and pressed the roll of tape against my face, hard. 'Your very last warning! Do you understand?'

Svanhild Olsvik had moved over to her daughter. She had taken a paper tissue and dried her tears. 'Stop crying!' she snarled. 'You've done this before.'

The daughter looked up at her mother with lifeless eyes. I could feel myself flinching inside. I had met fathers who abused their daughters. But a mother...?

'Fuck her,' Svendsbø said. 'It doesn't matter if she cries. It just makes it more realistic.'

Bratteli went to the door of the far room.

'Where are you going?' Hårkløv bellowed.

'Outside for a piss. Is that not allowed or what?'

Hårkløv glanced at Svendsbø, who shrugged. 'As long as you don't fall into the toilet out there.'

Bratteli went out.

I watched Svanhild Olsvik with new eyes now. A rogue lioness? 'So this is what you offered your clients. Free access to your daughter.'

This time Hårkløv kicked me with such vehemence I fell back and almost knocked myself out on the concrete floor. Semi-concussed, I heard Svanhild Olsvik say: 'Shouldn't we shut him up once and for all?'

'Mummy!' Astrid screamed hysterically.

Her mother spun round and slapped her daughter so hard it echoed all around the hall.

Haugen said: 'Listen…' I noticed he had started to look uncomfortable as well.

'This game stops right here,' Bratteli said from the doorway.

The others in the room gaped at him. Even Astrid stopped crying with a half-stifled gasp.

'Says fucking who?' Hårkløv said, and moved away from me.

Sigurd Svendsbø looked around, suddenly unsure what was happening.

'I do,' Bratteli said. 'I've done a lot of bad things in my life, but I'm no murderer! And I'm not planning to become one, either.'

If I'd had my arms free I would have applauded. Hårkløv turned to Svendsbø, and I watched them exchange wordless reactions to the new situation.

'You can count me out, too,' Haugen said, demonstratively moving away from the others. 'This has gone too far.'

Bratteli held up his phone. 'The police are on their way.'

'What!' shouted Svendsbø. 'For Christ's sake. Bønni…' He pointed to the door.

Hårkløv gesticulated towards me. 'And this pain in the arse, what shall we do with him?'

'He'll have to wait. This is about us now. They can stop us at the bridge.' Svendsbø headed for the door. Hårkløv stared unhappily at me. Then he followed Svendsbø.

Bratteli stepped aside. As they passed, Hårkløv sent him a stern glare. 'Your time will come, too. You can be dead sure.'

Svanhild Olsvik walked towards the door as well. 'Wait for me!' Without a look back at her daughter, she disappeared out of the door, on the heels of Svendsbø and Hårkløv.

Bratteli watched her leave, open-mouthed. From my position on the floor I said: 'She knows she'll lose her parental rights to her daughter now. This will be a social-services matter.'

Haugen and Bratteli looked down at me, a perplexed expression on their faces. 'Might be an idea to cut me free?' I said.

Haugen freed me while Bratteli released Astrid from the chair.

I stood up, my muscles aching after the battering Hårkløv had given me. When Astrid was free she looked from Bratteli to Haugen with obvious fear in her eyes. Then she ran straight to me, wrapped her arms around me and hugged me tight, her sobs long and painful, and her body trembling with despair. The two other men in the hall turned their backs, as though ashamed to be in the same room as us. I held her tight and gently stroked her shoulders. 'There, there,' I said. 'It'll all be fine now, Astrid. Everything's going to be fine.'

But everything is a big word. I was frightened I had promised her too much.

43

The police came, if not with bugles and fanfares, then with sirens blaring, which fell silent at the gate. Not long afterwards we heard running feet outside; Bjarne Bratteli was standing in the doorway to receive them.

Immediately he was led into the hall by uniformed police officers, two of them with secured weapons. Right behind them came Bjarne Solheim and Annemette Bergesen, both in civvies. They soon had an overview of the situation. Bergesen walked over to where Astrid and I were. The little girl clung to me even more tightly. Solheim guided Haugen and Bratteli into the opposite corner and motioned for the officers to take charge of them, then he turned to me, stroked his crew cut and raised his eyebrows. 'Veum?'

'Did you manage to stop them at Sotra Bridge?'

'Stop whom? We weren't given any info about the car or the individuals concerned. Just an emergency call to get here as fast as possible to this address, and there was a small child involved.' He looked at Astrid.

Bergesen said: 'That's why I'm here.'

I said discreetly: 'A few days ago we talked a little about a woman. This is her daughter.'

'And the woman?'

I whispered: 'Escaped in the getaway car.'

'Have we got a description of the car?' Solheim asked.

'I assume it was Bjørn Hårkløv's.' I looked questioningly at Haugen.

'Yes. It wasn't mine. I've got the key on me.'

'Then it was Hårkløv's. A black Audi. I assume it's registered in his name.'

Solheim beckoned to one of the officers. 'Find the registration number and put out an alert.'

'There are three people in the car. There were, anyway. Bjørn Hårkløv, an old acquaintance of yours, Sigurd Svendsbø and...' again I lowered my voice '...Svanhild Olsvik.' I gave them Svanhild's address in Fyllingsdalen and noticed that Astrid had let go of me. She had lifted her hands to her ears when her mother's name was mentioned. I gently held her close to me.

'Svendsbø?' Bergesen queried. 'Wasn't he the one involved in the previous abuse case? The one who was presumed drowned?'

'Yes.' To her quizzical gaze I said: 'Not everyone waits until Easter. People wake from the dead at Christmas, too.'

Solheim came over to us. 'Well, we'll secure the place and take some photos. Could you tell us what actually went on here, Veum?'

'Luckily I arrived in time to break it up, but you can see the camera. They were going to make a video with...' I nodded silently towards Astrid. 'When I arrived, I was spotted before I had a chance to contact you, and the most hard-bitten of this bunch were all for depositing me in the sea. You would've been rid of me for good, Solheim. But one of those two over there – Bjarne Bratteli – reached a point where he didn't want to be part of this, neither as an accomplice, nor as a passive spectator. He was the one who rang you.'

'And the other one?'

'Knut Haugen, son of the late Per Haugen, whom you might know.'

'And this Bratteli, who's he?'

'He was the one who would do the filming. At any rate, it's his equipment over there. He works in a kindergarten.'

Bergesen shook her head in resignation. Solheim's face hardened even further. He said: 'They'll have to be brought in and charged.'

'Of course.'

'And what was your role this time, Veum?'

'It's the same case we've been discussing several times over the last week. I was still after a potential murderer. A man or woman. What's more...'

'Yes?'

'He's admitted it now. It was Svendsbø in the grey Golf who tried to run down Sølvi and me. Have you found it?'

'Not yet.'

Solheim turned to Bergesen. 'What shall we do with her?' He looked down at Astrid.

'I'll take her with me to child welfare.'

'We can go in my car,' I said. 'She seems to feel safe with me.'

'Yes. Wonders will never cease,' Solheim said with a crooked smile and turned to his colleagues. 'Folks! Supply the two gentlemen over there with a pair of top-quality cable ties and take them to the station for questioning.'

Bratteli opened his mouth to protest, but caught himself and then accepted the situation. Haugen didn't protest either and followed him out. Both were accompanied by a police officer.

As they were about to pass, Bratteli stopped and turned to me. 'I hope you'll tell them what my role was in this.'

'For good and ill, I have to say.'

'At any rate I'm not a paedophile, like …' He glanced at Haugen. 'But they forced me. Even when Laila was living at home, she got into debt to them and I didn't have enough bloody money. Then they contacted me directly.'

'Who did?'

'Him … Hårkløv. He said they would cancel the debt if I did them a favour. And so I took the photos in the kindergarten.'

The officer beside him signalled that she was getting impatient. 'Come on now!'

'Afterwards they had a hold on me. I could've lost my job.'

'You definitely will now anyway.'

'But I saved your life. Don't forget that.'

I nodded. He pinched his mouth shut and walked on.

We waited a little before following, Annemette Bergesen first, Astrid and I behind. The little girl had her hand firmly in mine. I thought I might have to go to wherever child welfare placed her as well before the evening was over, so that she would feel secure.

Fortunately it didn't turn out like that. One of the women in the child-welfare office, which was just off the street where the main police station was, managed to gain her confidence in the hour we chatted, to such an extent that when I finally made a move to go Astrid just looked up at me with her big eyes and raised a hand in a little wave. I left her with a heavy heart, but I felt confident she would have expert help where she was going.

Before going home I popped by the crime squad to hear how it was going with the search for the black Audi and the wanted persons. I heard that Svanhild Olsvik had been arrested at her home address. She hadn't opened the door when the police rang her bell, but she was stopped when a taxi pulled up in front of her block an hour later and she tried to leave the building with two suitcases and a rucksack. The Audi and the two others hadn't been seen yet.

I drove home and had a nervous night's sleep. Before going to bed I called Sølvi and warned her that someone might still try something against her or Helene, even if the chance of this happening was probably less now than before. I asked if she wanted me to go over, but she said no. In a weary voice, she added: 'We can manage fine on our own, Varg.'

At eight o'clock the next morning I received a phone call from Annemette Bergesen. She told me that the grey Golf had been found abandoned on the island of Bjorøy, by a holiday home, which under closer examination turned out to have belonged to Sigurd Svendsbø's late parents and therefore in reality was his. Svendsbø and Hårkløv were still at large, both of them.

When I went down to the office and switched on the computer there was a message from the Tønsberg police. Mørk had sent me the passenger lists for the Widerøe routes between Bergen and Torp on the relevant days the previous week. They were in attachments and he asked me to report back as soon as I had been through them, to tell him if there were any names I recognised.

I opened the attachments and combed through them systematically. I scrolled down the lists until my fingers stopped in mid-air over the keyboard and the mouse lay as lifeless as if it had been caught in a trap.

There was a name I recognised. I moved a tiny bit up the list to see what the date was. From Bergen to Torp on Wednesday, 7th January. I moved to the list of passengers on the day after. Return from Torp to Bergen on Thursday, 8th January, the same day Foyn informed me that Slåtthaug had been reported missing.

I didn't call Mørk back, as he had asked me to do. Instead I grabbed the phone, found the right number on the list and dialled it. Not long afterwards we had arranged to meet.

44

I crossed Sotra Bridge on this day too, but drove past the side road I'd taken the previous day and continued south. All depending on the volume of traffic, it would take me between forty-five minutes and an hour to reach where I was going. Sund was the most southerly of the three districts forming the island kingdom west of Bergen.

Temperatures were still wintry, only three to four degrees, but the cloud cover had broken and the golden January sun angled in low over the countryside. The light breeze sweeping over the bonnet didn't have the slightest effect on the motion of the car. The roads were dry and fine, with occasional patches of snow at the edge, like filthy putty.

Passing the white wooden church in Fjell, I had to brake for a scruffy, grey dog crossing the road with its nose in the air, as though it personally owned this stretch. When I accelerated again, it walked along the stone wall around the church, sniffing, as though searching for hidden scents.

Further south, I branched off to the east and then drove south again. After some kilometres I came to a chapel on the right-hand side, also white, but with blue window frames and ledges. On an impulse I pulled in, stopped in front of the noticeboard by the entrance and got out of the car to read the notices. One of them prompted a nod of recognition: *3rd Sunday in Epiphany, 18th January, 6:00 p.m. Congregation meeting. Children's choir. Sermon by Pastor Storebø. All heartily welcome.*

I got back into my car and drove on. From the description he had given me, it couldn't be far now. A couple of kilometres further south a gravel track led off from the main road. Only a green post box on a stand set back from the road told me someone lived there. The low, white house stood behind a screen of trees at the end of the track. It was a typical west-Norwegian smallholding, probably dating back to the

1920s, with a plain, grey farmhouse. As I pulled up in front of the house, the door opened and Hans Storebø came onto the stoop. 'Welcome to my farm, Veum,' he said with a warm smile.

When I first met him, at Tora Haugen's, the heavy folds around his mouth reminded me of a bloodhound. Here he reminded me more of a good-natured farm dog. He was wearing a blue-and-white traditional sweater, grey trousers hanging loose around his legs, and around his neck protruded the collar of a brown, checked flannel shirt. 'I have some coffee and biscuits for us,' he said, beckoning me to follow him.

Through a small porch, where a steep staircase led up to an attic under the pitched roof, he led me into the kitchen and what in bygone days had probably been the parlour. It was a little room that would then only have been used on holy days. There were still remnants of the old carved furniture. On a chest of drawers along one wall was a big wireless, where I could imagine they collected once or twice a day to listen to the weather forecast and the news. The weather forecast was more important. But this scene was broken by the TV in one corner and the large, black, leather Stressless chair, which was strategically placed at the correct angle for the screen.

A single picture hung on the wall: a print of the French painting I thought was entitled *L'Angelus*. It showed a peasant couple standing in silent prayer over a basket of potatoes, with a low sun in the background. It could equally well have been a January day somewhere in the surrounding areas of Bergen as a field in nineteenth-century France, and I knew why it was there.

He had set a small, round table, next to the closed door to the adjacent room, with cups, plates, a dish of biscuits, a bowl of sugar cubes and a black Thermos in the middle, all placed with meticulous care.

He pulled a chair forwards. 'Take a seat. Do you have anything in your coffee?'

'No, thank you. I like it black.'

He nodded, apparently satisfied with the answer, and poured coffee for both of us. He took three or four sugar cubes and dropped them in his cup one by one. Once that was done, he sat down and fixed his

gaze on me. 'When you rang you said you had something to talk to me
about. Does that mean you've discovered something unnatural about
how my brother-in-law died?'

'Yes and no.' I took a sip of the coffee. 'I passed the chapel on my
way here. When I pulled in and read the notices on the board outside
I saw that a Pastor Storebø was giving a sermon this coming Sunday. I
assume that's you?'

'Yes, it's me. It's an open congregation and we like to use the term
pastor for leaders in the parish.'

'You might remember that when we talked last week I asked if the
term pastor meant anything to you. You asked if it was the parish priest
who officiated at the funeral I meant, but it wasn't. It didn't occur to you
to tell me you were a pastor yourself … out here?'

The warm smile faded. 'No, I must admit I didn't link it with the
questions you were asking.'

'No?'

'I can't see that it had anything to do with the case. It was my brother-
in-law you wanted to talk to. Not me.'

'But we've talked several times since. On the phone, mind you. Last
time you told me about a woman who was supposed to have visited
Haugen the day before he went missing. It's struck me that this is something you just made up.'

'Made up? Why?'

'To lead me up the garden path. And off your trail.'

'And why on earth would I want to do that? Lead you up the garden
path, as you put it?'

'I'll come back to that. Now listen to me. I've had some passenger
lists sent to me. Last week you went on a quick trip to Tønsberg. From
Bergen to Torp and back again the following day. Wednesday and
Thursday, to be absolutely precise.'

He nodded slowly and scratched one of his big, bushy eyebrows.

'How do you explain that?'

He deliberated for a moment. Then he smiled weakly. 'Explain? I was
invited there. A private matter.'

'Invited? Who by?'

'Well, as a pastor, on an occasion such as this, I have to invoke our oath of confidentiality.'

'Which can be very useful to hide behind.'

'That's not its intention.'

'No, but the person you were going to visit there was Karl Slåtthaug, wasn't it?'

'Karl Slåtthaug?'

'Yes. He told a colleague he was meeting a pastor on Wednesday evening.'

'I see. I'm not the only one in the profession, however.'

'The following day he was reported missing and a few days ago he was found in the sea at a place called Ollebukta Bay. In the same state as your brother-in-law.'

He nodded. 'I see.'

We sat looking at each other. I recognised something in his eyes, something I had seen in other interviewees on earlier occasions. It invariably comes to a point in such situations, when the person on the other side of the table starts to calculate: *How much does he actually know? How much is guesswork? How long can I stick to my line?*

'I'm sure you'll realise this has given me cause to ponder. The first death, in October, that was your brother-in-law. So, linked via family to a pastor, which I didn't find out until today. The second death, in December, was the late Mikael Midtbø – he was supposed to have met someone he called the pastor. The third death, this January, was Karl Slåtthaug, who was also meeting a pastor, on the day he disappeared. All these three were in prison eighteen months ago, convicted of the same crime: child abuse, or to be precise, possession of sexual images of children.'

He listened, rapt with concentration. I could see it now. The gradual realisation that there was no way out was slowly emerging. As he said nothing, I continued: 'At the beginning there was someone else accused of the same charge. That was me. But the charge was withdrawn and I was released.'

'I know.'

The two words hung in the air between us, like almost visible electricity. I could feel my heart beating, as it sometimes did when I was near the endgame. 'I may've been on your original list, too?'

Again the weak smile, as if he was reminded of a fond memory. 'I didn't have a list,' he said then.

I looked at him. He was a few years older than me, three or four, from what I could recall. He was stronger and had probably done more physical work than me, on his smallholding. But if he chose to turn rough, I had no particular worries about not being able to defend myself against him. All the signs were that he wasn't the type to use a weapon, not even whatever might come to hand. Apart from the fact that he had a view of life that was miles from my own, I'd had a positive impression of him from the beginning, when I met him in Brunestykket at his sister's place.

He extended a hand, lifted his coffee cup, drained it the way that Jesus, according to legend, drained His chalice at the last supper, set it down and leaned back in his chair.

I said: 'Shall we talk this through?'

'Talking can be good therapy. You look like someone who could do with it,' he answered with the same warm smile.

I could feel that my smile was a lot tauter as I went on: 'Then let's start in October. Your brother-in-law, Per Haugen, died in what might appear to be a drowning accident. I wouldn't say you talked about him with any great respect when we discussed him. You were shocked at what you'd heard in court and not only concerning his activities on the net; but also by the accusation that he'd sexually abused his daughter – made by Laila herself.'

He listened seriously to what I had to say. Only a few tiny nods of the head revealed that he understood and perhaps agreed with what I said.

'Then you yourself contacted me on Saturday. You told me about this woman who'd supposedly visited Haugen on one of the last days before he died and who, you more than suggested, might've been behind what happened in Frøviken.'

A brief nod.

'I've tried to find this woman, but in vain. It could be that she's someone we've never met or for that matter heard about. In fact, though, I've come to the conclusion that you made her up. I've always had a theory that there was a connection between these deaths. This was reinforced by the murder of Karl Slåtthaug.'

'Murder?' he queried softly. 'I thought you said he drowned ... too. Is it being categorised as ... murder?'

'That's what the police in Tønsberg are investigating it as.'

'I see.'

'Back to this woman. The only female I've met with sufficient ferocity to do anything like this is someone called Svanhild Olsvik. Does that name mean anything to you?' When he shook his head, I told him who she was: 'Mikael Midtbø's partner.' He nodded and threw up his hands as if to emphasise that it still didn't mean anything to him. '... One of those who survived this ...' I said, without going into detail about what she had on her own conscience.

I poured myself a cup of coffee from the Thermos and glanced at him. He held up a palm and shook his head. I took a swig of the lukewarm coffee, then went on. 'On receiving the passenger lists this morning and thus having a direct link between you and Karl Slåtthaug – at least circumstantially speaking – I began to put two and two together. Perhaps you'd begun to feel the heat and so, to mislead me, you threw in the lure of a mystery woman. But in so doing you showed me even more clearly that what happened in Frøviken was unlikely to have been an accident.' I let the words sink in before going a little further. 'Are you willing to give me the details now?'

Once again I seemed to see the scales tip in his eyes. Pro – contra. Yes – no. A couple of times he opened his mouth as if to say something, then caught himself.

I gave him all the time he needed, took another swig of coffee, stretched out my legs, cast another glance at *L'Angelus* on the wall and thought to myself: why are they actually praying? For the potatoes to have a long and useful life? For the working day to be over and for it to be time to go home to the children? A divine peace rested over the old painting, a type of peace I myself didn't feel I had experienced that many times in my life.

I shifted my gaze back down to the thoughtful expression on Hans Storebø's face. And him? How much peace had he experienced? Prayers and blessings, or doomsday sermons in the chapel? Memories of Televåg as a sombre backdrop to his childhood and, for all I knew, other things, which still weighed on him to this very day? The responsibility for his big sister Tora, who was so terribly deceived by her own husband, his brother-in-law? What was it ultimately that made a person take the most important decision in life, the one between life and death – not only their own but the lives and deaths of other people?

'We hadn't agreed to meet,' he said all of a sudden.

I gave a start. 'You mean … ?'

'Per and I.' I nodded without saying anything. Now it was important to let him choose his own words, tell the story as he remembered it. 'But I knew his morning habits. He got up early and went out to do some fishing. So I did the same. Got up early, drove to town, parked nearby and, when I saw him pass by, waited before following him. After all, I knew where he was going.' He paused.

'Yes, and then? You met him down by the sea?'

'Yes, he was standing on a rock, he'd cast the line and was slowly reeling it in, with small jerks of the rod, in case a fish was about to bite. He was quite surprised when I appeared. That has to be said.'

'Surprised in the sense of … annoyed?'

'Well.' He shrugged. 'It was more like … "What are you doing here?" And I said: "I wanted a chat with you, Per." "A chat? About what?" "Well, what do you think?" "We've got nothing to chat about. Nothing!" Then he turned away and cast again.'

Now he had raised his head, as though he was looking at the door behind me and half expecting someone to come in. Yet he had a faraway look in his eyes and I was fairly sure he was no longer in the here and now; he was back in Frøviken that morning in October.

'I talked to his back. I told him there was forgiveness for everything, but he had to turn to God himself, throw himself onto his knees in front of Him and pray that when his time came he could go in the knowledge that what awaited him after death was nothing but heavenly peace.'

'And how did he react?'

'He suddenly swung round. He stared at me with evil flashing from his eyes. "Get thee from me, Satan!" he said.' Now Storebø was back in the little sitting room and looking at me with a desperate expression on his face, as if I could arbitrate in this case. He laid one hand on his chest and said in an almost accusatory tone: 'That's what he said to me! He called me Satan!'

I opened my mouth to make a comment, but he carried on: 'I reacted with righteous fury. I shoved him away as hard as I could – well, it was a reflex action. He lost his balance, slipped on the bare rock and tumbled into the sea. I slid down after him and stood in the water up to my knees. When he tried to get up I pushed him down hard and held him under – under the water – not for long, because a spasm seemed to go through him and then he went still.' After a short pause he added: 'That's what the doctors said too, according to what Tora was told. There were signs suggesting he'd had a turn, which led to him drowning.'

'But that turn had been provoked by external circumstances. By you.'

Once again his eyes met mine. 'You could put it like that.'

I agreed. I could put it like that.

45

For a long time we sat like this, each on our own side of the table, as if we, too, were performing some kind of silent prayer. I didn't feel like any more of the coffee. I was afraid the biscuits would be too dry for me now. And he didn't seem to want any more, either.

In the end, it fell to me to break the silence. 'But it didn't stop there, Storebø.'

'Yes, it did. I went straight home without meeting anyone.'

'Exactly. You were lucky not to be seen, but you left him in the water without making any attempt to save his life, without calling for help. It was only later that you found out what had happened.'

'Yes, you can put it like that.'

I was still agreed. I could put it like that, too. 'And you didn't feel any regret afterwards? After all, you widowed your sister.'

He raised his head fully and straightened his back. 'I think on the Day of Judgement she will thank me for that. I freed her from the yoke. She can look the Lord straight in the face now.'

'Well…' He spoke in figurative terms I recognised well enough, but with which I wasn't that familiar, despite a long life and many encounters with people holding a great variety of beliefs and doubts. 'But as I said, it doesn't stop there. In December you were in Fyllingsdalen. What took you there?'

He was physically restless. He pulled at the lobe of his ear. Then he ran his hand through his dark, grey-streaked hair, rubbed his thumbs against his bushy eyebrows and rolled his shoulders, as if to ease some stiffness he had there. His whole body seemed to be bristling with resistance to what was coming.

'It … I had their names. I hadn't been able to make Per fall to his knees, but…' He looked at me with his big, blue eyes, with clear red streaks in the whites, as though someone had scratched him with something sharp. 'I'm one of the Lord's servants on this earth, Veum. My calling is to save souls. Every disciple of Satan I lead onto the true path is a victory for God, but also for me. Then I have fulfilled my role here on earth. That's why I rang this Mikael Midtbø, said I was a pastor and I had something important to discuss with him. He refused at first. But then I could hear he was hesitating. Perhaps he needed someone to talk to, as well, bearing in mind his stage of life. Then we agreed I would go to his home, in Fyllingsdalen. It turned out to be a high-rise building.'

I nodded. 'And what happened there?'

'He received me, let me in and we began to talk. But … firstly, he'd been drinking. He was far from sober. Secondly, he wasn't particularly attentive to what I had to say. And thirdly, evil shone from him. I think he must be one of the most disgusting people I've ever met. Ten times worse than Per! Gradually I realised he'd invited me there to jeer at me. "You bloody … You damned Jesuit!" he called me. And then he began to accuse me. "How many priests have committed sexual abuse?" he said. "At home … and in the Catholic church, protected by the Pope." As if I had anything to do with Catholics or the Pope. I'm a Lutheran of the most transparent kind! I said that to him. "Hah, you're no better, you lot," he continued. "How often do we read about sexual violation in chapel communities?" He said he had a partner, and what she could tell you about priests and preachers, it was impossible to ignore. "So don't you come here getting on your high horse." In the end he opened the balcony door, dragged me out and pointed across the valley. "Do you see all the people living here?" he bawled. "How many pigs are there among them, do you think? How many secrets are out there, among these people who are usually considered decent?" Then he turned to me again and said: "I'm a pig. You're a pig. The world is full of pigs." And then…'

Storebø was lost in thought. He broke off and stared into the distance, as if in a trance. I watched him, at first a little anxious that he might be having some kind of fit. But nothing else happened. He just sat there, in the beyond, his eyes neither open nor closed, as though he were trying to see inside himself, but with nothing to fasten his gaze on.

At length I raised my voice. 'Hans? Are you there?'

He gave a start, as though I had woken him from a midday nap. He looked around, recognised his own sitting room, locked his eyes on me and mumbled: 'Veum? Yes? What was it you wanted?'

I coughed gently. 'You were telling me what happened to Mikael Midtbø in Fyllingsdalen in December. That is, you hadn't reached the end. What happened on the balcony before you left?'

'Was I? Well, I … Did I tell you how he shouted at me?'

'We'd just finished that bit.'

'Again I reacted with righteous fury. He was so repugnant. I think you'd have spewed if you'd seen him.' As soberly as if he had been saying how he had washed up the coffee cups after a visit, he continued: 'I bent down, grabbed him around the ankles, lifted him up and threw him off the balcony. Afterwards I felt the joy of the Lord pump through me. I left his flat borne on angels' wings, got into my car, drove home and prayed to the Lord for forgiveness. And He forgave me! He knew that I was His servant. That it was His tasks I was performing on earth. Amen.'

Again there was a natural hiatus. There was a strange atmosphere in the cramped room. Inside, I was dizzy with shock at what he said so openly, yet I had – for good or ill – a sort of understanding of what he had done. They had been child molesters, both Per Haugen and Mikael Midtbø, but they had been to court once and would perhaps have landed there again if they had continued their activities. It was the job of the police and the law courts to take care of people like this, not self-appointed mortal servants of the Lord. I could already imagine how the situation would develop in the interview room at Bergen police station when Hamre and Solheim, or whoever, questioned Storebø about what he had done and, not least, about why. Both prosecutors and judges would have their hands full if he ever ended up in court, which I was gradually beginning to doubt.

But there was another canvas to paint. 'And then you went to Tønsberg to have it out with Karl Slåtthaug?'

He nodded and flashed me a sincere smile, exceedingly pleased with himself. 'Yes, but you do understand, don't you? He was the biggest pig of them all. He ran organised crime, sent innocent children out of the country and to the very worst places, and organised abuse of children here in Norway and abroad.'

'Can you document this?'

'What he was doing? It was clear enough at the trial. The only problem was that they couldn't prove anything. He'd been much too smart for them. But I talked to a police officer in the recesses. Several times. He told me about their suspicions – well, what they were sure about, but regrettably couldn't prove. And then he complained loudly about the defence counsels and how they distorted everything that was said.'

'Do you remember this officer's name?'

'No, it … But he was past his prime.'

'Hamre?'

'Mm … maybe. But I'm not sure. I can't give you a name.' Then it was as though we were back talking in completely neutral, natural tones – two men who had finished their silent prayer and were conversing politely over coffee.

'Can you tell me what happened in Tønsberg?'

'Well, we agreed to meet. Slåtthaug refused to see me in his home, so we met in the town centre somewhere. He took me to a pub, in what had once been the fire station. He drank beer. I kept to mineral water. I didn't feel any need to provoke him. On the contrary. I knew all about him, didn't I. This time it was more like a … well, a trap. To complete the task God had set me. He drank quite a lot – first beer, then shorts. But this pub, there were two good-natured women who ran it. They kept an eye on their clientele. When they considered he'd had enough, they refused to serve him and we went on, to another place, closer to the river or whatever it's called there.'

'They call it Kanalen.'

He nodded in an absent-minded way. 'I have no idea what he thought about why I was there. After a while he began to boast about all the things he'd done and got away with, and especially more recently, with all the reception centres for refugees, several of them only for children. It was like stealing sweeties from a jar in a shop, he said and looked at me expecting me to agree with him. In a way he was a charming fellow, Veum. But I saw through him. He was a demon, one of Satan's human minions. Recognisable, like a thistle in a rose bed.' He smiled dimly, pleased with his choice of image. 'Later, after we'd left the bar, we strolled along the quayside. He had to relieve himself, of course, went to the edge, undid his flies and readied himself.' He shrugged his shoulders. 'I just gave him a shove. What happened next, I'm not quite sure. Perhaps he hit his head on something on the way down. Perhaps his heart stopped, too. If he had one, that is. It was cold, Veum. There was a thin sheet of ice on the … Kanal. I watched him sink into the water and stood waiting for him to come up again. But he didn't. He stayed down. It was deeper there than in Frøviken, if I can put it like that.'

Once again Storebø managed to shake me with the way he described such dramatic events as though they were everyday incidents he was talking about, not actions that would lead to a dead man being pulled from the sea in the same place a couple of days later, when he was safely back in his sitting room.

He leaned across the table. 'What about you, Veum? Are you a child of the Lord or a disciple of Satan?'

I straightened up. Automatically I flexed my muscles. What was this? The opening phase of another attack, on the last of the original four accused men? Perhaps he didn't accept the police decision not to prosecute? It was just the proof that was lacking in my case, too? Was that why he hadn't protested when I rang and invited myself over a couple of hours ago?

'I'm not a believer, no. I may as well admit it.'

He looked at me rather sadly.

'I mean, who can believe in a god when you look around the world today? I know you believers say we humans have a choice, that we can choose between good and evil, that we have to carry the responsibility for all the misery ourselves. But I find it difficult to imagine a so-called

merciful God who sits quietly watching small children die in their thou-
sands because of a drought in Africa or other places. Are the children
responsible; are they to blame? Children being killed and maimed
when the homes they live in are bombed by people from the neighbouring country or their own government forces. Have they chosen
that? And what about the children who are abused and whose lives are
ruined by close relatives, in their own homes, in their own beds? Why
is there no one holding a celestial hand over them? No one is so safe in
danger as a flock of God's children, we say. Is that true? Unfortunately
not. I heard someone say once: "God might have created the earth. But
then he rolled over on his side and died. Afterwards we had to manage
as best we could."'

'The small children, they're victims of something much greater and
more dangerous than them. I've said it before – pure evil.'

'You believe in a personified devil as well, do you?'

He had become serious now. 'The devil exists, Veum. Don't doubt
for a second about that. He's sitting like a dark power behind all the evil
that takes place – war, famine, abuse – and life is a long, futile struggle
against him and his disciples. Do you remember my mentioning that
Tora and I come from Telavåg?'

'Yes, I do.'

'Even though I was only three years old when our village was razed,
I've heard it described many times since and I've also studied what
happened in great depth. What we had to go through there, all of us,
was the result of systematic, bureaucratic evil. What Terboven and his
colleagues did in Telavåg can be compared with what Eichmann and
others carried out from their desks, so to speak, single-handedly admin-
istering the whole of the Holocaust. They were "desk murderers" and in
my eyes they represented pure evil. There's simply no excuse for what
they did. Six million lives they had on their consciences, if you include
only the Jews. And here in Norway. The consequences of what happened in Telavåg formed the rest of our lives – Tora and me. Our father
died in Sachsenhausen. Our mother was never the same.'

'But you're saying it yourself. It was bureaucracy, desk planning.

Created by humans with a clear, political end, a basic ideology and contempt for those of other races and opposing political views.'

'Yep, you've got a mouth on you, I'll give you that.' He made a movement with his hands, as though brushing them clean. 'But someone has to do the dirty work too, Veum. Someone has to drive out the demons, purge the world of vermin and complete the task they've been sent here to do.'

'So, is this the motivation for what you did?'

'Have you read the Revelations?'

'Only in part.'

'Then let me refer you to chapter 22, verse 15: "For without are dogs, and sorcerers, and whoremongers, and idolaters, and whosoever loveth and maketh a lie." They deserved their fates and I say that, even though one of them was my brother-in-law.' Suddenly he raised his arms as if to bless me. 'Praise be the Lord! Hosanna in the highest!'

Then he sank back in his chair and sat watching me with the same amiable smile with which he had greeted me. I had to accept what he said was true, but even now I found it difficult to imagine him in the situations he had described, as an avenger on earth for a raging God. To all appearances he was more a case for psychiatry than for the police.

After a while I stood up. 'Well … I don't think we're going to get much further now, Storebø. But there are some surviving relatives – not grieving exactly, I have to admit – but nevertheless without answers. I recommend you contact the police and tell them what you've told me. I daren't say what will happen. It's also outside my jurisdiction, insofar as I have any.'

He eyed me from a distance, as though only partly taking in what I said. 'You're leaving?' He got up, too.

I kept him in my field of vision as he came round the table, still unsure what he might do. Once again, consciously or unconsciously, I flexed the muscles in my stomach, thighs and arms.

He held out a hand. 'Thank you for the talk, Veum. God bless you. May Jesus be with you. Drive carefully.'

Again it felt as if we were two old boys who had just had a cup of coffee together and now were leaving to go our separate ways. I was relatively pleased. I had found out what I had come to hear. In that sense, my goal was achieved. But it didn't feel as if I was on my way up to the podium to receive the applause from the crowd. On the contrary. It felt more like I had been caught taking illegal substances and had to travel home in shame, without a single medal on my chest.

He accompanied me out onto the steps and stood watching me as I got into my car. He raised a hand in a farewell wave as I started up the engine and turned back onto the main road. In the mirror I could see him standing there until he was lost behind a clump of trees.

46

I passed the chapel with the noticeboard by the entrance. I thought to myself that they might have to bring in cover for Pastor Storebø this Sunday. If he followed my advice he would be busy elsewhere.

I followed the main road north. After a few kilometres I noticed a big, grey SUV had appeared behind me. It accelerated, then braked and stayed at a suitable distance from me, ten to twenty metres. In the rear-view mirror I scoured the windscreen, but the reflection made it difficult to see who was behind the wheel.

On a slight upward incline, the SUV accelerated again. It occupied the left-hand lane as if it wanted to overtake, but when it was alongside me it swung hard in the opposite direction and thumped into my door. It was a sudden movement, but subconsciously I had been prepared and I twisted the wheel away so that we remained side by side up the slope. I glanced across, but there was no one in the passenger seat and it was impossible to see who was driving.

Before we reached the brow of the hill, the SUV braked and I broke free from its hold. I put my foot down and drove way over the speed limit. In the mirror I saw the driver do the same and come after me with much more horsepower, like a motorised knight chasing an outlaw down a country lane – Robin Hood in a grey Corolla.

Soon we were on an arterial road. We passed a mall, but it came too quickly for me to consider turning in. Now he was at my shoulder again. But this time he didn't try to overtake. He drove straight into me from the back, with such an impact that I had difficulty steering and lurched forwards. There he was again. Another big bang. My car swerved, skidded sideways, I twisted the wheel to straighten up while pressing the brake pedal softly to retain control, like driving on ice. We went over the crest of a hill, and now the road descended into a valley. In the middle of the hill I saw another car coming towards us. It braked and veered to the side as far as it could go. I managed to straighten my car just in time and raced past. I just had time to think, now at least someone will warn the police, when the SUV smashed into my rear end again, with an even greater impact this time. At last I caught a glimpse of the driver. It was Svendsbø.

It was lucky it was early in the day and there was little traffic on the roads. He powered up alongside me, wrenched the wheel round and hit me as precisely as possible in the bonnet. There was a loud bang and my car skidded to the right. I tried to wrest the wheel back, but there was something wrong. It wasn't obeying.

I stamped on the brake pedal again while feverishly pulling at the wheel, to no avail. I just saw the passenger's door of the robust vehicle next to me. We were approaching the bottom of the hill. To the left of us was a large lake, to the right an open field, which met a tract of forest. Up on the hill in front of us a juggernaut was starting its descent.

Several things happened more or less at the same time. The SUV on my left lurched to the side and skidded forwards with its brakes screaming. My car hit the high concrete kerb on the right with a bang, the Corolla rose into the air and was hurled over the edge of the road. I managed to grab the door handle before the car rolled over, once, twice. Then it met something hard and came to a quivering halt, I heard a hissing noise around me and everything went black, for how long I had no idea.

Opening my eyes, I found myself wrapped in an airbag. It lay like a duvet against my face and in a way it seemed as if I had been asleep, for a long time. There was a strong smell of petrol, but the car was upright, with the front of the bonnet concertinaed against a huge rock. I tried to move. The seat belt was hard against my chest, like a collar, but I was unable to locate the buckle. My whole body ached and a piece of music was playing in my head; it was like nothing I had heard before – atonal and shrill and much too loud.

One leg was stuck, as in a vice, but I could feel it tingling and move my toes up and down. The window beside me had shattered, but I wasn't able to get myself into a position to squeeze through. I tried to stick out my head to see up the road, but I couldn't find the right angle, and when I tried to turn a little bit more, my neck locked. Then I heard a terrible explosion from above me. I peered up, but all I could see was black smoke rising into the air and filling the sky like an ink blot spreading across a sheet of paper. In the end, the whole sheet was covered.

In the distance I heard a voice shouting something I couldn't quite catch. Even further away I heard the wail of sirens.

47

The paramedics strode over the concrete kerb and ran down the gentle slope. They were two young uniformed ambulance staff, one sturdy lad with short, blond hair and a red-haired woman with her hair gathered in a ponytail at the back. I was still stuck in the car, but they managed to prise open the door on the opposite side and were clearly reassured by what they could see and the way I reacted. 'We'll have to get you out,' they said. 'The police and the fire brigade are on the way. Looks like we'll have to lever you out somehow.'

'How's the other car?'

They ignored my question. The young man said: 'My colleague, Elise, will stay with you. I'll go up to see the rest of the crew.'

Once again I heard sirens wailing in the distance. After he had gone I repeated my question: 'How did the other car get on?'

She looked at me with a serious expression. 'Did you know the driver?'

Everything seemed to stand still. 'The driver?'

'Yes.'

Then it struck me who she was talking about. 'Yes. I mean no. But I know who he is.'

She went quiet.

'What happened, I asked you.' For the third time actually.

'We'll talk about it later. Try to relax now.'

Up by the edge of the road more uniformed officers appeared, this time from the fire service. I saw them exchange a few words before two of them came down the same slope. One had a crowbar in his hand, the other metal shears. I began to suspect that my old Toyota would never be the same again.

The two firemen introduced themselves by their Christian names: Lars and Harald. They went to work with a will. They cut the seat belt. Using the crowbar, they managed to free the leg that was stuck, and while Lars was carefully loosening things around me, Harald grabbed me under the armpits and slowly pulled me through the open door on the opposite side. It took them barely two minutes to complete the job. Then, on trembling legs, I was outside, gently moving one bit of my body after another, and with growing relief able to confirm that most still seemed to work. If it was Hans Storebø's valedictory blessings that had done the trick, it was possible I would have to rethink the influence of higher powers. For the time being I ascribed my survival to good fortune.

I looked up at the road. The black smoke was thinning, but still hung there like a storm warning. Two police officers I didn't know were standing around waiting as I plodded up with Elise, the paramedic, behind me as a backstop. As no one had answered my question, I would have to find out for myself.

Right at the top, I stopped. There was a fire engine and a traffic police vehicle, as well as an ambulance. The fire engine's hose was out and what remained of the big, grey SUV was still dripping water. It stood with the bonnet wrapped round a solid tree trunk on the other side of the road. The whole of the front was black, as though someone had drawn a tightly-fitting mask over it, and there was a stench of burning everywhere. The blackened tree looked as if it had grown through the bonnet, which was sliced in two. There were still glowing embers in the trunk above the roof of the vehicle. Several firemen, two police officers and the young paramedic from the ambulance stood in a semi-circle around it, deep in discussion. Further away was the juggernaut that had been coming towards us, now at an angle to the road. A big, burly man in dark-blue overalls was giving a statement to a uniformed officer and gesturing.

A civilian car approached from the north. It was waved on past the rapidly growing queue of traffic and it pulled up behind the police car. Two old acquaintances stepped out and quickly took stock. Hamre and Solheim. When they caught sight of me, Hamre muttered something and they came in my direction, both of them.

'Veum? Out getting some fresh air?' Hamre said, with a wry smile. But he turned serious when he stopped in front of me. 'Everything alright?'

'Seems so. Bit rickety here and there, and I've got a kink in my neck, but everything seems to be where it used to be.'

Solheim looked down the slope. 'Is that your car down there?'

'Yes.'

'Looks like you might have to get a new one.'

'Can I have that in writing?'

Hamre looked in the opposite direction, at the SUV on the other side. 'We got the reg numbers and realised you were involved. That one must be a rental vehicle. Do you know who was driving?'

'Sigurd Svendsbø, from what I could see.'

He nodded. 'Bjørn Hårkløv was stopped by the Hønefoss police this morning, after a brief chase. Svendsbø was the only one left.'

Solheim added: 'Doesn't look like he's going to be much of a problem.'

We followed his gaze. The firemen had opened the side of the SUV now. The whole of the cab was blackened. Hanging in the seat belt with the punctured remains of an airbag, like a burnt pancake over his shoulders, were the equally blackened remains of what appeared to have been Sigurd Svendsbø. This time there wasn't going to be any return. Flames are more lethal than water, when all is said and done.

'I don't understand how he could know where I was.'

'He might've been tailing you,' Solheim suggested.

'Unlikely. I would've seen him.'

'These guys are pros,' Hamre said. 'My guess is we'll find a transmitter under your car, if we have a look. It might even have been there for quite a while. They knew where you were last Sunday, for example.'

I nodded. 'It's not impossible.'

'So, what were you doing in these parts?' He looked at me from the corners of his eyes.

'Clearing up three murders for you.'

He was silent as he allowed the information to sink in. 'And by that you mean…?'

'The case I mentioned and discussed with you lot at the beginning of last week.'

'And you omitted to mention when we were talking last night?' Solheim said.

'In a way there were other cases in my head then. What led me to the solution was on my computer when I went to my office this morning.'

'And as usual you forgot to ring us?' Hamre said.

I coughed and nodded. But I was willing to concede the point. I might have looked slightly abashed.

Hamre rolled his eyes and looked heavenwards. 'Lordy, Lordy, I'm so happy I've only got a few weeks left.'

'But I haven't arrested anyone.'

'Really? You don't say. Did you think perhaps that we would take care of that?'

'If you don't mind, of course. He was explicit enough, but … he has a special background, so you'll have to see what you can get out of him.'

Once again he rolled his eyes. Then he addressed Solheim. 'Take down a name and an address, and we'll go there as soon as we've finished here.'

Solheim took out his notebook and biro and looked at me. I gave him the name, address and a detailed description of how to find him. He made notes. 'You'll be there in twenty minutes at the most,' I added.

'My sincere thanks, Veum,' Hamre said, the sarcasm as thick as syrup. He gazed around at his colleagues from the various departments. 'You'd better ask them who can drive you home. It won't be us.'

He nodded to me and motioned to Solheim to accompany him to the second car. The questioning of the lorry driver had finished. The traffic police were busy now, taking photos of the wrecked SUV and the dead man in the front seat. In the end it was an officer from the local police force who drove me back to Bergen. I asked him to drop me off at my office and went upstairs to lick my wounds as best I could. The first person I rang was Sølvi.

48

The ensuing days came to be subsumed under the heading 'recap'. I was summoned to the police station and questioned about the conversation I had with Hans Storebø, including my own detailed description of what he had said about the three deaths. We also covered the original intended hit-and-run incident at the beginning of January, the one that had led me to investigate this case. We agreed that it had been Sigurd Svendbø behind the wheel and not Hans Storebø. The grey Golf told its own story, and there was no doubt about who had been driving, even if he called himself Svein Sløvåg when he rented it. In addition, it had apparently been him who had been making the silent calls.

I phoned Foyn and brought him up to date. I asked him to send my regards to Mørk and to apologise for not ringing him back earlier. 'Heh heh,' Foyn replied. 'I'll invite him over for a good cognac, then he'll probably t-take it with equanimity. After all, the most important thing is that the case was solved.' We agreed to keep in touch in case we needed to give each other a helping hand on a later occasion.

On Friday Sølvi called and invited me to lunch at Enhjørningen – 'The Unicorn' – just round the corner from where she had her office in Bryggen. The sloping floors, the old paintings on the wooden walls and the fresh spring cod served with potatoes, roe and Sandefjord butter made me feel I was in the eighteenth century, far from Golfs, SUVs and other lethal weapons on four wheels. But Sølvi looked conspicuously serious, from start to finish. After the events of the previous week it hardly came as a surprise that she had taken an important decision. Out of consideration for Helene and the sole responsibility she bore for her, she could no longer expose herself or Helene to the burden it was to have a relationship with a man who had a profession like mine.

She liked me very much, as she said with a sad little smile, and I was genuinely welcome back after I had called it a day and joined the ranks of pensioners. I answered that I was afraid I couldn't afford to do that for a few years yet and thanked her for the offer. She gripped my hand and said: 'I'm going to miss you, Varg.'

'And me you,' I said.

When the meal was over, we walked together down the narrow stairs. In the hall she gave me a quick peck on the mouth before going to fetch her car from the multi-storey car park under Dreggsallmenningen.

I walked back – not home, but to my office. I had also taken a decision. Without any further hesitation, I picked up the envelope from the Public Health Institute, tore it open, took out the sheet of paper and began to read.

The answer was unambiguous. Almost half an hour ago I had lost a lover. Now I had lost a father as well. That is, I had also acquired a new one. One I had never met, but whose name and identity I knew.

I opened the lowest drawer, took out the office bottle of aquavit, filled up the waiting kitchen tumbler and sat leisurely drinking it. I did nothing with any greater urgency than this and at length I went home.

How many answers did you need actually? Was it perhaps enough now? Time to close the office door for good? To find something else? Beekeeper, could that be something for me?

It was a freezing-cold January evening. Above me, the sky was studded with stars. Too many to count, too many to keep watch over. I had to contact a decent accountant; perhaps he or she could help me. Or I would have to cope on my own, as I had always done.

The stars accompanied me all the way home. But it was all the company I had. And my car? It lay somewhere in Sotra, a wreck waiting for its final anointing with oil. No more roundabouts for the Toyota. No more stop signs. No more miles on the clock. Its time was up, once and for all.

For me it was different. My clock was still running. In Telthussmuget I let myself in and went upstairs to the first floor in the darkness. I didn't need any light. I knew where I was going. Home. Home sweet home.

=⊫=